Deadly Motives

Ann Girdharry

(previously published as Killer Motive)

Nurse Mandy Jones

Nurse Mandy Jones had been trying hard not to do another pregnancy test. She'd been trying so hard, the effort made her ache. This morning she could not bear it any longer. Three weeks was long enough

That's how it was when you desperately wanted a baby. And after too many disappointments and one terrible miscarriage, they didn't keep any test kits in the house. Her husband had banned them after he came home to find her crying again, a stick showing a negative result abandoned on the bathroom tiles.

She decided to buy one on her way into the hospital. Then not actually use it until she got home in the evening. It would be a difficult promise to keep.

She tossed her blue nurse's uniform onto the bed. She wouldn't tell her husband until she was absolutely sure. Not until she had the positive result in her hand. The idea of it made her giddy.

There was one other thing she had not told him. He didn't know she was a volunteer on the treatment team for the convicted killer, Travis. Definitely he would have objected. But she figured what her husband didn't know wouldn't harm him.

Travis was a multiple murderer. In the past, he'd strangled at least five women. With their own tights. Twenty-five years earlier, the South Coast Killer was hated by the whole country. But it happened well before Mandy's time. She knew the story, yet to her he was simply a sick old man with terminal cancer. A monster, yes, and also in need of treatment. And that was her job.

When they asked for volunteers, her hand went up. It was a mixture of passion for her work, and an understanding of how the senior nurses still remembered the Travis days. They lived through it, and as far as they were concerned, Travis was as dangerous and evil now as he was then. Which meant Mandy, as one of the younger ones, had a chance to help out her colleagues. It was usually the other way around, so this made a nice change.

The closer it got to seeing him, the more wound up she felt. In a few hours she would face him. What would Travis be like? What would she see in his eyes? Would she feel he was a calculating killer? Would his soul be cold? The idea of it made her sweat. Maybe she was too addicted to crime series because it was nerve-wracking and sort of exciting at the same time.

She applied a little of make-up and did a final check in the mirror. On impulse, she swiped up her amethyst necklace. Her sister had given it. For good luck, her sister said, and Mandy knew it was meant as good luck for a baby coming along soon. Wearing jewellery at work wasn't a good idea but she decided to make an exception, for the test. She fastened the clip and slipped the cold, purple tear-drop inside her uniform.

Several hours later, nurse Mandy Jones knew she had made a mistake joining the Travis team.

As soon as she entered the supplies room, someone sprang out from behind the shelves. Taking one look at the face in front of her, she flung herself at the door, wrenching at the handle. She screamed and kicked as she was dragged backwards. Her attacker pulled her to the floor. She tried to sink her teeth into the hand held over her mouth.

Though she fought with everything she had, her attacker was stronger. She was punched, and pulled by her hair into the corner. He took off her shoes. Ripped off her tights. The vinyl floor was cold against her bare legs. Something was being put around her neck. She brought up a hand. It was her own tights. They were being wrapped around tighter and tighter. Shutting off her air supply.

She tried to twist. Her fingers tore at the material and at the flesh of her own neck. Staring at the light in the ceiling, her vision started to dapple. Darkness moved in, as she felt the life being strangled out of her.

Time slowed. Everything was going black. Oh God no, these were her last moments. Her life was ebbing away. Soon it would be down to a trickle. And then. Nothing. Her body convulsed.

Her last thought was of the second life inside her. She imagined a tiny being, its heart beating. She'd done her desperate best to fight not only for herself but also for the new life she nurtured. And she would never be able to tell her husband the wonderful news.

Chapter One - One day before

Detective Inspector David Grant sat one side of the desk. He wore a dark grey suit and a crisp shirt. He had grey hair and steely grey eyes. Strangers often knocked years off his age and clocked him, wrongly, as under fifty. Friends said he didn't look lined, he looked experienced and seasoned. He was a man who had aged with grace. They wanted to know how he pulled it off.

On the other side of the desk, the doctor sat trim and straight. She seemed small in comparison to the detective. She wore her white hospital coat unbuttoned to show a chic, chocolate-coloured dress. Her hair was tucked neatly behind her ears. What she lacked in stature, Doctor Susan Hawthorne made up for in authority.

'Mr Travis might be a convicted killer to you, Detective Inspector. To me and my staff, let me be very clear, he is first a patient. And the treatment he requires can only be provided by this facility.'

Grant wasn't fazed. He spoke softly, a habit of his to detract from his height, his experience and his rank. He gave the doctor an apologetic smile.

'I completely understand.'

He didn't intend to bully her. What he wanted was to build bridges. After all, this was her domain and he needed her cooperation. They had already batted it backwards and forwards several times. In fact, the other two in the room, the

4

Hospital Manager and Grant's sergeant, had both fallen silent a good ten minutes ago.

'The prison hospital has limited facilities,' she said. 'As you well know, Travis is in his final stages of cancer and I won't have his treatment schedule messed around by you.'

'That's not my intention, doctor.'

She tapped her finger on the desk. 'He will get the same level of care as all our patients and your request to interview him on hospital premises is out of order, DI Grant.'

Her lips were pressed together, signalling this was very likely her final word.

'Doctor Hawthorne, I have to say I respect your principles. The last thing I want is to interfere with his treatment plan and I don't want to cause Travis unnecessary distress. I'm asking for a short interview, that's all. You, and the entire nation, know his brutal history, and I've always been certain he killed more than the five he was convicted for. It might be my last chance to get information. You said yourself that Travis knows he doesn't have long left and I believe this might be the right moment to get a confession.'

The doctor's eyes fell to a photo on her desktop, where a little girl rode her bicycle, stabilisers sticking out on either side, her red coat flapping. Contemplating a family photograph was always a good sign. Grant hoped Hawthorne was thinking about the young women who had been lost, and the suffering of the mothers left behind.

'She's got a lovely smile. How old is she?'

Doctor Hawthorne glanced away and out the window. Grey clouds hung low. She sighed.

'They're predicting snow before Christmas, aren't they, Inspector? Flora is four. Would you believe how excited kids get about building their first ever snowman?'

Grant let the idea of it hang in the air.

He had taken the precaution of doing his homework. Susan

Hawthorne might have the appearance of being a tough cookie. He knew better. At age nine, her best friend had suffered an asthma attack on the playing field and died in front of her. It was the event which inspired her to pursue a career in medicine. Before she married, she spent three years at a refugee camp in Kenya, working with a skeleton staff and next to zero facilities. Oh no, she might play it cool but the doctor had a liquid compassionate centre, and he was counting on it.

'This is a nightmare,' she said.

'A quagmire, doctor. I don't envy you.'

She had already told him the difficulties she faced briefing her staff and how one technician refused to treat Travis, two of her best nurses had cried and Susan now had a counsellor on permanent standby to help those of the team who had agreed to do it. Doctor Hawthorne intended to be there to personally oversee the session and support her staff.

Even with two prison officers escorting Travis at all times, and the man in handcuffs, she told him her team didn't feel safe. He didn't blame them. The fact Travis was now a frail sixty-year-old man didn't change much.

Travis was a shell of the person he had been, but Grant knew his mind was the same and it was the calculating cold mind of a killer. A psychopath who had murdered multiple times and almost got away with it.

Grant glanced at his new young sergeant. Delaney seemed relaxed. At the time, Grant hadn't been much longer in the job than Sergeant Delaney. Twenty-five years earlier, Grant had nailed Travis, except not for everything. This case was exceptional. Grant could never let this one go, because for him it was personal, and it had been personal for twenty-five years.

The doctor shuddered. 'Damn it, and just before our busiest time of year. I don't understand why can't you interview him at the prison.'

'As I explained, he's comfortable on the prison hospital

ward. He's spent years in the same place. Here at the public hospital he'll be on unfamiliar ground.' Grant gave her a smile. 'It's basic psychology, doctor. I've more chance here than anywhere.'

The atmosphere in the room was getting less tense. Doctor Hawthorne was starting to thaw.

'Those young women and their poor families – I really hate to think about it. It must have been dreadful. There's no medical reason to refuse your request. It's simply not protocol.'

'It's your call, doctor.'

She gave him such a direct look, he couldn't help but admire her. She must be a great team leader.

'Correct, Inspector, and as senior consultant in charge of his treatment, I have full discretion to adapt to the circumstances.'

The Hospital Manager, Tony Tanner, cleared his throat. He was against allowing the police access to Travis on their premises and he had said so loud and clear.

'Tony, do you have any final comments?' the doctor asked.

'As I said, I d-don't recommend we agree. Travis is enough of a s-s-security risk as it is.' Mr Tanner was having difficulty controlling his emotions and Grant was glad the manager didn't relaunch into another obstructive rant.

'And I have two families who have never known what happened to their daughters.'

Tanner shook his head. 'Not our problem, detective.'

'This is going in circles and Mr Tanner is right,' Hawthorne said. 'Christmas and New Year is our worst period. We're going to be bursting at the seams. And to make it worse we've got the threat of a flu epidemic. In two weeks' time it'll be crazy.'

'Then let me see Travis straightaway, before your peak. He's due for his first visit tomorrow.'

Susan Hawthorne tapped her fingers on the desk. She took another look at her daughter's picture.

'All right, Detective Inspector. I'll give you access for a *short* interview. And only one.'

'Thank you doctor, thank you very much indeed.'

The wave of relief Grant felt was almost physical. His palms were sweaty as he shook hands with the doctor and he was glad to be out of the small office.

'That went well, boss,' Delaney said. 'She warmed to you.'

'It's always important to build genuine trust, sergeant. Colleagues respond to it and it makes your life easier. Remember that.'

Outside, a wintry wind blew as Grant and Delaney got in their car. Grant didn't talk on the way back to the station. His mind was on the serial killer. Only Grant's wife, Lily, knew what Travis' conviction meant to him. Most people saw it as the one which made Grant. Only Lily knew it was the case which almost broke him.

Chapter Two

Ruby Silver was working her way up the climbing wall. She moved from hold to hold, her fingers practised and her legs strong. She was almost at the top and her muscles had the half-burn half-ache of a good climb. As she stopped to shake the fatigue out of her free arm, her best friend Soraya called up from below.

'Your phone buzzed.'

Ruby waited for the circulation in her shoulder to do its job. Then she took the strain again with both hands. She didn't glance down. One foot was dangling in space and the other was perched on a tiny hold.

'A few more moves and I'm there,' she called back.

This was the most difficult part of the whole ascent. It required a seeming leap across in mid-air to grab a tiny lip on the other side.

On the ground, Soraya had her legs firmly planted and both hands on the rope threaded through the carabiner, which attached to the harness around her waist. Securing a climber needed all your concentration. It was the same at a climbing wall as on a rock face. One mess up and your partner could be dead. Soraya pulled any slack through the carabiner to secure Ruby, who had one hell of a long way to fall. But this was no sweat. They had been climbing together since they were at the children's home and they knew how to keep each other safe.

Ruby inhaled the familiar scent of the climbing space. It was a mixture of other peoples' sweat and the tart resin they all used to stop their grip from slipping. Gathering her strength, she lunged, catching the lip with one hand. She felt a buzz and a spike of elation as she pulled herself across.

'Yay, way to go,' Soraya called out.

A few minutes later and Ruby abseiled down. She swept dark strands of hair from her face, smearing white resin across her temple. Soraya wiped it off.

'That lunge at the end is a tough one,' Ruby said. 'You'd better watch yourself.'

'Yeah, I saw you struggling.' Soraya grinned.

'Like hell you did.'

Taking the chance on the last lunge made Ruby happy and she was even happier for having made it. She was better at taking risks on the climbing wall than Soraya. In real life, it worked out the other way around – Ruby was the cautious one.

Since their days together in the children's home, Soraya was forging ahead building up her own beauty business. Soraya seemed fearless, whereas Ruby had stalled. She was the first to admit how in real life she lacked confidence. Which was why she was mouldering away at the university, stuck as a research assistant while her professor took all the credit for her work. When she'd always dreamed of so much more.

Sometimes Ruby felt she was a pot boiling and boiling, but the lid was firmly stuck on and there was nowhere for all the passion to go. She couldn't break out of needing to be safe and needing to be careful. Soraya knew why. And she understood.

Once they unlatched the rope, Ruby snatched her phone out of her backpack. The message was from Professor Caprini. Could she make it back for an important meeting even though she was on her day off? Texts from him were getting so regular sometimes she felt like his nursemaid. She never protested, though she knew she should.

'Please don't tell me it's Caprini again,' Soraya said.

Professor Caprini was one of the world's leading experts on criminal psychology. Over the course of his career, he had been called in on the highest-profile cases in the UK and across the Atlantic. It was his worldwide reputation which first attracted her to study with him.

'That bastard,' Soraya said. 'How dare he spoil your time off. What's he want this time? Help in the restroom?'

'He's not that bad.'

Ruby avoided her friend's eyes. They both knew exactly how bad the professor could be. After Ruby graduated in criminal psychology, Professor Caprini had taken Ruby on as one of his two assistants. She and her colleague Mark had taken on more and more of Caprini's work. Until it got to the stage where Mark got fed up and left, and the professor now used Ruby as his prop whenever he needed to. She and Mark had written Caprini's last research paper on serial killers, but their names weren't even credited.

'He's not well,' Ruby said. 'The professor can't help it.'

Soraya snorted.

Only those closest to Caprini knew how much his brilliance had faded in recent years. Ruby suspected dementia or some other degenerative disease, but Professor Caprini never confided in her.

'I'm sorry. I'll have to go.'

'How about I come with you and knock some sense into him?'

Ruby didn't rise to the argument, because she knew Soraya was right. She was about to toss the phone back in her bag when a name jumped out from the screen.

Travis.

Oh God.

Her mouth was suddenly dry and she felt like gagging. Her hands started shaking. Ruby's body overheated like she'd stepped straight into a steam room and sweat ran down her face.

'Rube?'

It was difficult to breathe as she fought the wave of panic. Ruby's heart beat fast enough to burst. Black dots danced in front of her eyes. She knew she might pass out. Or scream.

She'd spent years overcoming her panic attacks and she fought for control.

Soraya recognised the signs. She waited, toying with the ends of the rope. When they first met as little girls, Ruby had been crippled by panic. She would bolt for no reason and lock herself inside a wardrobe or inside a cupboard. Once, at the children's home, Ruby got stuck in the freezer and almost died.

Then came the years when Ruby vomited and shook and passed out in front of people at school.

These days Ruby could deal with the panic on her own. It had taken years of effort and therapy and it had been a long and hard-fought battle and Soraya was proud of her friend for having got this far.

It was a few minutes before Ruby took a deep breath. The sweating died down. She slowly retied her ponytail though her fingers still trembled. When she was ready, Ruby returned to Professor Caprini's message.

The police wanted to reinterview Travis and they were asking for Professor Caprini's input.

The South Coast Killer. The one man Ruby had spent her whole life dreading ever seeing and yet wanting to meet.

'It's important. Professor Caprini has been contacted by the police. A Detective Inspector Grant has read the professor's latest research and he wants an urgent meeting.'

Soraya had her hands on her hips. 'Great,' she said sarcastically.

'There's a convict who's dying. It seems the inspector wants to get information from him before it's too late. He's asking for Caprini's help.'

'Of course Caprini wants you there, the treacherous toad.

He's going to be clueless otherwise, isn't he?'

'The professor is ill,' Ruby said, though she was fed up making excuses for him.

'Yeah, and he needs to own up to it because meanwhile he's a fraud. You and Mark are the ones who did every scrap of the serial killer research. And it's Caprini's name all over it. How I wish you'd drop him in it one of these days.'

Ruby could feel Soraya getting angry.

'And you've got more brains than Caprini ever had, haven't you, sweetie? And he takes full advantage of it.'

She blushed. Soraya was right. Soraya was always right.

'I'm sorry, I'll have to cut this short to get back in time.'

'Bloody hell, who am I going to climb with now?'

But Ruby knew her friend's annoyance would be short lived.

She still remembered how lost she'd been when she arrived at the children's home. She was put to share a room with Soraya. It had been her one bit of luck.

They'd each lost their families in horrible circumstances and they both had their secrets. They didn't talk about any of that for a long, long time. For reasons which Ruby never knew, Soraya took the new girl Ruby under her wing. Soraya who was strong and tough and who stood up to the other girls. Soraya who had guts and could give it back as good as she got. Soraya was followed around by a funny little boy called Hawk and yet Soraya never made fun of him like the others.

Over the years, the three of them formed an unbreakable bond – Soraya, Ruby and Hawk. A strange trio who learned to rely on each other. Without them, Ruby would never have survived.

She started packing away her things, while Soraya watched, huffing and puffing and tossing back her hair.

But her friend wasn't someone to be knocked off her stride as easily as losing her weekend climbing partner. She was already checking out the rest of the possibilities, and the talent. That was another thing Soraya was much better at than Ruby.

Her friend caught the eye of a gorgeous looking man over the other side of the room. Dressed in tight leggings, which didn't leave much to the imagination, he was smiling back. Unlike Ruby, Soraya was never short of admirers.

'I don't think you're going to have much problem without me,' Ruby said. 'Looks like I'm already redundant.'

'You'll never be redundant to me, darling.'

Her friend was messing with her hair, a sure sign of serious flirtation. Soraya's eyes had a mischievous glint and Ruby almost felt sorry for the guy.

Soraya kissed her on the cheek and spoke close to her ear.

'And don't forget what I keep telling you, Mark is a bloodsucker too. I bet you're helping him out in his new job, aren't you? Well, you'd better cut it out.'

She gave a weak nod. How the hell had Soraya guessed Mark kept phoning for advice?

While her friend swayed her hips and wandered over to the other side of the room, Ruby went to take a shower.

She had more important things to concentrate on. Travis. The idea filled her with dread but this could be another chance to meet him.

Chapter Three

Here is a truth – you can never hide your inner nature.

I give myself as an example.

In my time, I've been subjected to countless hours of psychiatry. I've been paraded in front of a stream of psychologists, therapists and eminent specialists who've all attempted to change me. In short, they have all tried to exorcise my darker urges. To wipe me clean.

This has not been easy. This has not been successful.

The proof of this came when I set eyes on Detective Inspector David Grant. The man has not become bent in his senior years. He still holds himself broad-shouldered and upright, looking life in the face. I always hated that about him. How he could simply walk into a room and eyes would naturally gravitate towards him.

My hatred runs deep and dark like a black-blood river. I'd have liked to see Grant bowed down, worn out, the life crushed out of him by years of failure and toil.

Seeing the detective was like the flick of a switch. Everything in me, which other people had tried so hard to extinguish, came alive. The disguise I had so carefully constructed, was shattered. And I was exposed again as who I truly am.

In fact, I'm fairly certain the darkness in me sprang back with greater strength than before. As if it had been forced into a tiny box for too long, then, like a jack-in-the-box, it was released.

All those years of therapy wiped out in an instant.

All those years of pretending to be someone I have never been, evaporated.

I can't say I'm sorry.

I became again who I really am. And perhaps worse than I have ever been before. But we shall see if that is true or not.

And what am I?

I am a human being full of hatred and rage. And driven by a blood lust few can imagine.

Nobody sees me as I really am.

Let me put it another way, by telling you how some killers wear a mask. When they murder they become someone else. Whereas with me, my mask is the face I wear every day. That everyday face over which people's eyes flit when they hardly care to register me.

And here's my other secret. Underneath my everyday face, I am who I really am and only a few people have ever seen that. And none of them have lived.

Seeing Detective Inspector David Grant awoke my demons. Oh, I felt an excitement I've not felt for years. That detective made a serious mistake, thinking he can come back to taunt me.

But it's better than that. There's the inspiration of having the serial killer Travis coming to the hospital. Of having his DNA freely available for those of us with a desire to use it.

It's given me a wonderful idea. Have you guessed what? Yes, you probably have. And all my wonderful ideas require a victim.

So I set about locating one.

Eeny, meeny, miny, mo. I was spoilt for choice. Should it be a doctor? A technician? A member of the public? Or how about a nurse? Yes, a wonderful, caring soul who has agreed to care for a monster. Yes, I think a nurse would be fitting, don't you?

Chapter Four

Detective Sergeant Tom Delaney made sure he arrived early.

Tom's desk was in a corner. He shared the team space, or cubbyhole as they called it, with Detective Sergeants Diane Collins and Steve McGowan. Detective Inspector Grant had an office with a door opening onto the cubbyhole and he got a view over the back end of the car park, something Grant made sarcastic comments about whenever he mentioned the perks of seniority.

The boss was a creature of habit. He liked a mug of tea on his desk, with two sugars. On those rare mornings Tom arrived only slightly before Grant, he sprinted to put the kettle on while his boss parked his car.

Tom wasn't sucking up, he was simply grateful Grant had picked him. And a little confused about why. He had a decent track record but he didn't see himself as outstanding, and every detective in Sussex county had been fighting for the chance to be on Grant's team. Looked up to by everyone on the force, Grant was the top of the top.

Tom wanted to squeeze out every drop of experience he could before the inspector retired. Or, as Detective Sergeant McGowan dryly commented, before the boss dropped dead from a heart attack. Tom glanced at the birthday card collecting dust on Grant's shelf. It was difficult to believe the boss was fifty-five.

While he had the place to himself, Tom put in earplugs and

played back his notes on the Travis case. As he listened, he could imagine each victim – Edith, Grace, Diane, Sandra and Amy. He rarely read from the screen. Instead, he used text to audio software to listen to files. He didn't write that often either, and had a habit of dictating his own notes.

Perhaps his dyslexia was one reason Tom had such a clear memory. He had no problems recalling entire conversations and he remembered all the little details of cases, stacked in his brain in visual format. When he got taken on by Grant, the inspector hadn't commented on the dyslexia except to say how having an eye for detail was the mark of a good detective. For once, Tom hadn't felt embarrassed by it.

DS Steve McGowan came in wearing his cycling gear – lycra shorts even though they were in the middle of winter, fluorescent top and helmet, special shoes, the lot.

McGowan acted like he didn't notice Tom's difficulties with reading, though he definitely did because he had never mentioned it. That was McGowan's style, rough around the edges but basically solid. McGowan had been taken on by Grant after he faced a disciplinary charge. The gist was McGowan had been alone with a child rapist who had mysteriously fallen down a flight of concrete steps. It had landed the suspect a serious head injury. The details of how and why it happened were distorted by station gossip and McGowan himself was silent on the issue.

Collins breezed in. 'You listening to those original interviews again? I bet you know every word off by heart, don't you. Wow, it's cold out there this morning.'

Collins flung her coat over the back of her chair. 'You lucky beggar getting to meet Travis. I bet he's as sinister as the media always made out. They say he's got it all – hooded eyes and a look to chill you to the bone.'

'No such luck for us. It's you and me on the paperwork today,' McGowan said. 'Yeah Delaney, looks like you're the chief's new favourite. Or maybe he just wants to see what you're made of.'

McGowan gave Tom a slap on the back which might have cracked the rib of a lesser being. Tom laughed. He was used to McGowan's double-edged comments and he hadn't been on the rugby squad for nothing. He knew how to deal with the testosterone-fuelled jostling for position and he was relieved the older man was secure enough not to be properly jealous of the new recruit.

Tom popped out an earbud. 'Don't worry, I'll fill you both in on the juicy details when I get back.'

McGowan dragged his finger across his throat. He wasn't smiling.

'You'd better,' Collins said.

Tom had a lot of admiration for Collins. With three teenage children and a full-time job, it was amazing she kept her good humour. Underneath her motherly exterior, she was above all a cunning detective. She could easily have gone further up the ranks, but she told Tom she wasn't interested in more responsibility. She liked her job the way it was.

Grant came into the cubbyhole wearing one of his pristine grey suits. There was no banter and no start of the day small talk, which meant he wasn't in a good mood. Tom exchanged a glance with Collins.

She went to stand in Grant's doorway. 'Hello sir,' she said. 'Ready for the big one?'

Tom placed a mug of tea on Grant's desk. 'Today's the day then, boss.'

Grant gave Tom a sharp look. So sharp it made Tom's insides contract. It reminded him why Grant was feared by his enemies.

'I've been able to squeeze one interview out of the doctor,' Grant said, 'and I'm certainly not counting on a second. Which means, as you so rightly say, sergeant, today's the day. No cock ups.'

'Yes, boss.' Tom was relieved he'd not be saying much during the actual interview. Grant would take the lead.

Grant was swigging from his scalding-hot mug.

'McGowan and I will slug our way through the paperwork,' Collins said. 'Don't worry, sir, we'll have it down to half by the time you get back.'

'I wouldn't expect any less.'

Tom could see dark bags under the inspector's eyes. He didn't look in good shape. Had he slept? If Tom didn't know better, he'd say the boss looked like a man with several ghosts standing by his shoulder.

The inspector finished his tea.

'Let's get this show on the road. Why don't you drive, Delaney.'

As soon as he entered the hospital room, Tom could smell something unpleasant. It took him a moment to accept the stink was coming from the man on the bed. It was the convict's rank body odour.

Travis lay stretched out and his large bare feet poked out from under the sheet. Travis was near bald, his cheeks were sunken and his face had an ashen pallor. It was shocking. The illness must have been sucking the life out of him.

Before they entered the room, Doctor Hawthorne had taken Grant aside and told him the treatment had been more complicated than she expected. They'd encountered medical difficulties and Travis was exhausted by the session.

'You'll have to keep it as brief as possible,' she said. 'I can only allow you a few minutes maximum.'

Tom pulled up a chair, making sure he stayed out of the way. Grant would want to fill Travis' line of vision.

It was difficult to believe the man in the bed had been capable of multiple murders. Air rattled in and out of his chest and he was so gaunt, his bones stuck out. It made his six months' life expectancy seem optimistic.

Travis was handcuffed to only one prison officer, and flanked by another. Tom was a big guy and not easily intimidated, but he still felt one or two twinges of anxiety. This was a public facility. Wasn't Travis supposed to be cuffed to both officers at all times?

Travis didn't respond to them entering the room. His eyes were bloodshot and unfocused.

When he finally recognised Grant, Travis pulled his lips back in a sneer. He lifted his head slightly as if to protest before flopping it back on the pillow.

Inspector Grant introduced himself as if he and Travis had never met. He explained this was an informal interview and asked if Travis objected to them recording it.

'I'd like to ask questions about the two missing women.' Grant held up pictures of Meredith and Isabella. Though he positioned them in front of Travis' face, the man seemed not to notice.

'I have a new witness. She places you with Isabella the day of her disappearance. I've pieced together Isabella's movements that day, minute by minute. In fact, the testimony of my witness shows you were the last person to be seen with the victim.' Grant's voice was cold and clipped. 'You murdered her and we both know it. You murdered Meredith too.'

Travis fought for breath, yet he appeared unrattled and undisturbed, coiled like a snake with two red eyes fixed unblinking on Grant.

Tom watched carefully. The files detailed how this man was a master at deception. Twenty-five years earlier, the police had floundered. They had no idea who the killer might be. Forensic technology then wasn't what it was today, and detectives relied on interviews with witnesses and potential suspects to narrow down the field. It had been a fraught time, with the media and the public whipped into more and more of a frenzy as the bodies mounted up. Young women had been virtually housebound by fear.

'Is it comfortable at the prison hospital? I had an interesting talk with the warden yesterday. He reminded me how they kept you separate from other prisoners for years. In fact, it's the longest he's known for someone to remain in isolation for their own safety. Strange how inmates can react to another prisoner, isn't it. Being alone for that length of time must have taken a terrible mental toll on you.'

The prison officer cuffed to Travis jerked the metal cuff.

'Pay attention, Travis. The inspector's got questions for you.'

'Don't worry, officer. I'm sure I have his full attention. After all, if it became known we have new information linking him to Isabella, well, who knows if it would be enough to reignite the other inmates.'

Travis' red-veined eyes stayed fixed on Grant. They were cold and reptilian. This man was an animal and he hadn't changed. Travis was extremely ill, yet Tom could feel the power rolling off him. His stare was hypnotic. It was as if Travis was laughing inside – laughing at Grant, laughing at the parents of the dead girls.

'Despite the warden's best efforts, I understand one prisoner ends up in intensive care most years, from beatings or gang rape. Isolation is the only remedy.'

Grant looked at the picture of Isabella. 'Such a pretty young woman and she has a lovely smile. I think it's those blue eyes which are so appealing. I'd say she could be everybody's image of their ideal girl friend. What do you think?'

Travis said nothing, gave no reaction, and still his face and eyes seemed to be communicating. Was he winding them up? Was he being true to form, and acting like they said in the reports, by being a son of a bitch? No wonder Grant hadn't brought McGowan. McGowan would likely have planted his fist in Travis' face, given half the chance.

Tom marvelled at the inspector's patience.

'All I want to know is where to find their bodies.'

'You've asked me before.'

Like on the tapes, he spoke with a drawl and his lips barely moved.

'Is that all you've got to say, Inspector? What's the matter, you lost your touch?'

'I'll ask you one more time. Where did you put them?'

Grant folded his hands in his lap.

Tom sat listening to Travis' breathing.

Travis had come up on the radar after the first murder but not as a major suspect. He'd come up again on the third murder but the police only had some strange comments in his interrogation to raise suspicions.

It was those comments which convinced the young detective David Grant that Travis was linked to the crimes. He believed Travis was purposely taunting the officers and trying to obscure their judgement. Psychology wasn't highly regarded in those days but it seemed Grant had an instinct for it. Fortunately, Grant's senior officer gave him the benefit of the doubt and from that one small suspicion, Grant slowly and painstakingly pieced together a trail of clues.

After the fourth murder, Grant was able to convince the team Travis was their man. Grant was given free rein and he became the brains behind the operation. Travis was caught due to brilliant detective work by the newbie Grant. Tom sincerely hoped he'd be up to the same standard, he really did.

'Those young women fell within your catchment area. They fell within the timescale before your final arrest. And they went missing where you were most active.'

'You always thought you were so clever,' Travis rasped. 'Strutting around like a peacock. You were a sorry excuse for a detective then and you still are now.'

'I believe you did murder them, Travis.'

In the past, the care with which Travis treated each crime scene meant he was highly intelligent and scheming. He had led the original investigative team on a dance and seemed to extract pleasure by dropping hints about his activities. Playing with the police was as much a game to him as selecting and murdering his victims.

Tom was waiting for Travis to do the same thing. He wanted him to drop an enigmatic comment or two or make a sly remark.

Grant showed photographs of the last known locations of the women.

'Seem familiar?' he said.

In his smooth and even voice, Grant proposed a theory on how Travis had chosen each woman, how he stalked them and plotted their movements over the weeks before their deaths, just as he had with his other victims.

'Those women always meant something to you, didn't they, Inspector? How quaint.'

'You and I have played games for long enough. Make your confession while you can, or are you really prepared to spend your last days alone?'

Travis took a few rattling breaths.

'Have you any idea how exhausting these treatments are? Chemo, radiotherapy, endless punctures and tests, I've had the lot. Makes you sick as a dog. Isabella had beautiful blonde hair. She never wore it down. Except when she was strangled. Whereas Meredith, I couldn't tell you a thing about her.'

'Were they your first two?'

Travis coughed but there was no nurse at hand to offer water. Tom and the two prisoner officers stared at Travis with dislike and it was Grant who reached for the jug to pour out a beaker.

'Sorry, Inspector, the prisoner is only allowed to be offered assistance by hospital staff and you are strictly forbidden to make physical contact,' one of the prison officers said.

'Is that why you didn't flaunt about killing them when we arrested you? Because you used them to learn how to murder?? Is that why you didn't confess?'

Travis took tiny sips and swallowed with difficulty. 'Does everyone still think you're a hero?'

It was so unexpected and said so softly, Tom wasn't sure he heard it right.

Travis rolled his gaze over to the sergeant. 'I see no one's worked out the truth yet.'

Tom's muscles went solid, partly from the shock of looking into Travis' eyes and partly from the realisation Travis was lobbing shit in Grant's direction. How dare he. Grant had been brilliant.

'Come now, sergeant. You shouldn't believe everything you're told.'

Travis rolled his head back in Grant's direction. 'It's smart how you've covered up your mistakes.'

Then Travis made a strange sound, his chest jerking up and down. Tom stared. It was a very sick man's attempt at laughter.

'Cut that out Travis,' one of the officers said.

'This might be your last chance to set the record straight.' Grant sounded icily calm.

Travis pulled back his lips in a sneer. 'Reflect on your failings, Inspector Grant.'

Tom had to stop himself from reacting. Beneath the man's pain and his exhaustion and the ravages of his disease he was enjoying himself. He was enjoying Grant coming to talk to him. He was enjoying the efforts Grant was making. Of course, Tom thought, they had played a deadly game in the past and Grant had won. This was Travis' way of punishing Grant. His only way of getting his own back. Tom understood Travis had always and would forever withhold details of Meredith and Isabella for that one and only reason. To make Grant suffer. And he was attempting to dirty the inspector's reputation in whatever way he could by flinging out insinuations.

Travis fought for breath. When he managed to draw enough strength, he smiled at the inspector. All Tom's detective's principles and reasoning fell away. He suddenly loathed the man.

'I'll see you in hell,' Travis said.

Chapter Five

I can't tell you how wonderful it is to feel alive again.

The need has been like a hunger inside me. A hunger which eats at me and burns and flares white hot. And now it demands to be satisfied, like a beast. Oh yes, it shall have its fill. Today is the big day.

The hospital has assembled a select team – nurses, technicians and one doctor as physician in charge. They move around the hospital bed with practised professionalism, making a lot of eye contact with each other and I suppose it's for reassurance. Their fingers work the equipment. Gloved hands touch the patient's skin. There are needles, tubes, injections, monitoring.

I watch my chosen victim, nurse Mandy Jones. Her neat blue uniform is smartly zipped to the top. I wonder if she always takes it up so high, or is it especially for today? She's wearing sensible shoes and flesh-coloured tights. Her auburn hair is tied back in a ponytail which swings as she moves. I always did like young women with auburn hair, though appearance has never dictated my choices.

I've always been much more led by opportunity.

I bide my time. If I am to avoid detection, I must choose my moment to strike with care.

Chapter Six

The sergeant at the main desk, Wilson, had a box full of tinsel. He was taking the chance of a quiet moment to hang some Christmas cheer around the reception area, when David Grant and Tom Delaney returned to the station.

'How'd it go with that bastard Travis?' Wilson asked.

Grant kept walking. He was never a man to give much away and certainly not to Sergeant Wilson, the mainstay of the gossip tree.

'Okay,' Tom said.

'You know how to keep a man begging for details, don't you, Sergeant Delaney.'

At the cubbyhole, Grant told McGowan and Collins to gather round.

'You recorded the whole conversation?' Grant asked.

'Yes, boss.'

'Then let's watch it through again and see if we missed anything. Also, Delaney, I want you to become an expert on Travis. Study the man. Listen to all the tapes, watch the videos, until you know every detail of how he operates.'

'It was strange because he hardly spoke. But he was able to stir me up.'

'It's one of the traits of a psychopath, and don't forget Travis is a master at mind games. It's what he did to the whole investigating team. Everyone so loathed him we could hardly think straight.'

'He made me angry, even furious. He was laughing at us.'

Grant nodded. 'Anything else, sergeant?'

McGowan and Collins were hanging on every word.

'It seemed to me he got a rise out of stringing you along, boss and er, from making insinuations about you. He suggested you made some kind of mistake, didn't he. I suppose he means with the original investigation.'

Grant grunted. Tom Delaney had a nose for the job and he didn't even know how good he was. And he wasn't scared to say it like it was. He'd been right to bring Delaney into the team. He had the makings of a fine detective. Maybe one of the best.

'It's a good job I wasn't there,' McGowan said. 'I might have been tempted to–'

'Yes, it's a good thing you weren't there, sergeant,' Grant said.

He hung his coat over the back of his chair. Glory was what appealed to Travis in the past. Glory and recognition and national press coverage. The media interest had been fuelled by the nation's hatred but it had been perceived by Travis as a strange type of adoration. Yet Travis already lived all of it for the murders he'd been convicted for.

The problem being he had no lever to put pressure on Travis for this final confession. And Travis realised he could use withholding information on Meredith and Isabella as a method of punishing the man who put him away.

A dog-eared copy of Professor Caprini's research lay on Grant's desk. He had passed a second copy around the team. Delaney, predictably, had listened to every word online, probably several times. Very likely he knew the section on Travis off by heart. Collins had read it and McGowan had used it as a coffee mat.

Grant picked up the report. Criminal psychologists always had interesting things to say. Not always things which were right, or which fitted in with how a detective was trained to think, but nevertheless, it gave another angle.

Professor Caprini had delved into the early life of Travis. Might he know something? Might the professor have a nugget of information about Travis which could prove useful? Which might turn into a lever? Grant was hoping so. Professor Caprini had an uncanny insight into the minds of killers, that was for sure. His writing proved it and Grant was looking forward to pumping him for information.

'The video's ready, boss,' Delaney said.

Grant brought his screen to life and flicked through a list of emails, ignoring an urgent one from Detective Chief Superintendent Angela Fox asking for an update on Travis. Three envelopes lay in Grant's in-tray and he ripped open the first two and shoved the letters to the bottom of a teetering pile. When it finally fell over, he'd deal with it, most likely binning half of them as being out of date or no longer relevant.

That left the third envelope. Call it instinct or intuition, Grant hesitated before he touched it. It was perfectly ordinary looking, made of brown recycled paper, with a local postmark. This one he slit carefully with the letter opener. He tipped it, making sure not to touch the contents. Out slid a photograph.

It wasn't an ordinary shot taken in daytime. It looked like a night-time photograph of a house and it must have been taken with special equipment or some sort of filter.

Collins was the one with the best vantage point looking into Grant's office.

'You ready for this video, sir?'

When he didn't answer, she came to the other side of his desk.

'It looks like it was taken with infra-red technology or something like that,' she said. 'Or maybe with a specialised lens. Do you know the house?'

Grant noticed how Collins didn't reach out to inspect the

writing on the envelope. Collins had worked with him for the best part of ten years. Like him, she knew the signs. This was strange, this was important, and she didn't want to add her contamination.

Grant felt his pulse accelerating. He hadn't spent decades on the job to not recognise a bad omen when he saw one.

'DS Collins, please put gloves on, and get this straight over to the lab. I want to know all there is to know about it.'

'Yes, sir.'

Coming from the corridor, came the sounds of someone running towards the cubbyhole, followed by the thud of them tripping over McGowan's cycle gear.

'Who the hell put that shit–' Sergeant Wilson crashed through to the team office.

'Inspector Grant, sir, we just got a call from patrol.' Wilson was out of breath. 'They found a body. There's been a murder at the hospital.'

Chapter Seven

When they arrived at the hospital, the first thing they learned was the body had been found on the third floor. That was Doctor Hawthorne's cancer treatment area. Grant saw Delaney jerk.

An early response patrol officer was stationed at the entrance to the corridor.

'Tell me your name and give me an update, please,' Grant said.

'Constable Karen Smith, sir. The body is down the corridor , sir. It's in a supplies cupboard. We've been unable to isolate this corridor completely because there are patients undergoing essential treatment and the equipment they require can't be moved. But the supplies cupboard is secure.'

'Do we have a name for the victim?'

'She's been identified as Mandy Jones.' The officer consulted her notes. 'She's a nurse on this ward. Found by one of her colleagues. Been missing for around an hour before she was discovered.'

'Good work.'

'All hell broke loose when she was found, Inspector. Apparently it triggered some kind of mass hysteria amongst the staff. We've got a bunch of them in a room down the hallway. They're pretty shaken up.'

'That's to be expected. For your information only, a convicted killer, Travis, was on the premises this morning. Has any word of the murder leaked out to the public?'

'Not as far as I'm aware. We've tried to keep it under wraps. Patients are being led in and out of treatment rooms via a service stairwell and secondary corridor.'

'Well done, constable.' Further along the corridor, a second officer and a line of tape cut off the room where the victim had been discovered. Grant led the way. The patrol officer was averting his face from the body on the floor. The first thing Grant saw was Mandy Jones' toe-nails which were painted a pretty pink.

'Collins, please go to meet the person who found the body and see what she has to say. After that I want to know everything there is to know about our victim,' Grant said.

Of average height and weight and with auburn hair, Mandy Jones looked to be thirty-something. Her uniform had been pushed up to her waist. Her knees were twisted to the side to fit the body into the corner behind a stack of boxes.

Grant knelt and visually examined the woman's neck. She'd been strangled with a pair of tights, most likely her own, the same modus operandi as the South Coast Killer. Grant felt a cold shiver run up his back.

He took his time and did not allow himself to speculate. He was here for the facts and it was important to take in the scene as it had been freshly left.

Mandy Jones would have been nice looking alive, but the means of death had contorted her face. Her tongue was swollen and protruded and her eyes bulged. She wore a wedding ring. A trail of urine ran across the floor.

The room was lined with neatly labelled shelves. Nothing had fallen from them and not many of the boxes stacked on the floor had been disturbed either. It meant there had been a bit of a struggle but not much of one. Which was curious.

It looked as if she might have come here willingly and entered the supplies room not expecting trouble. With so many people on the ward, it would have been difficult to drag the nurse here without anyone seeing and she would have put up more of a fight to stay out of the confined space. Did it mean she freely came there with another person? Or had she been lured there? Or ambushed?

His mind kept going to Travis but jumping to conclusions at a crime scene was entirely wrong.

'We've got to cover all bases before the shit hits the fan. McGowan, I want you to check with the prison. Get the prison officers in for interview. You and Delaney see them separately. Find out if there were any windows of opportunity. Look for anything which seems off. Do full background checks on them. I want to know why they weren't both cuffed to Travis when Delaney and I interviewed him. Find out who Travis spends time with inside. And if anyone has been recently paroled.'

'Right, sir, onto it.'

Grant spoke over his shoulder to thin air. 'Any other witnesses, anything unusual reported by the hospital staff?'

The patrol officer spoke up. 'The nurse was on the treatment team for a man named Travis. The victim was noticed missing but colleagues assumed she was in the ladies toilet, or they assumed she might have found dealing with Travis too much to handle and taken herself off. She was discovered by accident when the other nurse came to get supplies.'

'Anyone else reported missing?'

'No, sir.'

'You're absolutely certain? You already checked on it?'

'Yes, sir.'

The pathologist, Luke Sanderson, arrived. Everyone cleared a space. Grant had punched through a text to Luke, hoping he'd be able to drop everything for this one. It seemed he had.

Luke didn't bother with pleasantries. He nodded to the inspector and began examining the body.

'Thanks for getting here so quickly, Luke,' Grant said.

He always used the pathologist's first name. The pair had been firm friends ever since Grant had caught a couple of officers snickering about the idea of the new pathologist being gay. Luke's predecessor had been one of Grant's oldest and most trusted colleagues and Grant had not been looking forward to a young replacement himself. But quite a lot of station jokes irked Grant, including the ones about sexuality. And Grant had made that clear. Afterwards, when Luke finally arrived, they naturally hit it off, which had been an unexpected bonus.

They both knew the time of death would be crucial.

'Delaney, make sure we keep all staff from this floor for questioning,' Grant said. 'Don't let anyone go home. As a priority, I want to see everyone from the team who treated Travis.'

'Let me through. I said, let me through!'

Grant gave a nod and Doctor Hawthorne was allowed to enter the corridor. She ran, her hospital coat flapping. Grant could see the whites of her eyes. It would take a lot to shake the doctor because she was used to remaining calm in panic situations.

'I got the news and I was caught in an emergency. I couldn't get away any quicker. Oh my god!'

'That's far enough. You can't cross the line, doctor. This is a crime scene,' he said evenly.

'They said it's Mandy. It can't be!'

'She's already been positively identified. Please stay calm, Doctor Hawthorne,' Grant said.

No one else said anything. It was best to let people absorb the shock in their own way. You could never predict how people reacted to the initial impact. Grant watched Dr Hawthorne carefully. It seemed she was about to vomit.

'Inspector, how can he have done it!'

Grant found a receptacle and pushed it into her hands.

'We can't draw any conclusions,' he said firmly. 'The

proximity of Travis to this crime is one factor amongst many.'

'But... but surely it must have been him!'

One look at Grant's expression stopped the doctor's protests.

Susan Hawthorne shook her head, as if she was trying to shake some sense into herself.

It was disbelief and denial, he had seen it many times before.

'We need to collect as much information as we can about Mandy Jones,' Grant said. 'Can you help us with that, doctor? And we need statements from all staff on this floor.'

'Wait. We were assured he was low-risk, Inspector. You promised me! You promised me my staff would be safe.'

Whatever assurances Hawthorne had received, they hadn't come from him. But Grant didn't bother to remind her.

The Hospital Manager arrived. He was pale and his tie was askew. He stayed well back from the yellow and black cut-off point. Grant thought he could see the man shaking.

'I told you! I said we should never have allowed him here.'

Doctor Hawthorne shrank back against the wall. 'Tony... I-I had a duty of care.'

'Our primary duty is to our regular patients and to staff. And now Mandy Jones is dead!'

The doctor started crying.

'That's enough, Mr Tanner. Recriminations won't achieve anything.'

'And you, Inspector, you encouraged her. The doctor trusted you.'

Grant motioned for Delaney to take Susan Hawthorne someplace else.

'This is a murder, plain and simple and as yet, we have not identified a suspect,' Grant said. 'No one could have foreseen this.'

'Are you stupid as well as arrogant? Of course it was him!'

'Calm down, Mr Tanner. This is my jurisdiction now and I understand how emotions are running high. Let us do our job. My sergeant will take your statement later, thank you. Why don't you go and get some fresh air?'

Tanner straightened his jacket and tie. He retreated, a little unsteady on his feet. When he reached the end, he took a glance back but his accusing gaze didn't quite make it to Grant's eyes.

Grant walked back to the supplies room. Luke was standing up slowly. He had finished his preliminary investigation. Now it would be photographs and swabs and it would all depend on analysis back at the lab.

Never jump to conclusions was a detective's number one rule. It was impossible for Travis to have carried out the murder. Or was it? He was a clever man. In the past, he'd been inspired in escaping his crimes.

Everyone did their level best not to crowd the pathologist. It seemed Travis had left the hospital two hours previously.

'What's your estimate on time of death?' Grant asked.

Luke peeled off his gloves and the rubber snapped as he tugged them over his wrists. It was unfortunate but, as he waited, Grant could smell Mandy Jones' urine.

'Within the last four hours,' Luke said.

The pathologist's words were measured and fell like a lead weight.

It put Travis squarely in the window of opportunity.

Chapter Eight

By the time Detective Inspector David Grant left the hospital, he had interviewed everyone who had direct contact with Travis, and his team had taken statements from staff on the third floor.

According to her colleagues, Mandy Jones was a young woman who led an ordinary life. She and her husband had recently bought their first house. She was happily married and trying for children. There were no rumours of an affair, or a problem marriage, or any financial difficulties.

Mandy's husband was an accountant. He arrived at the hospital before Luke got Mandy into a body bag. It was unfortunate for the poor man but it gave Grant a chance to see his first reaction.

The husband was distraught. One of the uniformed officers had to accompany him home and Grant sent Collins along too. Collins was superb with victims and terrific with upset witnesses. She was also a savvy detective.

It was a cliché the husband was always a prime suspect, but it was also the truth. Grant could rely on Collins to nose out any discrepancies in the husband's behaviour.

Whoever murdered Mandy Jones had been clever and no one saw a thing. It had been planned. The murderer had picked a little-used storeroom at the end of a corridor. The room was the back-up storage for the smaller supply cupboard kept on the main ward. The killer knew these facts. They knew it was unlikely they would be interrupted. Mandy Jones hadn't stood a chance.

He had a decent picture of the victim. What he didn't have yet was any idea why she'd been targeted. And why now? Find the motive and he would find the killer.

David Grant was the last to leave.

He had a nasty feeling in the pit of his stomach which wasn't anything to do with hunger. He hoped it wasn't anything to do with stomach ulcers either, which his wife and adult children kept warning him about.

He also hoped it was nothing to do with déjà vu and some kind of horrible link to the previous Travis crimes. It was difficult to think clearly because of how close Travis had been to the murder. Grant's mind kept linking the two together and the strangulation only emphasised it. But then a second killer, not Travis, would know that. They could use it as a smokescreen. The number one priority for Grant's team must be to eliminate Travis from the list of suspects. Then they would be able to concentrate on finding the real killer.

Starting the engine, he tried to ignore the little voice in his head, which kept saying, "But what if it was him?"

Detective Chief Superintendent Fox was demanding to see him. When this hit the press, it would explode big time and nothing he nor his superintendent could do would stop it. They were living on borrowed time. But there was something he had to do first.

Grant pulled in next to the local primary school. Decorations were up in the windows – giant elves and gold Christmas angels. He stepped out and quickly buttoned his coat and turned up the collar. Children were screaming and laughing in the playground, all dressed up in mittens, hats and scarves.

Meredith's sister, Carys Evans, lived in a bungalow on a quieter side street. Carys had a garden full of wintering rose bushes. Unlike the most of the houses in the road, she hadn't put out Christmas decorations.

On the doorstep, Carys blinked several times. Grant thought she swayed slightly at the shock of seeing him. He was careful not to rush her and he complimented her on the garden and then mentioned the snow forecast. By then, Carys had got herself back to normal and said how lovely it was to see him. It was a lie. The Evans family had always been so courteous. It was one of the things which felt like it turned the knife.

Sure enough, he was invited in as a welcome guest. Grant sat on the settee in a lounge full of bowls of old rose petals. They'd long since stopped giving off any fragrance and the musty smell reminded Grant of a funeral parlour. Carys pottered in the kitchen and Grant heard cups and saucers clinking onto a tray.

A while later, Carys was sitting in an armchair alongside him. She checked the contents of a teapot, wrinkling her nose as she peered inside.

'That monster was the one to blame for my sister, David, not you. And if he's killed again…' she gave a visible shudder, '…words fail me.'

The living room clock was ticking in the background. Then came the sound of tea pouring into his cup. It was true, Carys Evans never blamed Grant for the loss of her sister. Only she didn't need to blame him because Grant blamed himself.

'As I said, we don't have an idea yet who is responsible for the death at the hospital. But I thought it fair to warn you because I didn't want you hearing about it through the press.'

The parents of the Evans sisters had died a few years previously. He remembered their funerals and the deep regret he felt about not being able to bring them peace. Or was it more guilt than regret? Since then, Carys kept in touch. He tried to avoid meeting her too often.

The scent of earl grey tea wafted towards him. She was

always so full of politeness, just like her parents, who offered him tea and biscuits while their hands shook and their eyes filled with tears. They hadn't blamed him either.

'I hope you've let Isabella's parents know.'

Isabella Rees' parents had moved away from the area. Grant had already contacted the Devon police force to ask for an officer to visit Mr and Mrs Rees and break the news of the murder.

Carys arranged chocolate biscuits on a little plate and her façade slipped a little as she offered him one.

'He took my sister. He ruined my life. My brother went off the rails and then emigrated and we never heard from him again, my parents died without peace. Is the same thing going to happen to me? And Mr and Mrs Rees, what about them? Are they going to die never knowing? You don't know what it's like trying to carry on a life when...'

'Calm yourself, Carys.'

He reached forward and patted her hand. The same age as himself, Carys seemed so much older. She wore a dress for someone ten years her senior. She lived the life of a widow though she had never married. She was bereft, always waiting for the return of her sister.

'I'm so sorry, I didn't mean to... It was your terrible news, it's brought it all back.'

'I understand, I really do, and that's why I wanted to see you before you heard it from somebody else.'

'I know you did everything you could. You mustn't take it on yourself like you do.'

This was torture. Every senior officer he knew had regrets. Secret doubts about how they'd conducted an investigation. Or questions about the route they'd followed and how long it took. The choices they'd taken as the one in charge. The mistakes they'd made and the lives it cost.

Funny how the mind always strayed to it, rather than to the

successes. He supposed that was why he always carried such a terrible regret about Meredith and Isabella.

He took a biscuit and made a semblance of munching on a corner.

'I suppose you've had no news of your brother?'

Meredith's sister plunked two spoons of sugar into Grant's tea.

'Is it still two sugars you take? So bad for your health, you really should cut down.' She shook her head. 'There's been nothing from Edwyn. Not a word in twenty-five years.'

Edwyn Evans had disappeared without a trace, seemingly to Australia. The enquiries Grant made over the years had all come back blank. And yet he'd always had a small suspicion.

Carys' hazel eyes were fixed on the teapot.

'I'm sorry I can't stay longer, I really should get back to the station.'

'Of course, you mustn't let me keep you.'

She clutched a lace handkerchief in her lap and his heart twisted, knowing she would cry once he left.

Detective Chief Superintendent Fox sent Grant another urgent text and he knew, if he didn't get himself to Fox's office soon, he'd be in for more than a wrist-slapping. Fox was insecure, ambitious, and she didn't like to be kept waiting.

Grant was on his way back, when the night-time photograph suddenly popped into his mind. It gave him another nasty feeling in the pit of his stomach. Grant did a U-turn and drove straight to Mandy Jones' address. He sincerely hoped his guess was going to turn out to be wrong.

Pulling up outside a neat two-storey house, he cut the engine. It was a nice district. The houses in this road had their own garage and a driveway out the front.

There were two cars crammed into Mandy's drive. One of them must be the officer from victim support and another was a patrol car, which meant they were all still inside with the husband.

True to form, his technology-savvy Sergeant Delaney had already sent through a copy of the night-time photograph. Grant held up his phone.

The driveway Grant looked at had the same angle as the one on his screen. The line of bushes running along the side of the drive had the same shapes. A cold prickle ran down his arms.

The houses on this stretch were all pretty similar. He must make absolutely sure.

He looked up at the roofs. The neighbour's television aerial was identical to the one on his phone. And the same treetop showed above the roof line.

Grant's stomach dropped and he was glad he hadn't stopped by somewhere for a burger. It was the same bloody house.

Chapter Nine

Professor Caprini's office was tucked away in a quiet building at the back of the university campus, well away from the busier teaching blocks. It was plush and secluded and had its own dedicated parking space, which made Tom wonder if Caprini had the best office in the whole University. The professor was certainly treated as a VIP.

As they entered, Tom caught the mouth-watering aroma of real coffee, followed by the sight of an expensive tray of pastries. The professor invited Grant and Tom to take a leather sofa and offered them refreshments. Tom couldn't help comparing this set-up to the box-like cubicle they shared back at the station. This was the life. Criminal psychology must pay much better than police work.

Tom chose a brownie and took a deep breath of chocolate as he bit into it. He noticed how Inspector Grant helped himself to a brownie and a doughnut. His efforts to educate the boss on sugar overload had obviously been ignored.

Professor Caprini sat on a giant leather armchair. He was bird-like in appearance, wearing a dark suit which hung over a scrawny frame. His long legs and long fingers added to the effect.

A young woman entered. She softly closed the door behind her, and Tom's eyes followed her as she walked across the room. He couldn't help himself – she was athletic and wore a short skirt for a start. And she had dark attractive eyes and long lashes and dark hair swept back from her face, with a few wisps trailing down her temple. Her hair was slightly curly and it bounced as she walked. Without speaking, she pulled up a chair beside Caprini and opened her laptop.

The woman had a reserved air about her, almost shy. She'd barely glanced at them.

'This is my research assistant, Ruby Silver,' Caprini said. 'The other research assistant who helped me on this project, Mark Winslow, is no longer here. He recently got a job with New Scotland Yard.'

The man tended to run his words together. It almost sounded as if the professor slurred a little. Surely he hadn't been drinking?

Tom sat back, ready to memorise every word of his boss' tactics, for future reference.

'Thank you for bringing our meeting forward, Professor. I know I didn't give you much notice,' Grant said. 'I've long been an admirer of your work and your recent report on serial killers made fascinating reading. It's cutting edge.' He glanced at Ruby, waiting for her to react. What a strange young woman. And so quiet, as if she tried to hide the fact she was in the room. She hadn't even introduced herself. Ruby's eyes remained glued to her keyboard.

'Inspector, you're very kind,' Caprini said, accepting Grant's flattery with ease. 'Given the recent murder at the hospital, I'm willing to offer any assistance I can.'

'Our investigation is ongoing,' Grant said. 'As you can appreciate, I can't divulge any information today. As I said, your recent work was cutting edge regarding the mindset of killers. What I'm hoping for is some help on strategies and lines of attack for interviewing Mr Travis.'

At the mention of the name, for the first time, Ruby looked up and met Grant's eye. She had a direct gaze, he thought. Very likely, she was switched on regarding her work. And yet she was guarded.

'Travis has a terminal diagnosis and I intend to requestion him before it's too late. I want him to tell me about the women we never found. Any insight you can give on the man might help me get a breakthrough.'

Grant smiled at Caprini and at Ruby and then he took a huge bite of brownie.

Caprini's hands rested on his lap and he began tapping his fingers. He gave Ruby a sideways glance and indicated her laptop.

'You seem to have all our work at your fingertips, Ruby. Would you mind giving the inspector an overview?'

'Of course, Professor.'

Grant turned his full attention to Ruby. He liked her voice. It had a musical quality to it. And she had a quiet air of mystery, which made her intriguing.

'I'm looking forward to what you have to tell us, Ms Silver.'

They talked for almost two hours. Ruby was thorough. First, she went through Travis' early life. She told them about his family and about the people and events which influenced him as a child. Then she listed the special characteristics of his mind which made him a psychopath and how these had been formed and developed by his upbringing. Ruby gave explanations as to how his impulses impacted his need to kill. She used plenty of examples from the interview Professor Caprini had carried out with Travis. Every time she used an example, it was detailed and specific to the point she wanted to illustrate.

Ruby Silver clearly knew Travis in depth and Grant was impressed. He was also impressed by how she drew insights. And he noticed how she was careful to always refer back to the research, as if she was hypersensitive to not stepping on the professor's toes.

Then Ruby compared Travis to the other killers in the professor's report, defining his similarities and his differences. It wasn't only Travis she knew inside out, she knew the whole of the work by heart.

Professor Caprini wasn't modest about joining in. After each of Ruby's points, he repeated what she'd said over again, as if they might not have understood the first time. It had the effect of always drawing attention and credit to him. It was Caprini who stood out and Ruby was the minion. But Grant wasn't fooled.

A little suspicion formed in his mind. Who had been doing all the work? Who had really written the cutting-edge report? Grant felt certain it had been Ruby Silver and not Caprini. How else had she been able to quote from the interviews with such precision? And the professor had not added one bit of new information, in all the comments he'd made.

What Grant wondered at was why Ruby allowed herself to be used like that. It meant Caprini had been manipulative to be able to get a hold over her. But then wouldn't the country's top criminal psychologist naturally be a master manipulator? A man used to the limelight would do whatever necessary to keep his own name at the top of the list.

By the time they stood to leave, Grant had made a decision. He wanted to bring Ruby in on the team. She had expertise he wanted. Expertise which might prove vital in cracking this case. A couple of hours wasn't enough, no, he wanted her live contribution as the case evolved. And he knew how he would go about getting what he wanted, after all, Caprini wasn't the only one who knew how to be manipulative.

The professor's desk was huge. A fancy glass plaque sat to one side. It was probably some prestigious award. As they walked to the door, Grant admired the plaque, then as he continued on his way, he allowed the end of his coat, draped over his arm, to brush the plaque to the edge of the desk.

Caprini lunged to stop it falling. He had quick reflexes, beating Delaney, who leapt forward from several paces behind.

'I'm so sorry, how clumsy of me,' Grant said. 'I really must apologise.'

'No harm done,' Caprini said, tightly.

'Oh yes, another thought occurred to me. I was wondering, given your expertise on Travis, if I might invite you to join my team back at Himlands Heath? Only for this investigation, of course. It really would be a great help.'

It was an old and effective tactic – spring a last-minute surprise just as your target thinks they're rid of you. It was one of his favourites.

Caprini floundered for an excuse.

'That's not possible, Inspector. I have commitments here at the university, not to mention my international obligations. I simply don't have time in my schedule.'

'Of course, of course. Then perhaps you might be kind enough to lend me your assistant.'

He was careful to not use her name and not give her any importance, as if he was asking Caprini to lend him a book. In the mirror facing him, he caught the excitement on Ruby's face and saw how it was quickly chased away by a terrible shadow of sadness. The sadness was so private, it made him uncomfortable to have seen it.

Caprini had his back to the mirror and hadn't noticed anything.

'Co-operating with ongoing investigations has always been one of the university's priorities except I don't think…'

'We really could do with all the assistance we can get. I'm sure the Detective Chief Superintendent would agree with me – the media will be all over this case once they get hold of it.'

Grant let the idea percolate around Caprini's head. Of course, the professor would be interested in as much attention and name-spreading as he could get. Being involved in such a high-profile case wouldn't be something the professor could resist. The natural step would be to send Ruby. He couldn't get involved himself because Grant was pretty certain she was the one who wrote that damn report. Being on the ground like that would threaten to expose him.

Caprini laid a claw-like hand on Ruby's shoulder. Grant resisted the urge to shove it off.

'If you'd agree, Ruby?' Caprini said, in a paternal tone which set Grant's teeth on edge. 'I can be on the end of a phone at any time. When you're out of your depth and need help, all you need do is ask. I'm right here.'

Ruby was smiling for the first time and not at Caprini.

'Detective Inspector Grant,' she said. 'I'd love to join you.'

On the drive back, Grant wasn't the only one who was happy.

'You're in a good mood, Delancy. Is it anything to do with Ruby Silver?'

'Of course not.' Tom blushed and concentrated on the road.

Grant chuckled. 'Did you notice anything unusual about the professor?'

'Other than he's got a great set-up and he thinks a lot of himself? Not really. His hands seemed to shake a lot of the time.'

'Exactly. Did you see how he held them in his lap to make it less obvious? And if I'm not mistaken, he slightly slurred his words. If you ask me, the professor is suffering from an illness. Perhaps Parkinson's since his motor abilities don't seem to be affected.'

'That's why you pushed his posh plaque? I wondered what was going on. Doesn't Parkinson's affect thinking ability?'

'It does. Which is why I suspect Ms Ruby Silver will turn out to be the real brains at Caprini's end.'

'Yes sir.'

Grant smiled to himself. It definitely looked as if he wasn't the only one who liked the idea of Ruby Silver joining them.

Chapter Ten

I wish I'd seen the look of horror on his face. The look of dread as he realised history was repeating itself.

Did the great Detective Inspector Grant shit his pants? Or hasn't he realised yet?

It's cold and dark out here. December is getting colder as the days go by. A chill dampness seeps through the seat of my trousers as I keep myself low amongst the ornamental shrubbery. The shadows are deep and streetlights don't penetrate to my hiding place. It's lucky for me how people find it important to live in nice decorated surroundings. How they enjoy beautifying their driveways and their communal spaces. How they've spent money on tall grasses and bushes and other shit like that where someone like me can crouch unseen.

I'm at the back of the house. My next victim is in her bedroom. It's up on the top floor, directly in front of me, and there are no obstacles to my view, though it's some distance away.

She crosses the room again. Net curtains obscure the details but with my naked eye, I see the curves of her body, the shape of her breasts. She's slow and relaxed. What's she doing up there? Getting ready for a bath? Preparing herself for an evening of intimacy? She really shouldn't leave the light on like that. Anyone could be watching.

Preparation is the first key to success. That's what my

mentor said. I've had it drummed in to me.

I start setting up my equipment. Camera, lens, tripod. When will I send the next photograph? I'd like it to arrive like last time and give them a feeling of suspense. To give them an idea of impending doom and a ticking clock. And the fact they will be too damn late.

That's not as easy to organise as you might suppose. I can't use special delivery. It risks leaving a trail that could, however remote the possibility, lead back to me. No, I have to rely on the normal postal service. It's anonymous but also annoyingly plodding.

I've done my research. I know the postal delivery times at the police station. And I know how the desk sergeant greets the postwoman and exchanges a bit of banter before he even gives each day's deliveries his attention.

Sometimes he can let the pile sit on the side for up to fifteen minutes before he gets around to sorting it. Then again, I expect he'll learn to jump as soon as he sees one from me.

I lift my camera to get a good view of the rear of the house. I use infrared technology and it makes the window glow and I need to adjust the settings so it doesn't spoil the picture. After all, they've got to be able to recognise the place and I know the police are a tad on the stupid side.

The excitement is making me want to rush. It's almost making me want to piss my pants.

Just as she reaches to draw the curtains, I take my snaps. Perfect.

What could be better? Not just the victim's house but the next victim herself caught in the frame.

Chapter Eleven

Detective Sergeant Diane Collins was busy setting up the incident room. Grant had managed, as usual, to get one of the best ones. It was light and airy and big, with plenty of space for the four of them. Well, it would be the five of them with Ruby Silver.

Diane knew how Grant liked things done. He liked one huge whiteboard in the middle of the front wall for the victim. Diane started a map with the victim's name in the middle and lines linking to possible suspects. So far, the husband was the only name she could fill in and all the other lines leading out went to question marks. She pinned up photographs of Mandy Jones' body in the storeroom. Diane added up a headshot of the victim when she had been alive.

On another wall, a second whiteboard was devoted to Travis. Tom Delaney was adding details down the side about the prison officers and a list of paroled prisoners. Meanwhile, Diane began writing up a list of the five original victims and a map of where they'd each been found.

Meredith Evans and Isabella Rees had a board to themselves.

The night photograph of Mandy Jones' house was on fourth board on its own.

Each officer had a desk in the incident room and the technicians had linked up the technology. Diane put Ruby

Silver's place next to her own. Why shouldn't the two women club together? It would make a nice change having another female working with them.

Diane felt the adrenalin rush she always felt at the prospect of a long and difficult investigation. This was where it was all going to happen. This was where they would find Mandy's killer. And they would need refreshments. She picked up the phone to order in the first round of doughnuts.

Detective Chief Superintendent Angela Fox had a longish nose and auburn hair. David Grant often wondered why she didn't dye it another colour. Or change her name. It would have been worth it to avoid the station jokes. Not least to avoid the inevitable, myriad photographs of her tacked in secret places, such as the inside of lockers.

In those shots, her face was superimposed by the face of her namesake, or pointy ears had been added on, or the tail of a fox, or more likely pointed fox teeth. Dead chickens were a frequent feature. Often the faces of other officers had been added in place of the chicken's head, for instance an officer who she had recently reprimanded. Or someone whose head was due for the block. DCS Fox had a reputation for having a mean temper and a vicious bite.

Grant knocked on the door. In her three years at the station, Fox hadn't endeared herself to anyone, though she showed a grudging respect for Grant which he tried to return.

There was no pause to acknowledge his entry. No friendly greeting. She launched straight in.

'When I send a text, I expect a prompt reply.' Ice laced her words.

Grant took his time pulling out the chair. He caught a glint of teeth and tried not to think of the desk sergeant's most recent caricature of Fox standing over Grant's limp body with her mouth dripping blood.

'She's after you,' Sergeant Wilson had said. 'Good job you're in early. You'd better get yourself up there double sharp.'

Grant had come in at half six. He left Collins and Delaney setting up the incident room and plodded up the stairs. Under his wife's instructions, he wasn't supposed to be using the lift. That is, not if he wanted to have a Christmas full of mince pies and Christmas pudding and lots of helpings of turkey – which, of course, he did. Under that threat, Grant had complied to Lily's no-escalator rule, though he did it with bad grace.

He'd been wheezing by the time he got to the third floor.

'Please, David, don't tell me I need to send you for a cardio check-up,' Fox said.

'What good will it do? Just work me until I drop dead then my wife can collect the insurance.'

The Superintendent gave a malicious grin. 'If you say so. Now fill me in on the Jones murder. I've already got press interest and I need the facts.' She gave him a hard look. 'I don't like being kept in the dark.'

Their exchange was short and efficient. Fox was sharp and she was ambitious. Grant could see her predicting the worst outcome and the best-case scenarios, just like a politician. It was the part of her he didn't like and why officers at the station didn't feel comfortable with Fox. The problem was they could never be sure she was watching their backs, rather than putting her own as a priority.

At the end of his account there was an ominous silence. Grant could feel his heart still thumping from the stairs and he anticipated what she was about to say, steeling himself for it.

'Are you sure you're the best person for the job?' Fox asked. 'This is going to be intense. You nailed Travis the first time and that was a long time ago. Are you sure you're up to it?'

Despite himself, Grant felt Fox's words go in and leave a wound.

'Let's face it, keeping a distance on this one is going to be hard, David. I could always assign DI Crocker to the Jones murder and leave you to concentrate on the Travis interviews.'

Crocker was a decent detective. Grant liked his outspoken nature but Crocker had a reputation for rushing cases and blaming his team if things didn't go well.

'It has to be me on this case because I know Travis better than anyone. If there's a link between Travis and the Jones murder, I'll find it. And if there isn't, then we've a regular murder enquiry. My age has nothing to do with it.'

This wasn't the first time Fox hinted he was past it. Did she feel threatened by him and his clout and reputation? Was that why she took these opportunities to get the knife in? She was always asking the same questions - did he want early retirement? Was he ready to slow down? It was the only thing she had on him. Probably Fox was trying to wobble him. She needed to let him know who was boss. Maybe she thought he was after her job? Which he wasn't.

Grant didn't fall for it. Fox had no chance of undermining him. Yes, he would soon be fifty-six. And he certainly wasn't as fit as he used to be. Then again, with Delaney and McGowan around he didn't need to be. They had enough health lectures, diet and fitness advice, and high energy, to make a man feel exhausted. And he wasn't ready for retirement yet. Oh no. He had murders to solve. And he had a successor to train up.

Grant waited. Fox wasn't prepared for an open confrontation with him and perhaps she'd never be. Besides, it was his team who brought in all the good statistics. He felt confident Fox wasn't ready to get rid of him yet.

'And this Ruby Silver you've asked to join us as a consultant criminal psychologist – you think she can help?'

'I'm sure of it.'

'All right but I want to be *kept properly informed*. And I'll want you in for the press conference. No, please don't annoy me with excuses. And don't try to get out of it, and don't pull your usual trick of turning up late either. I expect you there. On time.'

'Of course, ma'am.'

On the way down the stairs, Grant passed Sergeant Wilson.

'How'd it go? Foxy eat you for breakfast?'

Grant laughed. 'Not a chance. She called me old and she wasn't wrong on that one. But I'm tough old meat and just like always, she had to spit me out.'

Ruby arrived at the police station as Grant entered Fox's office. It was unfortunate. It was also unfortunate Collins and Delaney were occupied in the incident room because she found herself sitting in the cubbyhole with a scowling Detective Sergeant Steve McGowan.

'Nailing killers is something you learn from years of experience in the field,' he said. 'Not from sitting behind a desk making up fancy theories.'

McGowan dragged Caprini's research report across his desk and plunked his full mug on top of it. Dark liquid sploshed over. When he gave her a glare, Ruby felt herself floundering. She'd not expected hostility from Grant's team. It had been stupid of her.

Ruby had travelled down the previous afternoon. She'd booked herself into a bed and breakfast room at a local pub, called The Nag's Head. She'd been so wired up it had been impossible to sleep. Whether by the prospect of Travis or by being part of the investigation, or both, she wasn't sure. She was better as a loner. People always scared her too much. And DS McGowan was proving to her why.

Minutes before leaving The Nag's Head, nerves overtook her, as usual, and Ruby vomited in the toilet. Now she felt like doing it again. More than anything, no one here must know what a gamble it was for her coming back to Himlands Heath. This was the place where it had all happened. She must be careful not to trip herself up or give herself away. As far as Grant and his team were concerned, they must think this was her first time in the town.

'I'm here to add what I can about Travis' mindset and a killer's psychology. I'm not here to tread on anyone's toes.'

McGowan gave her another rude stare. He crossed his arms in front of his chest so his biceps bulged.

'As long as you don't get in my way,' he said. 'And I'm sure you'll be running back to the university in no time.'

Ruby silently prayed for Inspector Grant to walk through the door. Or for anyone to. It didn't happen. Instead she had to sit in silence with DS McGowan, who seemed hell bent on treating her like the outsider she was.

By the time DS Collins came back to the cubbyhole, Ruby was almost ready to give up before she started. Collins shot McGowan an accusing look.

'Welcome to the team, Ruby. I hope McGowan's been making you feel at home.'

McGowan briefly met Ruby's eyes. Ruby had seen that look many times at the children's home. His meaning was clear – snitch on me and I can make life hell for you.

'Yeah, sure he has.'

'I'm DS Collins but you can call me Diane if you want. Why don't you come on down to the incident room and get settled in? Inspector Grant will be joining us there any minute.'

Ruby watched how the team operated. They seemed to know each other well. They didn't try to score points off each other and McGowan was the only one she got a bad vibe from. Ruby did her best to ignore him and get a grip on where she might fit in.

Diane Collins was cheerful and friendly. Ruby had not dared take a doughnut offered by Diane, because, for certain, it would be coming straight back up.

As she'd seen at the university, Tom Delaney had the build

of a sports player. He was tall and broad-shouldered and damn good looking, with dark hair falling into his eyes which he kept brushing away. And they were friendly eyes too, dark brown and warm. Just the sort of man Soraya would make a bee-line for.

And then there was Grant. He stood quietly at the front through Diane's report on Mandy Jones' life. During Steve McGowan's report on the prison, Grant waited by the side of McGowan's desk, intent on every word. Like in Caprini's office, Grant commanded respect without really doing very much. In fact, what he seemed to be very good at was listening.

'Full checks on the two prison officers pan out,' McGowan said. 'They both have excellent employment records and they both say they were with Travis the whole time, even in the toilets. They uncuffed one wrist because the doctor told them it was getting in the way of his treatment. He needed to have one arm free for shots and stuff like that.'

'You checked it out with Doctor Hawthorne?' Grant asked.

McGowan nodded.

'So we can rule Travis out?' Collins asked, her pen poised over the whiteboard.

'For now he seems an unlikely candidate,' Grant said. 'It seems highly improbable both prison officers would be involved in some kind of conspiracy with Travis. Strike Travis' name through, DS Collins, but don't remove it.'

All eyes turned to Ruby. She was the only one who'd said nothing so far. She licked her dry lips.

'Go ahead, Ruby. This is a free for all,' Grant said. 'As I explained at the beginning, we all chip in and you shouldn't hold anything back. Everyone's angle is important. Having an input from a criminal psychologist isn't an edge we usually have.'

McGowan cracked his knuckles and Ruby's stomach flipped. She risked a glance in his direction. What she saw was a dusting of sugar clinging to his moustache. Everyone must have seen it – Diane, Tom, Inspector Grant, and they'd decided not to let him know. It helped take the edge off McGowan's hostility and made him much less intimidating.

Diane gave Ruby a smile.

Ruby took a breath and plunged in.

'It seems to me Travis is an influence on the killer, whether it's remotely or directly. Or perhaps he's been an inspiration. For sure, Travis has a place in this somewhere even if he isn't a suspect.' As she used her voice, she felt more sure of herself.

'Good,' Grant said. 'The pathologist's report tells us the victim had Travis' DNA on her. He can't say if it was transferred at the time of the murder or when Mandy Jones touched Travis as his nurse. So that's inconclusive.'

'Any potential suspects amongst the prison parolees?' Collins asked.

'There've been two people released for parole in the last year,' Delaney said. 'They could both be of interest. I've already contacted their parole officers and organised interviews. Both were in for manslaughter and both had contact with Travis on the inside.'

'And their motive would be what?' Grant asked. 'Why would they risk their freedom again?'

'Might Travis have threatened them in some way, or bribed them?' McGowan said.

Collins shook her head. 'Seems unlikely to me,' she said, without making it sound in the least bit critical. 'And you said Travis went twenty-five years with no visitors. So I don't see him as someone with much influence in the outside world.'

'A debt to be repaid?' Delaney suggested.

'Maybe. We'll check in on that tomorrow. I'd like you to go ahead with the interviews on your own, Delaney. Nice work,' Grant said.

The inspector walked across the room and tapped the board

with the photograph of Mandy Jones' house. 'Any thoughts on this?'

'The lab report on it will be ready later today,' Collins said.

Ruby felt the inspector's eyes on her. She tried to quell her anxiety at the idea the inspector might be able to guess her secret. That was impossible. The inspector couldn't see inside her skin, nor inside her head. He didn't know anything about her. And she had the upper hand because she knew all about DI Grant. Ruby knew every detail of how he'd captured Travis. In fact, she'd used her position as a university researcher to gain access to all kinds of records which were not strictly necessary for the analysis of Travis and his traits.

She knew how Grant had put together the pieces of the puzzle. About how the police had tracked the trail of carnage for years, lagging behind the killer, with no leads. Women's strangled bodies were turning up every few months and the media were plunged into a frenzy every time. Grant had been inspired and he'd been the only match for Travis, who was skilled, and crafty and who'd got away with it. Oh yes, Ruby had all the information on David Grant. After all, she needed it to make her feel more secure.

Tom was offering her a doughnut. Ruby took one and left it on her desk.

'Er well, one house photograph doesn't say much about the killer.'

She was pleased her voice sounded steadier. Work was always where she felt strongest. 'We know taking photographs wasn't one of Travis' traits. In assessing killers, I always look at common habits...' She used the word "I" deliberately and made sure she was looking at McGowan when she said it. The sugar was still there.

'Because habits tell us a lot about a killer. For instance, the setting of the crime scene or the items a killer deliberately leaves behind. In this case, they used the victim's own tights to strangle her. They sent a photograph of her house to you. The killer gained something by doing those two things. If we can work out what the killer gained by each one, it will help build the profile. And that way, we can narrow down the field.'

'Yes, carry on,' Grant said.

'Though we tend to think of killers as lacking in intelligence, actually many serial killers have a high intelligence, though they don't have developed social skills. And er, another common trait is they plan meticulously.'

She hesitated, wondering if she really should put her next thought into words.

Inspector Grant had come to sit on the edge of Diane's desk. Ruby could feel his full attention on her. His grey eyes were kind.

'As far as I can see, the planning, the selecting of the victim, the taking and sending of the photograph, they were all meticulously carried out,' she said. 'The photo is especially important. And it says this isn't some random killing. The motive of the murderer may well have very little to do with Mandy Jones. For me, this has the traits of a serial killer. Mandy Jones was simply a convenient target.'

'You think this isn't going to be the only murder?' Delaney asked. 'Is that what you're telling us?'

'Yes, that's exactly what I'm thinking. I think we're looking at the beginning of a pattern.'

Detective Inspector Grant was nodding.

'Well, aren't you the clever one,' McGowan said, under his breath.

Chapter Twelve

Doctor Susan Hawthorne lived in a leafy district of Himlands Heath. Her nearest neighbours on one side were lawyers who worked long hours, and on the other side, a retired pilot who spent most of his time running a charity bookshop in the town centre.

As senior consultant on the cancer ward, the buck stopped with her. Calls in the middle of the night were common. Everyone looked to her to know what to do and make the hard decisions, even when she sometimes didn't know herself. On days like today, the responsibility could feel suffocating. 'Come on, Susan, get your shit together,' she muttered to herself. 'People are counting on you.'

Susan's husband taught Spanish at one of Himlands Heath's sixth form colleges. He usually left early and, like he planned to do that morning, he dropped their daughter Flora at pre-school on his way in. As he bent to kiss Susan goodbye, she enjoyed the scent of his aftershave and of him. She caressed his jawline with her fingertip.

'Was it a bad phone call?' he asked.

'Not one of the best.'

Then Susan gave Flora a kiss on the forehead, thinking about the roller blades they'd bought Flora as her Christmas present. Soon they'd be able to teach her, and the three of them could go out to the park at weekends and skate along the cycle path.

'Have a great day, sweet pea.'

'You too, Mummy.'

It was Doctor Hawthorne's one good moment of the morning and she enjoyed it because she knew that day she would need all the grit and stuffing she'd got.

She went upstairs to get dressed. Overnight, a message had come through from the prison hospital. Travis needed to come in for more treatment.

They would have to accommodate him. The next nearest hospital with suitable facilities was hours away. Oh God, she would have to ask her team again, with Mandy not even cold in the ground. What the hell could she say? How could she face them and even dare to ask? The thought filled her with dread. Made her legs go weak. They were all good people but this was asking too much. If every single one of them refused she wouldn't blame them.

Susan was used to pressure but this was off the charts.

She had a small office at the back of the house, equipped with video link up, so she could talk to her junior doctors on site whenever she needed to. It would turn out to be one of those days with no time except for dealing with Travis and running from emergency to emergency, she could feel it already. If she didn't deal with her emergency messages and eat something decent she'd never make it through the next twelve hours.

She made her go-to breakfast for bad days and carried it through.

Desk Sergeant Wilson felt jittery. He was a man with his finger on the pulse and rumours were circulating – a new serial killer case, Grant's team taking on a major investigation.

The house photograph from the first victim had arrived in a standard, brown envelope. Sergeant Wilson had imprinted it on his brain and retina – the size, shape and feel of that type of envelope. Just in case. Like a whippet on the scent, he gave the new pile of mail a once-over. And that's why he immediately spotted a brown corner sticking out amongst all the other brown corners.

Two seconds later his brain kicked in. Grant's team were still on their morning briefing.

Sergeant Wilson crashed into the incident room, his gloved hand thrust out.

'It's the same. I swear it's the same.'

It looked like every other brown envelope, yet the tension in the room notched up.

'Make a space,' Grant said.

They swept everything from one of the desks and Grant donned gloves. He made a conscious effort to keep his mind calm as he slit the envelope.

Out slipped a night-time shot of a house. Like the first, it had been taken with light sensitive equipment. His team clustered around. This time, they could see a silhouette in an upstairs window. It was a woman. Grant heard Wilson swallow.

'What are we looking at here? Are we looking at the next victim?' Collins asked.

'We must presume we are.' Grant glanced around the circle. 'I want ideas on how to narrow down the field.'

'The first victim came from the hospital. It wouldn't be a bad assumption the second one could be from there as well. Perhaps even from the same team,' Ruby said.

'Could we circulate a copy of this through hospital personnel?' Collins asked. 'What do you think, Delaney? Could it be sent around via social media?'

'It could if we can get the cooperation of their HR department to start a phone cascade. What do you say, boss?'

'I think we risk triggering mass panic and I don't think we're ready to take that step yet. We don't even know for sure if this is the next victim,' Grant said.

Yet he felt in his guts it was. And there was another worse feeling he didn't want to put into words. That they were already too late. The murderer was ahead of them on every count. How likely was it a killer would send a clue if they thought Grant and his team could actually beat them to it?

'Take this over to the tech guys, McGowan, and tell them its top priority. Delaney, contact Doctor Hawthorne. Tell her it's urgent. Send her a copy and ask her to check discreetly with her staff. And you and Collins get over to the hospital to liaise with her, in case someone recognises it.'

Grant pushed aside a feeling of hopelessness. They must do their best and put the puzzle together, piece by piece. 'Ruby, you're with me,' he said. 'Let's brainstorm all the possibilities we can think of and come up with more source points for potential victims.'

Delaney got off the phone. 'Doctor Hawthorne isn't in yet and her secretary can't get hold of her at home.'

David Grant stopped what he was doing. 'Is that unusual?'

'The secretary said no, not really, but, I dunno, she didn't seem convinced. I've an idea the two of them know how to get hold of each other at a moment's notice. She said maybe Hawthorne was in the shower and I got the feeling that's pretty much the only time the doctor wouldn't respond. And Doctor Hawthorne, she'd be a likely candidate, wouldn't she?'

'Too right,' Collins said. 'First off, she works at the hospital. Second, she's had contact with Travis…'

Wilson was glued to the tension, his eyes still on the photo and the quick working of Grant's team.

'What's Doctor Hawthorne's address?' Wilson asked. 'If we've got a patrol car in the area, they can be there within minutes.'

'Get it, Delaney, pronto,' Grant said. 'And check satellite images on the internet to see if you can spot any correlation with the photo.' Grant clapped his hand on Wilson's shoulder. 'And let's ask patrol to do an urgent check at her house.'

Ruby thought the inspector sounded amazingly calm and collected. He must realise they'd be too late. Even if Doctor Hawthorne were the target, the killer would never allow them to get there in time. No, they were being played with. As a cat plays with a mouse. And she realised how badly she wanted to do everything she could to help Grant beat the killer at his own game.

Chapter Thirteen

The death of the dear doctor went without incident. Or, to be more precise, it went exactly as I planned.

The woman sat alone in a little room on the ground floor. I watched the husband and child leave. The neighbourhood was quiet. The doctor even had her back to the French doors and was tapping away at her keyboard.

Accessing the garden was child's play. When it came to the house, the Hawthornes were more security conscious. All their doors and windows are double-glazed and intruder-unfriendly. Then again, as I well knew from my research, Susan had a silly habit of airing her office while she worked. She'd opened the French doors a crack and, as I crept closer, I could smell the unmistakable scent of bacon.

I waited a few more minutes, savouring the moment. Enjoying the anticipation. Revelling in my power over life and death. This was beyond any drug. Beyond any other human emotion. It made me feel like a god

My victim was surprised when I stepped up behind her.

And then she was terrified.

I have to tell you, Doctor Susan Hawthorne was a fighter but she was no match for me. She wore a short dress and dark tights and ankle boots. I had the boots and tights off within seconds. With her tights in my hand, I looked into her eyes and drank in the terror, as a greedily thirsty man sates himself at a fountain. Then I twisted the band around her neck and watched as life slowly left her.

Before they dulled, her eyes flicked to the desktop and a picture of her daughter. In the photograph, the girl was grinning ludicrously. Two front teeth were missing. Her legs and cheeks were fat. I suppose the doctor was thinking how she'd never see her daughter again. How the child would never have a mother to love her. It gave the moment a delicious twist.

With her body limp under my hands, I let go of the tights. I'd been gasping, my breathing jagged and wet. That's a true rush. One which makes any other seem sordid and worthless. You see, I have the power to take life. And not give a damn about it. I think of it as my inheritance.

I check the room to make sure I've not made any careless mistakes. Then I hunt for my trophy. It's a minor risk but I can't resist. I don't think I told you before how I like to collect mementos.

I select my prize from the desk. It's glittery and pretty and precious. It would remind me forever of the desperation in her eyes. And of how much I enjoyed it.

Chapter Fourteen

Ruby had never seen a dead body before.

Doctor Hawthorne was sprawled on the carpet. She lay in slats of sunlight glancing through from the French windows. Her legs were bare. And her tights had been used around her neck. The woman had such a horrible expression on her face and Ruby had to drag her eyes away from the doctor's lifeless ones. Ruby rubbed her arms to get rid of the goosebumps.

'First time?' Collins asked.

Ruby nodded.

'Take it slow. No pressure,' Collins said. 'It takes a while to get used to this sort of thing. Not that I can say I've ever got used to it.'

The room smelled of death. The doctor had dug her nails into the pile of the carpet. Two of them had ripped off, leaving her fingers bloody.

The little office was full of technicians. They were patiently waiting for the pathologist to finish his preliminary examination. Meanwhile, he was on his knees dictating his findings into his phone and to the room in general.

Ruby listened to his voice as she swept the rest of the room, taking in the details. There wasn't much to see – a desk, a chair knocked over, a bookcase stuffed with medical journals and fiction paperbacks. It looked like the doctor was a historical romance addict, as well as a workaholic.

As she got used to the feeling of being at a crime scene with a real dead person lying not far from her feet, Ruby's professional brain kicked in. Ever since forever, she'd had an obsession with killers. Of course, she kept this to herself until the right moment came to apply for a professional training. Criminal psychology had suited her like a hand fitting a glove. She loved it and she had a feel for it – the way crimes were committed, their location, the choice of victim, the timing, any communications from the murderer, the story told at the crime scene – it was all information about the mind of the person committing the act. And she loved to unpick the trail and delve into the psychological make-up of the suspect. Up until now, it had all been theory and after-the-fact analysis. This was the real thing. And it definitely had an appeal.

The pathologist had finished dictating his notes and he issued instructions to the technicians. Coming back to Himlands Heath was a risk. Could Ruby control her own memories? Would her emotions overwhelm her? Would the past snatch her back? And perhaps it was the shock of the body, but right at that moment, a terrible recollection of her brother came to the surface.

Ruby wanted to screw her eyes shut. She fought not to, breathing through her mouth, hoping no one noticed she was suddenly sweating and afraid. She pushed her brother's memory down as hard as she could. They were all so concentrated, she thought she was safe. Then she noticed McGowan had his eye on her. Shit.

Ruby took a walk around the room, ignoring the wobble in her legs and willing her emotions to settle. The memory was pushed back into the depths and she slowly let her working mind take over. *Concentrate*, she told herself. *Ignore McGowan, he hates you anyway. What insights can this room give about the killer?*

The computer keyboard had fallen from the desk. So had a plate and what looked like the remains of the doctor's breakfast.

One item deliberately left by the killer was easy to identify – the tights. The same as with the first victim. There was no message or writing left in the room or on the body. There was no small item lodged in the mouth. The killer had not done any cutting or left any obvious marking on the skin. Nothing had been left around the victim. Ruby continued scanning the area.

Inspector Grant was by the pathologist's shoulder. It looked as if the two of them got on well, despite their age difference. They spoke as friends and equals and she could sense the trust between them. Luke Sanderson must be very happy to be on such good terms with David Grant. It must be nice to have colleagues, maybe even a mentor, like that.

Ruby took a slow walk around the room. Apparently, the patio door hadn't been locked, suggesting the killer had got in via the garden. The forensics team were already working the area outside. They were crawling around the lawn clad in their puffy white suits.

Ruby stopped beside the framed certificates on Doctor Hawthorne's wall. There were several of them listing the doctor's medical credentials.

'When you're ready for me to lift her, I'll take Doctor Hawthorne back for examination,' Luke said to Grant. 'I've done all I need to here.'

Grant came to stand at Ruby's shoulder.

'Is there anything you'd like to add to the crime scene notes?'

She shook her head. 'You've already covered it all, except…'

He raised an eyebrow.

'I was wondering about the personal stuff on her desk. She has a photograph, I guess of her daughter, and the rest of the things are practical. No keepsake from a holiday? No art work brought home from school? No Mother's Day gift? Is there nothing missing?'

'Good point. I'll ask Collins to check with the husband. She's still with him.'

They all knew Diane was still with the husband, because they'd heard him wailing for the last twenty minutes, even through the closed lounge door.

'Poor man,' she said.

As Grant turned to read the certificates, she sensed him freeze.

The inspector raised a finger and pointed. He was staring at Susan Hawthorne's initials.

'Delaney.'

Luke looked up from his notepad. The technicians stopped what they were doing. A small silence fell in the room. The inspector's tone was unmistakeable.

Grant's sergeant was at his side in an instant.

'What's Doctor Hawthorne's full name?' Grant asked.

'I don't think we've got that,' Delaney said. 'Shall I go and check with the husband?'

Ruby's skin was crawling – it was a mixture of excitement and anticipation. Grant had identified something crucial. She also realised he already guessed the answer to his own question and only wanted confirmation from Delaney. A confirmation she felt sure would not be good news. Her estimation of Inspector Grant went up even further.

She thought Tom looked pale when he came back.

'You're not going to like it, boss. The doc's full name was Susan Grace Hawthorne.'

Grace, thought Ruby, of course. It was the same name as Travis' second victim.

Chapter Fifteen

'I thought I should let you know, ma'am,' Grant said. 'We double-checked and Mandy Jones' middle name didn't figure on her employment records. Her husband said she hated it and never used it. Her middle name was Edith. The same name as the first of Travis' victims.'

Detective Chief Superintendent Fox steepled her fingers. 'I don't like the sound of this. What exactly are you telling me?'

'It seems the middle names of our first two victims tie in with the names of Travis' victims in the past – Edith and Grace.'

It had been a grim discovery. What was he dealing with? A copycat killer? Someone intent on working their way down the whole damn list?

'What the heck! And you're telling me the hospital is the epicentre? We've got a maniac spreading carnage at a public facility and he's working his way along a list of names?'

'The next in line are Diane, Sandra and Amy.'

'And if this gets out every single one of them will be banging on our door demanding protection.'

Fox got to her feet, not a good sign. 'I hope you don't think I'm mad enough to sanction the release of this to the press. How many women with those names even work at the hospital? Have you any idea? Or live in Himlands Heath? My God, we'd have mass panic.'

'Not to mention the Diane on my own team.' He noticed

how Fox pressed her lips together. 'And then there's all the women with matching middle names.'

'Yes, I've got the idea thank you, Inspector.' She glared down at him. 'Please send Sergeant Collins on a leave of absence. And we're on borrowed time. Some bright spark in the press is going to work out the names link to Travis sooner rather than later.'

'I'll leave handling that one to you.'

'Please tell me you've got a main suspect.'

'It's not Travis. Aside from that...'

'Oh bloody hell. I'm counting on you, David. We need to get this under control.'

He could see her mind working furiously, clicking through the ramifications. He nodded several times. In his experience, this often had a calming effect.

Fox sat down.

'Understood ma'am. The house photographs are our best bet and we're working flat out to get ahead on the next one. And we do believe there will be another one.'

'This is bad. Very bad. All right, keep me up to date. And I want somebody in custody by Christmas Day, you understand me?'

The hesitation was so slight, he almost missed the chink of concern in her shiny armour. Ah-hah, so, she was driven to protect and serve after all.

Fox quickly brushed over it. 'I'll delay the press conference as long as I can. Give you time to get some results.'

'Thank you, ma'am, I appreciate it.'

David Grant kissed his wife, Lily. He saw her wrinkling her nose. She was a true copper's wife and always recognised the end of a bad day.

'Things not going well on the Travis case?'

'I think it's only the beginning,' he said. 'Reminds me too

much of last time.'

'Looks like I'll be eating supper alone.'

He hugged her again. 'I'll try not to come to bed too late.'

Going straight to his study, David Grant closed the blinds with a *clack*. The desk chair sagged as he plonked down in it. He knew this feeling. He'd known it more than once in his career. It was a deadly cocktail of dread and anticipation. The feeling of facing a hidden, clever enemy. An enemy who played a game in which innocent people would die until he worked out what the hell was going on.

And the house photographs were being sent to him.

Why?

To get the killer he must crack the code.

A bottle clinked as he pulled out the desk drawer. It was a cliché, but this was where he kept his stash of booze for emergencies. He was a whiskey man and this bottle had been given to him by his son, Daniel, two Christmases earlier.

The liquid gurgled as Grant poured a double.

When it had gone down the hatch, he wheeled himself over to the filing cabinet, where he kept his ghosts.

Over the years, he'd thrown the files which haunted him into the lower drawer. There weren't many. Hiding at the bottom of the pile was a buff folder.

He dragged it out and threw it onto the desk. It fell with a *slap*.

He scanned each page and examined the photographs. It was a copy of his notes on the Travis case.

At the hospital, Travis had accused him of making a mistake.

Of being a fraud.

The page he wanted was at the back. At the very end. A faded photograph of an infant boy.

The child was two years old when his mother, Amy, was killed by Travis. Travis took the boy, or killed him, Grant had never been able to find out which. He knew the age of the child because it was the same age as Daniel.

You can't do everything in this job. He was one man. A human being with limits of time and police resources. He had large hands but they weren't large enough to keep hold of all the cards. Sometimes one fluttered to the floor. Like the boy. And then got buried under the mountain of new priorities.

After Travis' arrest, there'd been the work of putting together a successful prosecution for five murders and the court case had been long and detailed. Not to mention the ongoing hunt for Meredith and Isabella. There had been new cases coming in, and the pressure to take on more urgent investigations. It had meant the slipping to the bottom of the pile of the cold trail on the boy. No body had ever been found. No trace of him had ever been uncovered.

In the end, he was forced to let it go. And it was deeply felt because he and Lily were enjoying their own young son. How can you forget an abducted child when you're watching another one fall asleep? How can you abandon one boy and then come home to take your own in your arms and be filled with wonder and love?

Grant stared at the photograph and his hand was unsteady. He wasn't a fraud. But he'd carry the regret to his grave.

On the little rise running behind Grant's back garden, Ruby was getting chilled. The cold and damp were seeping up into her body, despite the thermal matting she had under her bottom. Pouring herself a tea from her flask, Ruby warmed her hands on the cup.

She'd had years of practice at surveillance. Watching people when they didn't know she was, had become one of the habits she couldn't do without. Call it insecurity. Or call it collecting information which made her feel safer around other people – she didn't know what name it should have. Except it was embarrassing and awkward. And something she couldn't live without.

She told Soraya she'd given it up years ago.

Except she never had.

Squirming into a more comfortable position, she lifted her digital binoculars. There was hardly enough light. She really should go back to her room, this was stupid.

The habit had started when she left the children's home. It hadn't been a nice place. She had almost gone under from the day-to-day aggression from the other kids and the harshness of the staff. It was only her alliances with Soraya and the awkward little boy called Hawk, which kept her going. The three of them had made it together, and Soraya was tough, nobody messed with her, and by extension, nobody messed with Soraya's friends – not the mean girls and not the mean boys, and so Ruby was protected.

When she left, she missed that protection. At the university she felt vulnerable and exposed. As if they could see inside her soul and know the wound she carried. As if at any moment, her peers would find out the truth about how she had failed her little brother. How she'd never been strong enough. Her weakness and her desperation always came back to him.

And that's when she started spying – spying on her fellow students, spying on her tutors. She followed them and found out where they lived. Then she would find a spot where she could watch and see them coming and going. It was all surprisingly easy.

She convinced herself she wasn't doing any harm. There was nothing wrong with simply watching, was there? Yet she knew it wasn't right.

Fifteen minutes later, she packed away her things and walked back to the pub. Spying on David Grant felt bad. What would he think of her if he knew?

The Nag's Head was in a quiet part of town. She'd taken a

room at the very top of the house, underneath a pointed roof, which was crooked on one side. The landlord told her it was made on purpose that way, which seemed to her absurd. It meant on one side of her room, the ceiling had a strange dent and she had to bend down to get into bed. It struck her how it was the first funny and non-life-threatening thing she'd ever experienced about Himlands Heath.

She pulled the duvet up to her chin. And in the quiet and the private, she cried herself to sleep thinking about her little brother, and how she had left him to die.

Chapter Sixteen

Twenty-five years earlier – Amy's story

Amy checked the recipe for the hundredth time. She didn't want to make any mistakes for Mike's special dinner. Giving the sauce a stir, she dipped in a teaspoon, blew on it and popped it into her mouth. *Hmmm*, perfectly smooth and creamy and cheesy. She gave a little squirm of delight. And it didn't have too much peppercorn either, important because Mike hated things too peppery.

In fact, he could be pretty picky about food in general and about quite a lot of things. He didn't like spices, nor food that had gone cold, or was too salty. And he complained if he saw dust or if the carpet had a speck on it or if the shower or sink wasn't sparkling. Which was why she always made a lot of effort to please him, even if it meant hoovering in the morning and then again before he got home from work. Or wiping over the bathroom taps several times a day as soon as she spotted a splash.

Mike was Amy's second husband. So far, this marriage was going well. Or, at least, it was compared to the first one, which she could only describe as a complete disaster. Her first husband had turned out to be someone who spent most of his free time drinking with his mates and then came home and shouted at her. Amy had been glad when he was arrested for drink driving.

Then he ran off with another woman, leaving Amy with a two-year-old and juggling child care and work and kid's sicknesses. She was a classroom assistant at the local primary school and it had been touch-and-go whether she managed to keep her job.

She was preparing a special dinner for Mike because she had news. She was pregnant. And she hoped Mike would take it well.

Meeting Mike had been a miracle. For a start, his interest in her was unexpected. Amy didn't consider herself attractive, though she made a lot of effort with clothes and make-up. In fact, she made a lot of effort for men in general. That had always been her problem. But not many of them were prepared to take on other people's toddlers. Which was why she really was determined to make this marriage work.

By the time dinner was ready, Mike came home. She heard him going upstairs to take a shower and she felt a buzz of excitement and nerves. She took a tiny sip of wine and reminded herself it would only be one glass an evening, now the baby was coming along.

Mike worked at a warehouse where they machined enormous metal parts for engines. Most of the work was done by huge robot printers commanded by computers, so the manpower was minimal. He was one of three supervisors. The machines worked through the day and night but they could never be left unattended, in case something went wrong. In fact, Mike usually worked the night shift. He said he preferred it quiet with only him and the machines, and the pay was better.

He'd swapped shifts. He didn't always want to do that when Amy plucked up the courage to ask, but this time he agreed to her offer of a candle-lit dinner.

Amy checked the chicken in the oven, leaving the door open a few extra moments so the scents wafted up the stairs. Then she took off her apron and went to light the candles in the main room.

The evening went well. Mike had been cautiously pleased at the news. And he made no complaints about the chicken, or the sauce, or the dessert, which were all good signs. Even her little one slept through the evening without disturbing them.

After dinner, Mike left her to clear the table. As Amy packed the dishwasher she felt happy and relieved. The new baby was going to work out well.

The last thing she did was pop into the laundry area to programme a wash for overnight. Mike had dumped his work clothes on top of the pile. She loaded in Rosie's little items first, and a couple of her own things and she was just about to stuff in Mike's shirt when she noticed a few marks running up the sleeve from the cuff.

She scratched at the rust-red splotches. They were dried and she felt sure it was a spray of blood. How strange. Mike worked in the office, with a huge window looking out over the work area. He rarely had any need to enter the machine room because it was all remotely operated. In fact, he had told her it was dangerous to go in there. Surely he couldn't have injured himself at work, so how could he have got blood on his sleeve? And it didn't look like it was drips, it was a spray going from large marks to small. It was a mystery. And Mike hadn't mentioned anything.

She didn't dare to ask him. Mike didn't like her asking questions because he said it gave him a headache. Ignoring the strange warning feeling at the back of her neck, Amy squirted on some stain remover. She told herself there was nothing suspicious or strange. Probably a nosebleed or something like that. She quickly started the machine and didn't think any more of it.

Chapter Seventeen

I read a lot. Especially about killers like me.

For instance, I've read Professor Caprini's most recent, startling research. The man knows what he's talking about when it comes to murder. And his report received international praise.

I've printed out the section Professor Caprini wrote on Travis. It lies by my bedside. The corners are grimy because I've studied it so much. My favourite chunks I know word for word.

I have to say, the author is a genius. Caprini knows the mind of a killer. He has written with clarity on the fake life we have to lead, the phoney smile, the hollow job, the meaningless existence we're forced to lead, day after day. Whilst inside, the fire burns hot for the taking of a life.

The report details the coldness and the calculation. The mind turned inwards. And it pulls no punches about the drive and the heat and the blood lust and the insanity of an insatiable thirst. Bravo. You have described it accurately.

My own demons have been temporarily quietened by the doctor's death. Yet I hear them stirring. They are restless. I hear their cry for more. They are demanding blood and justice.

So, guess what? I'm spending my time choosing my next victim. And it's divine.

You see, this isn't all simply random death. I have an end game in mind. A final target who must suffer. And I'm working my way towards them. But I mustn't do it too quickly. No, I want to prolong the anguish and the pain for my final victim as long as possible. I want them to feel me creeping closer and closer. I want them to reach the edge of despair at the trail of bodies, until they finally realise they are responsible for everyone who has died.

You remember I told you about rule number one, don't you? Preparation. Which brings me to rule number two, which is, out-think the lawman.

Something I am highly skilled at.

I consider my list of names. There are several potentials for my next victim. Who will have the honour of being the next step in my trail of breadcrumbs? They are all so enticing. In the end, I choose the one who appeals most to my sense of humour.

Want to know something even better? The press are starting to call me The Strangler. It has a nice ring to it, don't you think?

Chapter Eighteen

Detective Sergeant Collins had known Inspector Grant almost ten years. When he asked her to come to his office and then wanted her to close the door, she knew it was serious.

It had been hanging over Diane ever since they realised the significance of the victim's names. They'd already had an Edith. Then a Grace. Diane was the name of the third victim killed by Travis. Very likely their new murderer would be picking out his next target, which meant she was under threat.

'I want you reassigned to another team, Collins. Better still, why not take an extended vacation? Get away somewhere nice?'

Diane refused the chair the inspector offered. She needed to be on her feet to fight this one. She loved her job. It gave her a sense of freedom and purpose. It meant she was part of something important. And this case was turning into one of the darkest they'd tackled. There was no way she was going to be sidelined.

'With all due respect, Inspector, the killer has been choosing women with middle names which match the previous victims. Diane is my first name. It doesn't fit the pattern.'

'I don't care if it fits the pattern or not. This is a risk I'm not willing to take and you're off the case.'

Diane wasn't going to let herself get booted out. Or, at least, not the easy way. She argued her side. Assigning her to another team didn't take away any of the risk, she told him. All officers knew they were putting themselves on the line every day. She didn't see this as any different.

David Grant felt his blood pressure rising.

Their team worked well together, Collins said. Without her he'd have a massive hole which a new DS wouldn't be able to step into quickly. It would mean their efficiency would slip at a time when good teamwork was vital.

Collins was good at arguing her corner, Grant gave her that. She was very good at her job, point blank. Still, he wanted her gone. He wanted her safe. And preferably on a long vacation, far, far away.

She kept on at it. With Christmas time coming up, she insisted it couldn't happen. She had family coming. She had kids to cater for. She wasn't going to run away. A holiday someplace else was out of the question. And why did he think she might be safer shut at home like a sitting duck? Or running around Himlands Heath with one of the other teams?

Grant knew full well he could order Collins out of his team but he couldn't bring himself to do it. She was too loyal. Too fierce. Too good at her job. She worked well with Delaney, she got on with McGowan, who was a great cop but could be a real pain in the ass, she was drawing Ruby into the circle. He raised his voice again and saw how Diane wasn't going to back down. Damn it. He slammed the flat of his hand on the table.

Grant walked to his window and stared down at the back end of the car park. Grey tarmac and a grey sky and a madman on the loose, and a team second to none. It wasn't all bad.

'I don't accept all your points but you can stay on the case. And I mean for the time being only. On the strict condition you agree to a uniformed officer parked outside your house twenty-four-seven, and no arguing the toss on that one.'

Diane nodded and kept her mouth shut. He gave her a hard look and realised she was very likely overjoyed, which didn't do much for his blood pressure.

As soon as Collins left, Grant called in DS McGowan and told him he was to stick to Collins like glue. If McGowan left her alone for a nanosecond he'd find Grant's boot half-way up his backside and his career in ruins. DS McGowan wasn't happy and Grant knew Collins wouldn't be happy either when she realised she'd grown a new shadow. Too bad.

Inspector Grant then called Fox and asked for permission to pull in three detective constables to do the legwork on the investigation. She agreed. Then when he told her he was keeping Collins on the case, Fox almost blew a gasket. He had to hold the handset away from his ear until she calmed down. My God, thought Grant, this was turning into one hell of a day. And he still had the bloody press conference to get through.

The Inspector, Delaney and McGowan were standing together in a tiny room behind the auditorium used for the press conferences. The technical team were taking up most of the space and Ruby was a few steps away, watching the technicians make their last-minute adjustments.

Delaney peered through the crack in the doors.

'I've never seen it so packed. All the nationals have sent someone. The media are practically drooling over this one. They've already dubbed the killer The Strangler, did you hear about that?'

'Oh bloody wonderful.' Grant forced a finger down his collar and tried to wriggle himself a couple more centimetres Had the damn thing shrunk in the wash?

'By the way, nice suit, boss,' Delaney said..'

Grant wasn't in a mood for banter and he scowled. Making an effort for the press, hell even turning up to speak to that pack of hyenas wasn't his idea of time well spent.

Had he made his first bad decision on this case? Was he going to regret letting Collins stay? Grant was feeling the pressure. He knew better than anyone how a killer can come up with a hundred ways of sneaking up on a target.

'Let's get on with this bloody thing and get back to the real work,' he said.

It was too hot in there and too crowded. His collar was sticking to his own damn neck.

Detective Chief Superintendent Fox arrived looking fresh and neat. Grant's annoyance level crept up.

'Are you ready, David? And remember, don't provoke. This is short and sharp and to the point. And as we agreed, for God's sake, there's to be no mention of you-know-what. If there's any digging I'll be slapping it down.'

'Understood, ma'am. At least there's some good news on the forensics side. I just got word from Luke. There was no DNA from Travis on Doctor Hawthorne.'

. 'I was hoping it would come through in time. That's bloody wonderful. So he's definitively ruled out?'

'Yes.'

'Good. We'll approach this as a fresh investigation with no links to the past. Let me handle any questions about Travis, if you don't mind.'

The inspector gave a small nod, knowing he'd play that one by ear.

'DS McGowan, you're with me,' Grant said, and he and McGowan followed the Superintendent out onto the platform.

Tom and Ruby listened to the statement read out by DCS Fox. McGowan sat tight-lipped and muscular by Grant's side. He was often rolled out for press conferences because, quite frankly, he looked the part. He was like a film extra – the archetypal hardened detective, out for blood, and Fox liked to use him for window dressing.

Then came a barrage of questions from the press which Grant valiantly responded to.

It was less frenetic at the back and they had breathing space. The technicians were leisurely monitoring the audio-visual.

Tom wondered where Collins was. He and McGowan had been straining to hear the conversation she had with Grant in his office, but the inspector's space was surprisingly sound-proof and Collins hadn't been ready to share. Grant must have thought about getting rid of her. Why hadn't he? Tom trusted Grant's judgement but he couldn't stop a little bit of himself being worried about Collins. If he were in her position, how would he feel? And there was no doubt it put extra strain on the team to be thinking about her safety.

'Your Inspector Grant's good, isn't he?' Ruby said.

'Grant's one of the best,' Tom said. 'I can see he likes you. You probably don't realise but he's not like that with everyone.'

'He's the same with me as he is with you.'

Tom shrugged. 'Yeah, I've never been able to work that one out either. Seems he likes both of us.'

He was smiling at her and Ruby couldn't think of what to say. There was an awkward silence. They both filled it by listening intently to Grant and Fox.

'So where are you staying?' Tom finally asked.

'The Nag's Head, in a funny little room with a weird roof.'

'Right, yeah I know it. Not a bad choice. I suppose it's different for you down here. Did you always live in London?'

She immediately felt wary and hated herself for it. The university was in London. Why was he asking? Was he digging for information? Was he trying to find out about her background?

She kept it casual, after all, she'd had a lifetime of practice lying about where she was from.

'You can't beat London for the vibe. It's a bit quiet around here, but there's nothing wrong with that.'

He was nice and she felt bad for fobbing him off. How could

she ever get close to someone when she had to pretend all the time?

Next door, Fox was calling it to a close. People were still firing questions as Fox and Grant stood to leave. Ruby could hear the mad *click click click* of flashlights and the scraping of chairs. Then a man's voice shouted above the din.

In unison, the technicians looked up. One tried to speak. All of them were staring at Tom.

Tom pushed Ruby so hard she bit her own mouth..

'Get back! Tom bolted for the door. As it swung open, Ruby saw a stampede. Journalists were screaming and trampling each other. She saw Tom trying to get through them, barging people out of his way. At the front, McGowan leapt from the platform. Then came a blast which threw her to the ground.

Chapter Nineteen

Twenty-five years earlier – Amy's story

Amy went for an ultrasound scan and Mike came with her. They discovered it was going to be a boy and Mike had been pleased. He said he'd always wanted a son. Yet, in the months which followed, Mike did not become involved in preparations for the new baby. Which Amy found strange.

Even her first, hopeless, husband, had liked picking out clothes and toys. Her first husband had also indulged in the occasional, gift for Amy. Whereas Mike kept himself detached and slightly clinical. He left everything to her. Amy decided it was simply part of Mike's character to be very private. It was nothing she should be worried about. He had been pleased which was all that mattered.

With each passing month, she got more and more tired. It was difficult to keep up the enthusiasm for looking after an energetic little one, as well as juggling her job and cooking and the endless cleaning of the house. Mike hadn't let up on any of his demands for it to be super-clean and it was exhausting.

Dragging herself through each day began to feel impossible. Mike had taken to spending more and more time out. Out where, she wondered? She had no idea. As far as she knew, he didn't have any actual friends. She didn't dare ask him and she continued to do what he told her. She had always complied because she didn't want to lose him, and she realised how it gave him total control over her.

Perhaps he was working longer hours to save up for the baby? That's what, against all the odds, she hoped.

Of course, her real fear was he had lost interest in her. And in the baby. The two of them had become boring. She told herself it would be okay and things would get better once the pregnancy was over and she had more energy to devote to Mike. Mike was a man who needed pampering. He wanted attention and adoration, and she couldn't give it to him. It made her feel depressed.

Mike took to sleeping all day, then getting up and leaving for work without speaking to her. She still prepared meals for him, which sometimes he ate and sometimes he ignored, leaving them cold and abandoned on the counter in the kitchen. She had never felt more alone. Often, the sight of Mike's untouched plate reduced her to tears. She dreaded the sound of the front door slamming and the feeling of being the only one in the house, left to fend for herself and her three-year-old.

One day, when she hadn't seen Mike for what seemed like days, she made a horrible discovery.

It happened when she was sorting clothes for what felt like the millionth wash of the week. Little Rosie was three-and-a-half now and her clothes attracted food like a magnet.

The washing liquid gave off an overpowering flowery perfume as she poured it out. Wrinkling her nose, she rested her hip on the counter. Smells were getting more and more pungent. It was a side effect of her hormones.

She was about to stuff Mike's shirt in the washer when she froze.

A button was hanging from a thread.

But that wasn't the worst thing.

A horrible nausea welled up. She bent over and waited for it to pass.

Then she examined the shirt again. Yes, there was a ripped button and behind the button a single hair was caught. A blonde one.

Pulling away the hair, Amy held it up to the light. It was unmistakably blonde and long.

Amy's own hair was dark and so was her daughter's. She closed her eyes and waited to see if she vomited.

Was Mike having an affair? Was this the evidence of it? It had crossed her mind he was seeing someone else and she always pushed the vile idea away. But how to explain the hair and the little tear where the button was attached, as if there had been a struggle?

Her mind flashed to the blood splatter on Mike's sleeve. She'd forgotten all about it. Then, in a rush and before she could think about what she was doing, she ran to the kitchen trash bin, and pushed in the shirt. She pulled out the whole bag of refuse, tied it up and marched it out into the yard. The lid of the outside bin closed with a *thunk* and she saw her own hands were trembling.

The refuse would be collected soon. Then it would be gone. Out of sight, out of mind, she told herself. Forget it and never ask him. If he was seeing someone else there would be other signs and she must look out for them.

It took a long while for her to recover. At any slight sound, she jumped and her heart started racing, as if Mike might come home and discover her examining the shirt. She knew it would make him angry. Furious even.

Putting her hand over her tummy, she thought about the new baby. She must pretend she suspected nothing and wait for the baby to arrive. Then she could decide what to do.

This is stupid, she told herself. *It's your hormones messing you up.* But the blonde hair worried her and the little rip scared her. It's not an affair, she told herself mechanically, and she tried to pull herself together, ignoring all her instincts which were screaming at her to get out.

Chapter Twenty

It was pandemonium in the conference room. Tom fell over journalists. People were crawling along the ground as fast as they could to get away from the front platform. Others had run, only to trip over chairs and then be trampled by their colleagues.

DS McGowan had leapt from the platform onto the offender. A bunch of uniformed officers helped him tackle the offender to the ground. Detective Chief Superintendent Fox kept her composure and was directing people to the rear exits. An explosive device had been thrown on to the platform. Luckily, it gave out more smoke and noise than actual firepower.

Tom opened up both rear doors as the sprinkler system came on.

How the hell anyone had smuggled a device into the pressroom was another question. Fox was furious. She would have someone's head for this. Literally.

Eight members of the press had minor injuries, some expensive equipment had been trashed and Detective Inspector Grant ripped his jacket.

'That's what I get for making an effort to look smart,' he said wryly.

The man who hurled the device was frogmarched to the cells. He had come there to deliver a message – convicted killers shouldn't receive life-prolonging treatments – the National Health Service should save its money for everyone else.

'Just what we need,' McGowan complained. 'A loony.'

The man had more to tell. It turned out he wasn't the only one against Travis getting treatment at a public hospital. The man had come to the station as a spokesperson. Apparently, there was a bunch of people getting themselves organised to protest. The next time Travis came in for treatment, they were planning a big demonstration.

'I hope that damn idiot isn't so delusional he thinks he'll be there to join them,' Fox snapped. 'He won't be getting within ten miles of the hospital by the time I've finished with him.'

Tom rushed out to check on Ruby and Collins. Ruby had a swollen lip but she and Collins were both fine.

'Sorry I pushed you so hard,' he said. For the first time Ruby smiled at him and it made him feel a bit light-headed.

'Listen up,' Grant said to his team. 'McGowan and Delaney, well done. This could have been a lot worse than it was. But it's turning into a damn security nightmare. A demonstration at the hospital won't only be a mess, it'll be an opportunity. We're going to have a bunch of innocent bystanders waving placards and creating chaos. Without realising it, they'll be offering themselves up as bait to the killer.'

Doctor Hawthorne's neighbours had put up a string of fairy lights at the front of their house. They ran along the wall and decorated the gate. At night-time they probably flashed all kinds of pretty colours. Ruby pulled up the collar of her parka and pulled down her woolly hat. Her fingertips were already going numb.

She followed Collins and McGowan to the back of the house.. The killer had taken his night-time shot from the rear. They were going to scout around to see if they could spot from where exactly he took the picture. Perhaps they would find trace evidence.

'It's frosty underfoot. I don't think we're going to find

prints,' Collins said. 'Even if the killer was careless enough to leave any.'

Collins was less cheerful than normal. She was tense, which made sense, given she was a potential target, Ruby thought. McGowan was his usual untalkative self. It had made for an uncomfortable car ride.

As soon as they were at the back of the property, she clocked the various possibilities for cover and knew straightaway the shot had been taken from a stand of tall, ornamental grasses. Years of her own surveillance experience had left its mark. From the angle of the shot, it was the only possibility. That was where the killer had crouched when he watched Doctor Hawthorne in her bedroom.

Ruby glanced up at the doctor's window. The curtains were drawn. Permanently.

She made sure not to walk towards the grasses. They were the type which reached almost to head height. In the summer, they were probably topped by tufty ends. During the winter, the greeny-yellow stems remained dense, like straw. It would be a perfect hiding place.

McGowan was comparing the photograph on his phone to what they saw in front of them and sizing up the line on which the killer had been when he took the shot. He'd got it about right. Since they had no information on the equipment the killer used, he didn't know how far along the line to place the murderer.

'Along this line,' McGowan said, indicating with his arm. 'Ruby, you follow behind me and Collins, and don't trample the ground. We're looking for footprints, or flattened vegetation, or marks from equipment, stuff like that.'

My god, what a moron. He was treating her like some kind of idiot. What the hell did he have against her anyway?

Stuffing her hands in her pockets, Ruby obediently walked behind the two detectives. As they got closer and closer to the grasses, McGowan veered off course. He had his eye on a row of bushes further away, which ran along a fence line.

'With ground as hard as this, we're not going to find much,' Collins said.

McGowan was already at the fence. He was kneeling, scanning for evidence, about four metres from where the killer must have been standing.

Shit. Ruby was hoping he would be the one to find the patch. Now McGowan gave her no alternative apart from handing him another reason to dislike her. Why did she have to tie herself up in knots? Why couldn't she simply stand up to him?

After a few moments, she made her way to the grasses. As soon as she got close, she could see some of them were trampled. Yes, the killer had crouched in the middle.

'What about over here?' she called. 'I think there's something.'

McGowan made a show of rolling his eyes. He finished following the fence line all the way to the end before he came over. Then he saw the damaged stems. McGowan bent close. He got out his phone and took a shot of Hawthorne's window. Then he compared it to the one they had on file.

'Bloody hell, she's right.'

'Don't sound so shocked,' Collins said. 'There's more to Ruby than meets the eye.'

'The day I take advice from someone who keeps their nose stuck in a book is the day I–'

Collins cut him off. 'Stop strutting, McGowan, I'm freezing to death. Get on with taking the pictures. We're not going to get much else from the area. Still, we can requestion the neighbours. Someone might have seen him. And make sure you get good close-up shots. Maybe Luke Sanderson can give us an estimate of the suspect's height or weight based on what's happened to these stems.'

'I think that might be stretching it,' McGowan said. 'This isn't CSI you know.'

'Shut up and get on with it.' Collins started heading back to the car.

A neighbour pulled into his driveway. Ruby watched him get out. He opened the boot of his car and took out a kid's scooter. It was metallic pink and had a fancy bow tied around the handle. Likely a Christmas present.

It was bad timing. The scooter transported Ruby back to when she rode her own pink scooter to pre-school every day, her little brother beside her in his stroller. They had their own game. She would ride in front as quickly as she could, then turn around and zoom towards him. She remembered how the front wheel juddered as it rolled over the pavement, faster and faster. And he would kick his legs and squeal as she raced towards him as if it was the best game in the whole wide world.

McGowan was staring at her. 'What's up with you?'

'Nothing.'

He snorted. 'Looks like you've seen a ghost or something.'

'I said it's nothing.'

He was a hateful arrogant man. How she wished she could answer him back and, like Soraya and Collins, come out with an acid comment.

Instead, she turned and made for the car, fighting to keep in the tears.

Chapter Twenty-one

Did you know, us killers aren't the only ones who have habits?

Oh no, everyone has them.

In fact, having predictable habits and following a daily or weekly routine can bring about someone's downfall. How? It's obvious, isn't it? Because, for someone who's watching carefully, all those habits and patterns show the little chinks of opportunity. They show where someone is vulnerable. They highlight the places a killer can slip inside someone's guard. With ease.

My next victim is in the supermarket. She's wheeling her trolley down the vegetable aisle, passing the cauliflower and now the potatoes. I'm on the other side at the oranges. I lift one to my face and smell its sweet fragrance.

I'm tempted to pass right by her. I know I can do it. She won't even give me a glance, I bet you.

The daring of it makes me excited. My hands are sweaty on the trolley handle. Walking slowly, I ease closer, step by casual step. It's after work and the place is busy. I wait my moment and then pass right behind her. I'm close enough to touch her hair and I almost wet myself.

I think this means my confidence is building. I'm getting into the swing of it. I'm getting good at it. I can kill and I can stalk and I can get away with it. Two down and a third one almost in the bag. I'm becoming a master, just like my mentor.

But I mustn't make a mistake. I must not fuck up. Backing off, I disappear to the self-checkout. In a few minutes, I go out to wait in my car. All the time I'm aware of security cameras and that's why I'm wearing a baseball cap. I know they do it in films and it's cheesy but it works. No one will be able to see my face. Genius.

Naturally, I've parked in a dimly lit area and where I also have a clear view of her car underneath the bright lights.

Twenty minutes later, my target emerges, her trolley piled high. I watch her pack her shopping into the boot – groceries, gifts, Christmas decorations. Clunk, she slams it shut. Then wheels the trolley back to the trolley park. She doesn't even look around her. Not even a single glance over her shoulder. She really should be more careful. She's no idea who's watching her.

In my mind's eye I imagine the moment she turns. I'm going to take her in her garage, sneaking in before she has chance to close the outer door. Her husband won't be home when she gets back. There will be fear in her eyes. Then desperation. Followed by abject terror. The idea of it starts up the excitement again.

Preparation – check. Out-think the lawman – check.

She's starting her car and I follow her out to the exit. Then we proceed to her house which I know isn't very far away.

I stop on the opposite side of the road. One neighbour is home but they've already drawn the curtains. I wait for her to go inside. The garage door is electric and slow to rise and slide itself along the ceiling. Naturally, it's equally slow to close. I already did my research and I timed the number of seconds it takes.

She's gone in. She's cut the engine. There's a pause before the door starts to come down again. I sprint across the road and dart inside.

Chapter Twenty-two

Twenty-five years earlier – Amy's story

The baby was born. And baby Ryan affected Mike in a way Amy would never have imagined. He adored the baby. He stopped going out. Those were both good things, but they were accompanied by something which wasn't quite so good – Mike became hyper-attentive to Ryan's needs. And Ryan and Ryan's comfort and well-being became Mike's number one priority.

It all started to go wrong. Mike shouted at her when Ryan cried. He told her it was Amy's fault if the baby was upset. Mike didn't like it if Ryan's milk was cold. He would tell her off or complain if Ryan's bottle wasn't ready on time. He even set up a timer in the kitchen and if it rang and Ryan's food wasn't ready, he would get angry. Or angry if Ryan's nappy needed changing. Or when Ryan whimpered. She started to jump and stress every time the baby made the slightest noise.

Mike had always treated her like a servant to his own needs and now he treated her like a servant to Ryan's. She was trapped.

Was this normal behaviour for a father? She didn't think so but she really didn't know. Some days she could hardly think straight. Her first husband hadn't behaved in these extreme ways but then again, he'd not been a model husband either. Mike was probably under strain from being a father for the first time. Hopefully he would mellow as Ryan got older.

One day she sat slumped and exhausted on the sofa trying to find enough energy to get dressed. Her attention was caught by the television.

It was a news flash. The South Coast Killer had claimed another victim. There was footage of the spot where the woman had been found dead the previous night, strangled with her own tights. It was the third killing of the South Coast Killer. With one hand, Amy pulled closed the neck of her dressing gown and clutched Ryan with the other. As she listened to the reporter detailing how the woman died, Amy's back went chill.

The woman had been discovered in a car park. The police believed the killer might have marks on his face where the victim scratched him. Also, he might have oil on his clothes because the victim had been found not far from an old spillage.

The South Coast Killer was spreading fear. Women were terrified to go out of their own houses. The police believed the same man had killed all three women. They said, perhaps there had been other victims, as yet undiscovered. His identity remained a mystery.

The list of victims' names came up on the screen, along with the dates of their deaths.

She froze.

By her feet, Rosie was trying to get her attention. Four-year-old Rosie was insistent, waving a picture in front of her mother. But Amy ignored her daughter. She could not tear her eyes off the first date on the screen because it was the day she made the special dinner for Mike. How could she possibly forget the day she told Mike she was pregnant?

The same day she discovered the blood marks.

'Do you like it, Mummy?' Rosie asked again.

It's just a coincidence, Amy told herself. One stupid nosebleed. It's got nothing to do with the South Coast Killer. Still, she sat, unable to drag herself away from the voice of the reporter.

They were showing a picture of the second victim. Amy took a quick in-breath. The woman had blonde hair. The shirt with the ripped button flashed into Amy's mind. And the one blonde hair clinging on behind it. She remembered holding it up and how it had reflected the light.

She pulled Ryan close and so tight, he protested.

'Mummy! Do you like it?' Rosie shouted.

No, no, this was silly. It was only one stupid button and one hair. How she wished she could remember the date she found the damn thing dangling. Ryan had not arrived and she must almost have been at term, and now he was eighteen months old.

She stared at the screen. The woman's dead body had been found a year and a half ago.

Amy shook her head. No, it was another coincidence.

Rosie likely sensed a problem. She came to sit close. The little girl cuddled up, searching her mother's face.

'It's all right, darling,' Amy lied. 'There's nothing to worry about.'

A few hours later, she finally managed to get herself off the sofa. She managed to stop clinging on to her children for dear life. She almost managed to convince herself she was imagining things.

On automatic, she took a shower and got dressed.

With every fibre of her being, she wanted to avoid the laundry room but she knew she had to go there. She felt like a zombie as she walked back downstairs. Her steps led her to the washing area. Sifting through the pile one by one, she made herself sniff Mike's clothes. Her hands were shaking. She could hardly get herself to lift each item because she dreaded what she might discover. Each inhale she had to force herself to do it. But she found no stink of oil, no funny petrol smells, nothing.

She felt a huge wave of relief. She was simply being

ridiculous. From lack of sleep and the stress of caring for the children, everything was getting to her. It was as if, for a few moments, she struggled to fend off a weird kind of madness. As if reality had tried to warp into being nothing like she thought it was. It had been horrible. And now the bubble had burst. Things had gone back to normal. Everything was okay.

Mike could be cold and he shouted. But at other times, he was charming and attentive. He made her feel wanted. He wasn't a killer. That was impossible. He was an ordinary man and a father. A plain and simple ordinary man reacting to the normal pressures of babies and young kids. Everything else was in her imagination.

Life returned to normal.

Yet, a few days later, she was forced to ask herself why Mike's trousers had suddenly gone missing. Why had a perfectly good pair of trousers, and ones which he often wore to work, simply disappeared? By then, it was too late to check the refuse bin in the yard because it had been cleared for the week. She remembered stuffing the shirt in there. Had Mike done the same with his trousers? And if so, why? Was it because they had oil on the knees?

The thought made her feel ill.

Then a few nights later, when Mike was getting undressed for bed, she noticed a red mark on his neck. It was a mark that was starting to heal. A gouge and a thin trail, as if made by a fingernail.

She still tried to deny it. Maybe it had been made by Rosie or Ryan? Sometimes the kids scratched when they didn't mean to. Yes, that had to be it. She pushed away her suspicions and told herself she was being an idiot. But deep down inside, she felt very, very scared.

Chapter Twenty-three

When the envelope arrived at the police station, an entire crack team pounced on it. Grant's three detectives, the technology experts, and several lab technicians were there within moments and, in Grant's absence, so was Detective Chief Superintendent Fox.

Desk Sergeant Wilson knew each second counted and ran the suspect envelope through to the incident room. Like last time, Wilson knew he was right. The typing was the same and the envelope was the same. He would stake his reputation on it.

When Sergeant Wilson placed the envelope on Diane Collins' desk, she felt blood plummeting from the top half of her body, down into her legs. She pressed her hand to her temple.

'It's another one,' was all Wilson said.

She had been waiting for it. Or had she been waiting for the moment when someone came up behind her and manhandled her to the ground? When she felt someone ripping at her clothes? And then a restriction around her neck.

Now Diane regretted not telling her husband about the names.

McGowan was by her side. In fact, since she argued with the inspector, every time she turned around McGowan was there. He even insisted on accompanying her home and then had checked the premises before he left. McGowan swung by to pick her up in the morning, stood next to her at the photocopying machine, which was in the station for Christ sakes, hovered behind her in the queue at the sandwich bar, barging anyone out of the way who got too close. McGowan went as far as evil-eyeing her oldest son's friends which had been enough to send them packing. McGowan had been thorough. She knew Inspector Grant had put him up to it and she should probably thank him, if she wasn't so pissed off.

By the time she put on gloves, a circle of spectators gathered around the table. The team kept their distance and Diane tried to keep her nerve steady. She thought about her second oldest son and how, the previous weekend, she watched him scoring for his team. It had been the last basketball tournament before the holidays and a big match. In her mind's eye, she saw him leaping for the hoop in slow motion and the ball arching perfectly. It dropped through the net, and he flashed a smile her way as the crowd cheered and his teammates whooped with delight. It had been a fantastic moment.

Diane took a breath and slit the flap. She tapped the envelope and a photograph slid into the tray.

It was upside down.

Please don't let it be my house.

Diane wished Inspector Grant were by her side. It would make her feel better because he always made things seem better.

McGowan stood so close, she could hear him breathing. DCS Fox put a hand on her shoulder but she didn't feel the reassurance she would have felt if it been her own inspector.

Please don't let it be my house.

A lab technician offered her a plastic prong. She took it and carefully turned over the picture.

Everyone craned forwards a little.

'Do you recognise it?' Superintendent Fox asked.

Her vision became fuzzy. She heard a funny buzzing in her ears and her mind went blank. For a moment she really couldn't tell if it was her house or not. She ran her eye over the outline and tried to focus. Was it? It was so dark. She couldn't make out the details. There was a top floor with three windows. And a front door with some kind of porch. Then her brain caught up with the facts.

'It's definitely not my place.'

Her legs felt like they turned to spaghetti. Everyone who held their breath, which was probably pretty much everyone in the circle, let it go. The room was suddenly filled with noise and activity. It was all focused on the paper in the tray.

Within seconds, a copy of the house was up on each screen in the room.

The personnel department at the hospital had identified four women with Diane as either a first or second name. Officers were stationed discretely at each woman's workstation and outside where they lived.

To complicate things, it turned out Diana had become a much more popular name than Diane in the last twenty-five years. Grant had wanted to include them on the potential list of targets and the hospital had fourteen staff members with a first or second name of Diana. It had been a hard call. Fox lacked the resources to cover so many women on a twenty-four-hour basis.

Instead, they came up with a compromise. Delaney and the hospital personnel department invented a fun Christmas competition and hospital staff had voluntarily given photographs of where they lived to enter. Of course, the Dianas had all been targeted and they all applied. The house photographs of each entrant had been scanned using image recognition software.

In the incident room, the seconds ticked by as they waited to see if there would be a match.

Diane took the opportunity of eyes being off her and she sat down. She wasn't the next target. Thank goodness. She sent a quick text to her husband. She didn't tell him she loved him, which would be too alarming to a police officer's spouse, instead she asked him to get bread on the way home. He responded in seconds, with yes, and a kiss.

Now she could better concentrate on her job and help nail this bastard. Who the hell was he after next?

Delaney was doing a manual check on the Dianes and then the Dianas, while the program was checking through the hundreds of photographs donated by staff. It seemed to take forever. At the end of it, they were all still staring at the screen. The photograph Collins had taken out took up one side and the other half was still a black oblong.

'There's no match, ma'am,' one of the technicians called out.

'None here either. It doesn't belong to a Diane or a Diana,' Delaney said.

'You're seriously telling me nothing has flagged up from the frigging hundreds of photographs we got?' McGowan said.

Collins shared McGowan's frustration. There was a woman out there and this was her house. And they had no idea how the hell to find her.

'Get to work!' Fox yelled. 'I don't care how the hell you do it but find the person this belongs to.'

Inspector Grant had travelled to London to meet with Mark Winslow, Ruby's old colleague at the university. By the time he got back, the team had drawn a blank on every single lead and every single possibility they'd been painstakingly collecting for the last forty-eight hours. They did not have a clue who the killer was targeting.

As soon as he walked in, David Grant could sense the floundering. He felt his people anticipating another failure. That was the genius of the killer, he thought grimly. The sending of the photographs was the murderer telling them they weren't good enough. That they would never get there in time.

Grant had to stamp out the doom before it took hold.

He toured the room, making small remarks here and there

– a pat on the back, a nod of encouragement, a small joke. It pulled them up. They felt better and everyone started to feel more positive.

Grant put his arm around Diane's shoulders. For the briefest moment, she rested against him.

'Sorry I wasn't here. How are you holding up?'

'Perfectly,' she said. 'Oh, and your wife sent a message asking me not to let you have any more doughnuts.'

Collins said it loud enough for other people to hear. It was her way of helping the team, Grant knew it and he didn't mind them getting their spirits back at his expense.

'Have you been brainwashing my wife with your health tips again, Delaney? As long as she didn't ask you to make me run around the car park.'

A few people laughed. The atmosphere shifted and energy picked up again. McGowan stopped scowling. Delaney and Ruby stopped looking like the world was about to end.

His visit to London had been worth it. For a start, Mark had spilled the beans about the professor. It was as Grant suspected, Ruby was the real mastermind behind the serial killer report. It turned out she'd done most of the actual interviewing of killers too, including the interviews with Travis. Though he worked with Ruby for over three years, Mark knew squat about Ruby's private life and he only knew the minimum about her background. Which is why Grant had done some of his own research. It had been interesting.

He gathered his top team.

'Let's generate options. We need to know where else to search for this potential victim. And I want to know whether we've any other suspects coming up on the radar. I asked you to go wide on this one. Now throw out your ideas. It doesn't matter how crazy it sounds. You're the ones tuned in and I want to know what you're thinking.'

Collins and McGowan had been interviewing every man

paroled from Travis' prison in the last twenty-five years. Delaney had been interviewing all the prison officers. Everyone had their hands full. Grant had added three more detective constables to the team, making six in total, and set them the task of identifying members of the public who had contact with nurse Mandy Jones and Doctor Hawthorne in the last year. The constables had to speak to them on the phone or invite them in to the station for an informal chat. It was a mammoth task. On top of that, the press office had put out a request for witnesses who might have seen the suspect outside the victim's houses taking photographs. Calls were coming through.

'Thoughts on the next victim first,' Grant said.

'It could be someone from the group against Travis receiving treatment,' Collins said. 'There've been no demonstrations yet but they might already be on the killer's radar. I know they've got a website up and running.'

'Good. Put together a list of names and addresses. We'll get patrol and the constables to do a check on foot.'

'We've identified addresses of patients who were receiving treatment on the same day as Travis and constables took photographs of where they lived which were already added to the database,' McGowan said. 'Should we think about trawling the rest of the three hundred patients at the hospital, starting with the Dianes and the Dianas?'

'Get onto it,' Grant said.

'We're really stabbing in the dark,' Delaney said. 'All we've got is the list of previous victim's names and we can't go public with Diane or Diana. This is spiralling and we've nothing concrete.'

'I'm not so sure,' Ruby said. 'I think I've got something.'

All eyes turned to her.

Ruby tapped her pen on her notepad. She'd been considering the meaning of the photographs. She went through her thoughts with them – the killer spent time observing people in the dark, which meant they must have watched for hours. It said something about the killer. After all, she should know, she had nocturnal surveillance habits herself, though she didn't mention that to Grant's team.

And there was something personal about taking pictures of where people lived. What was the killer obsessed by? Family life? What went on behind closed doors?

She told them she thought this was someone with a wound, a resentment from the past which had festered and got bigger and deeper until it had driven them to seek revenge. If that was so, then as she said before, these killings were random and meaningless. The more important question was, who was the ultimate target?

Ruby didn't think the women who'd been killed so far were important to the killer. They were collateral damage to get the ball rolling. She also didn't believe the ultimate target of the killer was someone at the hospital, because the trail had begun there and you don't begin a trail where you want it to end. No, in her view, the most recent house would more likely belong to someone closer to the real final target of the killer.

'That's a big leap you've made to the idea of the killer having an ultimate goal,' McGowan said. But he stroked his moustache and didn't contradict her.

'Do you mean they're aiming at a person? Or do you mean some kind of big, mass killing like we've seen in terrorist attacks?' Collins asked.

'I'd say a person,' Ruby said.

That was the thing with tracking serial killers, Grant thought, you had to be prepared to go places no one in their right minds wanted to go. He watched as Ruby received appreciative murmurs from Delaney and Collins. McGowan wasn't on board yet, but then again, he was always slow to warm to newcomers, or new anything.

'Any idea who?' Delaney asked.

Ruby shook her head.

DCS Fox had been hovering at the edge of the group. She nodded at Grant and headed off. Grant could tell she liked the way Ruby thought, and he did too, though she was still a mystery woman. When he checked up on her, he had found some interesting details. According to the files, Ruby Silver lived in a children's home from age four, following the death of her parents in a car crash. Over the years, she stayed with a few foster families and Ruby always ended up running away. After each running away episode, her foster placements broke down which meant she was returned to the children's home.

There was also one curious record he came across. At aged only nine years old, Ruby went missing for two days. She was found on the moorland, a long way from her foster family, and not very far from Himlands Heath.

'What do you think, sir?' Collins asked.

'I think Ms Silver might be on to something, and if the next victim isn't going to be from the hospital, then there are two other places which seem high probabilities,' he said. 'The first is the prison. Delaney, you'd better contact prison staff to request pictures.'

'On it, boss.'

Grant knew they were all imagining the worst. He was too. That a young woman's life was already being taken. Perhaps it was happening even as they talked.

'And the second possibility?' McGowan asked.

Grant made sure to meet each person's eye and to keep his voice calm. 'Collins and McGowan, we need to do a name check and get photographs from everyone working from this station. And I want to extend it to include spouses and significant others.'

Chapter Twenty-four

Amy's story

Amy watched the news every day. She dare not miss it. She engineered the cleaning and the chores to give her enough free time to be sitting on the sofa for the beginning of the early evening programme. Months had passed with nothing new about the South Coast Killer. Then today it was all over the television again. The South Coast Killer had claimed another victim.

The dead woman's name was Sandra Knight. Amy mouthed the name to herself as the victim's picture came up on the screen.

Ryan was almost two. Rosie was chatting to him about her day at pre-school and showing him the picture she'd painted. Rosie loved to do paintings for Ryan. She drew flowers and dogs and cats. Especially cats because Rosie really wanted a kitten and Ryan did too. Today, Rosie had drawn an elephant.

Rosie loved her little brother. She told him about craft work and the sand pit and how one day they would hold hands and she would take him to pre-school. Then after, together they would go to big school and she would look after him.

'Shussh, Rosie,' Amy said. 'I can't hear what they're saying.'

Grabbing the remote control, she turned up the volume. Her eyes were riveted on the photograph of Sandra Knight. The reporter was saying this time the police got something. A camera captured a suspect leaving the scene. Reaching down, Amy clutched the edge of the sofa.

It had been a million in one chance, but the police believed the South Coast Killer had been caught on a security camera mounted outside a DVD shop. The owner of the DVD shop was being interviewed. A microphone was thrust into his face and he was telling the reporter how he had so many thefts over the last few years, he got fed up with his profits going down the toilet and put up his own security camera. She listened as he babbled on about how expensive it had been and how he fitted it himself. The interview was taking place at the end of the street. You could see the DVD shop's sign in the distance, the area all taped off and crawling with police.

Then came a shot of a different newscaster back in the studio. They were going to show the clip. The precious three seconds of footage was to be shared with the nation. The newscaster reminded them there would be a telephone number to call if anyone had information to give to the police. Amy's pulse began racing. She started to feel lightheaded.

Please let it be someone short or fat. Or bald.

There was a pause. Technical difficulties, she presumed. The newscaster was saying they were about to air it and people should be patient.

And then it started. It was a grey grainy blur, not at all in focus. She saw the brick corner of a building. Then a man appeared. He moved across the frame and his movements were choppy. He was wearing a short coat. In the first frame he was in view and he was looking away from the camera but his face was caught on the side. In the second frame, he walked a couple more steps. By the third frame he was out of sight.

For a moment, her heart stopped. The man was tall like Mike. His hair was short like Mike's. The side of his face was the same shape as her husband's. And there was something about the way he walked. It was only a few steps. But he had long legs and an overlong stride, and a slight slope down of his right shoulder.

Oh God.

She leapt to her feet and screamed at her daughter. 'Rosie!'

Rosie yelped and dropped her crayons.

Scooping up Ryan, Amy ran for the stairs. Rosie was panicked and she followed right behind, trying to keep up.

Amy was thrown into a blind terror. Running into her bedroom, she pulled a suitcase from the top of the wardrobe. Dumping Ryan on the bed, she dragged it into Rosie and Ryan's room. She threw things in at random – anything she could get her hands on – Ryan's nappies, clothing, anything she could grab.

She was almost too breathless to speak. 'Rosie, put in your stuff!'

Amy couldn't think straight. Back in her own room she grabbed whatever clothes she could scoop up in an armful. Rosie understood the urgency and did her best to add in some of her own things and Ryan's toys and some shoes.

Amy shut the case with a snap. With the case in one hand and Ryan under her arm, she almost fell down the stairs.

'Get your coat! And get Ryan's.'

In the hallway, Amy tried to stuff her feet into trainers. They wouldn't go because she was rushing so much. She dumped Ryan on the floor and grabbed her purse and money from the side. Then she suddenly thought of her passport and ran to get it in the kitchen. Pulling out a drawer, she scattered the contents on the floor to find it.

By the time she got back, Rosie had her own shoes on and Ryan's were on his feet.

'Good girl, Rosie!'

Grabbing them both, Amy flung open the door. The world was spinning. The street was a blur of green grass and red brick and grey tarmac. It was surreal because she could hear a song playing from a neighbour's radio. Was there time to go for help? No. She must get out. She must escape.

Her hands were shaking so badly she dropped the car keys and had to scramble for them on the driveway.

She slung the case in the back. When she opened the rear door, Rosie scooted over to her side while Amy strapped Ryan into his child seat. The buckle of Ryan's safety harness was stiff and she had trouble closing it. The slick sweat on her hands made it worse. Then she reached over and clicked in Rosie.

Amy was about to fling herself into the driver's seat when she felt a hand on her shoulder. The hand was heavy and large, and it gripped her like a vice. Amy felt such terror, her world started falling apart. As if it disintegrated into little fragments around her. She turned, flattening her back against the car, and found herself face to face with her husband, Mike Travis.

Chapter Twenty-five

Amy's story

'Get in and drive,' Mike Travis ordered his wife.

Amy wanted to scream for help but nothing came out except a gulping sound. All she could think about were the television reports of the murdered women. What had Mike seen? Did he know she'd put a suitcase in the back? Did he know she was running away?

'Wh-what's wrong, darling?' she managed to say.

'I said, get in and drive.'

He sounded reasonable. Maybe she was wrong. Maybe he didn't suspect anything. But then why was he behaving like this?

Amy wanted to cry but Ryan started kicking his feet against the back of the driver's seat. It was something Mike never tolerated. Her heart stopped. In the panic of facing Mike, she had almost forgotten the children were there.

'Stop that, Ryan,' she said.

She got in the car and twisted to look at her son. Ryan took one glance at his mother's face and howled.

She tried to get her brain to work. What was Mike thinking? What was he doing? Did he know she knew?

Mike slid into the passenger side.

Having him so close flooded her with more terror. Her

whole body was shaking. She wouldn't be able to pretend she wasn't in a state.

'M-my sister phoned. She's had an accident. I need to go to the hospital.'

It was a preposterous lie. Amy was estranged from her family. She'd fallen out with her parents and her sister years ago and vowed never to speak to them. In fact, she and her sister hated each other's guts and Mike knew it.

'Is that right?' Mike said.

She cut him a glance and thought she saw a ghost of a smile. But not a nice one. No, a nasty one she'd never seen on his face before. She tried smiling in return but instead found herself emitting a high-pitched squeak like a frightened child.

'Turn left at the roundabout,' Mike said. 'And then take the road out of town onto the bypass.'

Did the journey last two seconds or two hours? She felt so numb it was a marvel she controlled the car. It was as if she left her body and floated somewhere else, watching events unfold.

At every intersection, she did her best to catch the eye of another driver. No one looked her way. Silently, she prayed for a passer-by to notice something was wrong. They didn't.

Of course they wouldn't because she had no courage to try to attract attention. She was too frightened of Mike. And people were too busy. She was just another woman driving a car. Nothing strange. Nothing odd. Nothing else.

What about if she threw herself from the vehicle? Surely someone would rush to her aid? Then she could get away. But she didn't have the nerve. She was trapped. Incapable of shouting. Unable to move. Paralysed. Powerless to function outside of Mike's quiet commands.

From the very beginning, it had been like this with him. She was weak and dependent on him for praise and attention. She did everything he wanted. And now she was incapable of saving herself.

Her hopes faded as they passed traffic light after traffic light. The streets became less busy and there were fewer houses. They were heading south east from town, towards the heath and moorland around Himlands Heath.

'Mummy, I'm scared,' Rosie said.

Amy started crying. She tried to pretend to herself it would all work out okay. That Mike hadn't seen anything. That he didn't suspect a thing. That they were simply going on a family drive. She wanted to tell Rosie the same lie but she couldn't get it out of her mouth.

'Mummy?" Rosie pleaded.

The sound of her daughter's voice somehow stirred some courage.

'Please Mike, what's going on?'

'Just drive.'

'I-I don't want to drive. I want to go home. Can we do that? Can we go home? Please Mike, let's go back and I'll make us a nice supper.'

He looked at her. 'Where did you think you would go?'

Oh God, he knew about the suitcase. He must have seen it all. Witnessed her blind urge to flee. Again, her husband's voice was measured and yet she found it chilling. Was he reasonable or was he furious? Was he a killer or was he a normal husband? Was he going to let her live, or was he going to…

A few miles down the road and Mike directed them towards a nature reserve. They kept going until they reached a small car park. Amy's heart sank when she saw how deserted it was.

The heathland was used by ramblers and dog walkers, but who would come out on a freezing day like today? And surely most people were busy making their last-minute plans for the Christmas holidays? She was alone.

A few days earlier, she and her daughter had put up the Christmas tree and Rosie had decorated it. At the thought, Amy sobbed.

'Please Mike.'

'Get out of the car.'

The cold struck her and froze the sweat on her back. She shivered violently. Mike took her arm and pulled her away from the car. There didn't seem to be any path. Quite a way in front, she could see a stand of trees. Amy looked down at her own legs. Oh God, she was wearing a skirt. And tights.

'Mummy!' Rosie screamed.

Oh no, oh no, not Rosie and Ryan. Not the children. Please, please, surely he wouldn't…

Amy finally found her voice and she screamed as loud as she could.

'Get out of the car! Run Rosie! Run!'

They were almost at the trees.

'Rosie! Run!'

Mike dragged her into the middle. He was pushing her to the ground and pulling off her shoes. Amy kicked her legs. He pushed her face into the mud and she fought back.

She was looking up at him. He was like an animal, snarling, then grinning in delight. Rough fingers tore down her tights. She felt his hands on her neck and then a thick twist of material was tightening around her throat.

She twisted and bucked and he used his knee to grind her hips into the ground.

Amy fought her husband off for as long as she could, finally finding her courage and gouging her nails into Mike Travis' face.

Her last thoughts were of her children. Her beautiful baby boy. And her lovely daughter. Please let Rosie get away. Please let her run and run and never stop.

Chapter Twenty-six

Inspector David Grant discovered the identity of the third body a few hours later. A husband had made an emergency call and an ambulance had been dispatched to a three-bedroomed house. The house in the photograph.

The husband had returned home to find his wife dead on the garage floor. The victim's name was Eleanor Diane Vickers. She worked as a secretary. In fact, she was secretary to the psychiatrist responsible for the inmates at Travis' prison.

Delaney and Grant drove to the crime scene together. As they crossed town, it was late night shopping and the high street was packed. Grant heard Christmas music blasting from shops and Christmas lights hung along the roadside.

Delaney was driving. 'It's not exactly the season to be merry, is it, boss?'

'Dealing with the dark side is part of the job. You'll get used to it colouring everything but you mustn't let it drag you down. Life goes on. Usually it makes me appreciate the good things even more. I hope it'll do the same for you.'

'Yes, sir,' Tom Delaney said. He liked it when it was just the two of them. In those quiet moments, Grant had a habit of talking to him in a more private way and giving little snippets of advice. As if the inspector were pulling him closer. It made him feel proud and loyal and grateful. He would do anything to be Grant's right-hand man.

David Grant was thinking about his own holiday preparations. His son, Daniel, was coming over from America on a rare visit. Grant's daughter, Chrissie, would be bringing her new boyfriend for the first time. Damn it, he'd be lucky if he managed to snatch a couple of minutes with them. He wondered if his family would forgive him, though he knew they would, especially his daughter.

Delaney pulled in behind the pathologist's car. 'Looks as if Luke Sanderson got here ahead of us. How does he do it?'

McGowan, Collins and Ruby arrived soon after. The four of them waited outside the garage. The less people contaminating the area, the better.

'Go and speak to the husband please, Collins. McGowan, check the details with the ambulance crew. Delaney, speak to the neighbours. Ruby, you're with me.'

They pulled on plastic shoe protectors and went in.

The woman lay near the back, close to the entrance door to the kitchen. It looked as if she'd been unloading her bags. The boot of her car was open and spillage littered the ground – groceries, bits of paper, a smashed bottle. Grant could smell sweet sickly liquor and, sure enough, it had been a bottle of Baileys. The sticky mess was running across the floor.

'Hello, Inspector,' Luke said. 'Please be careful where you step.'

The pathologist was intent on his work. 'She was strangled using her own tights. No evidence of sexual assault.'

'Any footprints?' Grant asked, hopefully.

'Doesn't look like it. He's careful, and it was a short struggle. The killer easily overpowered her.'

Grant crouched down. 'We were right but we were too late,' he said quietly.

Luke didn't say anything, as if not knowing whether Grant was talking to him or apologising to the victim.

Ruby didn't want to look. It was too hard and too horrible to see the woman's last moments etched on her face. The fear was still there. And the desperation. Ruby turned away.

The forensics team were taking photographs and recording where each item had landed – a packet of ham, a tin of beans, pasta spilling from a split box. The sticky Baileys had pooled near a car tyre. Ruby bent to peer under the vehicle. And came face to face with a child's stuffed toy.

She screamed.

One of the lab women put a steadying hand on her arm. 'It's all right, detective,' she said. 'It's only a kid's cuddly animal. It must have been with the victim's shopping.'

The woman must have thought Ruby had been spooked by the two big eyes staring at her.

'I won't have anyone disturbing my crime scene,' the pathologist said. 'Get her outside.'

They led her away.

She leant against one of the police cars. The victim had brought home a stuffed animal. Not any old animal, but a tiger. The famous one from a children's story. It had two big eyes and a mouth in a permanent smile. In the story, it liked to jump all over just for fun. And it was exactly the same as the cuddly tiger her little brother had held close when he went to sleep every night. It had been his favourite.

That tiger. It had smelled of him too. Ruby knew it did because so often she snuggled right down next to him and watched him fall asleep, one of her own small hands on her brother. The tiger smelled of his sweet breath. If she breathed in deeply, she thought she could still catch the faint scent of–

'Ruby, are you okay?'

She snapped her eyes open. It was Tom Delaney.

'The inspector asked me to check on you.'

Oh no, she was making a right fool of herself.

'Sorry,' she mumbled.

'Don't worry, we've all been spooked by crime scenes. It's nothing to feel awkward about.'

He gave her a reassuring smile.

'The woman had some toys. Christmas gifts, I suppose. Did she have children?' Ruby asked.

The inspector and McGowan joined them.

'Feeling better?' McGowan asked.

To other people it probably sounded innocent. It made Ruby curl up her toes.

'I just spoke to the neighbours, sir,' Delaney said. 'They say she and her husband lived here on their own. They've no children. And they didn't see or hear anything suspicious.'

'The electric door of the garage was shut when the husband arrived,' McGowan said. 'No signs of forced entry. I'd say the killer got in after the victim drove in, and before the door had chance to close. It's confirmed her name's Eleanor Diane Vickers. As we were told, she's secretary to the psychiatrist who works with the inmates at Travis' prison.'

'Looks like you were right, Ruby,' Delaney said. 'He's veered off choosing his victims from the hospital staff. He's still going for the middle names – Edith, Grace, and now a Diane.'

Sergeant Delaney didn't finish the list. He didn't need to because they all knew it.

'Goddam that son-of-a–' McGowan said.

Ruby completed the list in her own head – Edith, Grace, and Diane... and then Sandra and Amy.

For the first time, Grant looked angry. 'Don't stand around yapping. Finish off properly here and let's get back to the station,' he snapped.

Chapter Twenty-seven

I'm watching the evening news.

There's a full report on The Strangler's latest attack. It seems I'm starting to get famous. Things are getting better.

They show pictures of the secretary making her look like everyone's favourite aunt or cousin. Whereas I know her as the condescending witch who always speaks down her nose at me while I organise my appointments with the psychiatrist. That's why I chose her. Because I hate her guts.

I'm eating my take away supper and the kitchen is full of fish and chips scents and vinegar.

I have to say I'm a bit disappointed. The journalists haven't tagged on to my brilliance with the women's names yet. Are they really so stupid they haven't realised? Or are the police manipulating them into keeping it secret? So much for journalists' independence. Either way, it would be even more satisfying if every Sandra and Amy in Himlands Heath, or better, the whole of the south of England, started gibbering in terror.

When the reporters have finished going over it again and again, I make my way down to the basement. The basement is my special place. I spend hours and sometimes days down here caressing and drooling and admiring. You see, it's the room where I keep my mementos.

The basement smells odd and I like to think it stinks of

death. And suffering.

They are showcased on special shelves. I move slowly from one item to another.

First, the teardrop necklace from the nurse. It's smooth to the touch. The colours of the amethyst are lovely. I like the delicate tracery of the silver around the stone. My fingers caress it. I run my tongue over the silver. And I can taste death.

Then the ornament I took from the doctor. It's an enamel goldfish set in a solid glass sphere. Very beautiful and doubtless special to her. It was placed right beside the photograph of the girl and I have an idea it was a gift from her or closely associated with her in some way. The girl in the photo looked like a stupid brat. But I remember the intensity in the doctor's eyes when she was drawn to the picture. The goldfish reminds me of her desperate pleading to live. And my own power to refuse.

Then there's the memento from the secretary. It's a miniature dream catcher I snatched from her key fob. It's worn at the edges, which means she's had it on there for a long time. It was precious to her. Most likely it represented something special in her life.

I take it and lift it to my lips. I smell it, breathing in deeply, drawing it into my lungs. I touch my tongue to the glass beads and I can taste the woman's terror.

I took her life. I took everything. And it makes me smile.

I don't want to let it go, but eventually I place it tenderly back in its place. Then I turn and face another shelf.

The souvenirs on this one were left to me by my mentor. The police never recovered them and that's a tribute to the cleverness of the man who taught me everything I know.

My mentor enjoyed collecting jewellery from his victims. I select the first small item from his row. Reverently, I bring it to my lips.

Chapter Twenty-eight

Inspector Grant received more bad news. Travis would be coming in for another treatment at the hospital. With the third victim's body lying in the morgue, Grant felt the pressure. To make the situation worse, the anti-Travis group planned to be out in force. They would be demonstrating at the hospital entrance.

'Looks set to be a nightmare,' Grant said to himself.

He walked into the briefing room and shook Inspector Mainwaring's hand. Mainwaring was from uniformed division and their two teams would be working together on this one. Mainwaring would be securing the hospital and Grant didn't envy him the job.

Grant wanted his team on the ground, scouting for anyone acting strangely. Suspects were often known to turn up and mingle with the crowd. It gave a certain sort of criminal a kick to be close to the detectives hunting them down.

Fox was clear with them how she didn't want Travis to have any contact with the public. His only contact would be with police officers, prison officers and a select team of hospital staff responsible for his treatment. Access to the ward and the hospital premises would be tightly controlled. Everything would be monitored. Travis wouldn't be able to blink without them knowing it.

Superintendent Fox was up on the podium. She made eye

contact with senior officers in the room – there would be no murders in Travis' wake, everyone would have to remain vigilant, her priority was to have as many officers on the ground as possible. No screw-ups. No chinks.

It was Grant's turn.

'This is another emergency pain control assessment. Four prison officers will escort the prisoner and he will only have access to areas where we've cleared out members of the public. As you can imagine, this is going to be a logistical nightmare. You all know a nurse was killed on that ward. Then Doctor Hawthorne was murdered. The doctor's deputy will administer the treatment to Travis herself. Only two nurses and two technicians will be in attendance. They are all volunteers and have been vetted by my team.' He paused. 'All four are men.'

Grant scanned the room for protests. This was going against everything he believed in on equalities issues. He was a firm supporter of women in all roles and he had left Doctor Patel to make her own choices. But he and Doctor Patel agreed they needed to minimise the risks as much as they could. And the killer had so far only chosen women. His team had run background checks on the four members of staff and seen no suspicious markers.

Doctor Priya Patel was level headed and calm under pressure. Grant couldn't have asked for anyone better to be in charge.

'That doctor woman must have guts.' An officer said in the front row. 'And she's not got any of the hit list names either, which is useful.'

'Doctor Priya Amira Patel? No, we're clear on the name issue there,' Grant said wryly. 'But that doesn't mean we're letting our guard down. Any one of the hospital staff could still be a target for the killer. Any one of them could be the killer. Which is why Doctor Patel will have an officer in her driveway for the foreseeable future.'

The next name on the list was Sandra. Hospital personnel had identified four members of staff with Sandra either as their first or middle name. All had been requested to stay at home and a uniformed officer would be stationed with each one.

'The treatment should last no longer than two hours. We aim to get him in and out as fast as possible.'

He handed the podium over to Inspector Mainwaring who began assigning duties.

Grant went to stand beside Collins. His team had already checked with the prison and they had no staff with the name Sandra. The next on the list was Amy and they had none of that name either. At the police station, they'd identified one woman with a middle name of Sandra. Superintendent Fox was keeping her well clear of the hospital operation and had assigned her an officer escort.

But what if the killer deviated? What if they picked their victim from a different pool? It hadn't escaped Grant's attention how with so many police resources trained on the hospital, now would be the ideal time for the killer to strike again. But in a completely different place.

Delaney, Collins and McGowan were ready to go, eager even. Ruby looked as nervous as she usually did. Inspector Grant decided to keep her close to him. He needed her expert eyes on the crowd but he couldn't risk her freaking out like she had in the garage.

'Keep your eyes open at all times,' Grant told his top team. 'The killer could be in the crowd. He could be watching from a distance so stay alert. There's a high probability he'll turn up, even if he doesn't take action.'

'But how are we going to recognise him if he's there?' Delaney asked.

It was the million-dollar question.

'Don't sweat it, Delaney. It's a copper's instinct,' McGowan said.

'Exactly. I can't tell you what to look out for,' Grant said. 'Except you'll know it when you see it.'

Inspector Grant asked Delaney to drive. 'Learn from this operation, sergeant. A public site like the hospital is impossible to secure. Uniform will set up a perimeter at the roadside and they'll keep the anti-Travis protestors back at that point. Patients still need to come and go, and so do emergency paramedic crews. Funnels will be created to check people entering and exiting the building. As you can imagine, the whole set-up will be a bloody mess.'

'Yes, boss. And you really think the killer might turn up?'

'A murderer once asked me for directions. We were leaving the crime scene and he was in the crowd. He couldn't resist it.'

'And you nabbed him straightaway?'

'Oh no, it took us weeks to work our way towards him. But that exchange was a mistake. In the end, it helped us nail him.'

Delaney whistled.

Grant continued. 'It's a strong possibility he'll turn up today. He's wanted to get our attention from the beginning. He sends the photos. There's something going on between him and us. Don't you think so, Delaney?'

'Who can say, boss? But if there's something going on, it seems to me it's *you* the killer wants to attract. You're the one involved in the original investigation. You're the one he sends the house photos to.'

'Good observation. A man like that, he's the type to want to look you in the eye. Let's make sure as hell he's not the only one to get something out of this morning.'

As they turned off the main road, they passed the protestors. It was a much bigger crowd than expected, almost sixty people. Uniform were keeping them behind crowd-control barriers.

David Grant turned his head as he spotted a familiar face. 'Stop. Drop me off here.'

Delaney wasn't happy. 'Is that wise, sir? At least let me come with you.'

The crowd were quiet and polite, awaiting Travis' arrival. Most of them seemed like perfectly ordinary people, yet they'd be capable of turning into a screaming mob once the prison van turned up. Not to mention the fact the killer might be amongst them.

'It's all right, sergeant. I'll see you shortly.'

Meredith Evans' sister, Carys, was right at the front pressed against the metal barrier. She wore a tweed-effect skirt and a winter coat. Carys' woolly hat and scarf were keeping out the cold and Grant wished he'd remembered to bring his own gloves. His breath misted as he spoke.

'Good morning.'

'Hello, Inspector. Cold, isn't it?' she said. She was clutching a placard. It said only one word – No.

'Is this really wise, Carys? We've an unknown murderer on the loose and–'

She interrupted him. 'Why should Travis get treatments which cost thousands? He's a monster. We're going to be speaking to the press later. Lots of people agree with us.'

'What I mean is it's a risk being in the open like this. I really would prefer if–'

'No, David, don't try to put pressure on me. I couldn't fight for my sister. At least let me fight for this.'

He didn't know what to say. He sincerely hoped she'd not been manipulated into turning up. Organisers of groups sometimes piled emotional pressure on people like Carys because they wanted the families of victims involved. It gave their cause more kudos.

'Please. I'm only thinking about your safety.'

He scanned the faces around him. Actually, there were quite a lot of elderly people. Perhaps they were the only ones with enough free time to come and stand there on a weekday morning.

Carys Evans didn't look like she wanted to be persuaded by him. Grant knew that as an officer of the law, it wasn't his place to convince her one way or the other. She was free to do as she wished. He could only be concerned about her as a friend. He was about to turn away when she grabbed his arm.

'I don't want revenge, you know that. But why should he die in comfort after what he did? I want justice for Meredith. I want to know what happened to her. I want Travis to say it. Say he did it. I know it shouldn't make any difference but I want him to say it before he dies. And to tell me where she is.'

He saw the terrible agony in her eyes. Her hand was on his arm and Grant covered it with his own and nodded. He understood, he really did.

Inside the hospital, Doctor Patel was waiting for him. She was authoritative and calm, and with her manner, she reminded him rather horribly of Doctor Hawthorne. He shook her hand warmly and marvelled at how she seemed so collected in such a pressured situation, whereas the hospital manager, Mr Tanner, was a bag of nerves and emotion, his stutter more enhanced than usual.

'I t-tell you he's dangerous and no one will listen.'

'Mr Tanner sir, we have not yet identified a suspect. Travis is not under suspicion.'

'I don't care. I t-t-tried to divert Travis to another facility.' A bead of spit flew out. 'At the last moment, the hospital board got involved and so did our Member of Parliament. I couldn't believe it when Doctor Patel rejected our proposal to divert him elsewhere.'

Grant wanted to tell Tanner to shut up. He didn't like the way Tanner liked to undermine his colleagues, worse still how he discussed it in public.

The hospital manager threw his hands in the air. 'It was

crazy. She argued how the next nearest hospital with the right expertise is over four hours away. She said it would involve too much s-suffering on the part of the patient to have to be transported so far. It was unbelievable.'

Grant gave the doctor a sympathetic look. 'Sir, we really don't have time for this.'

'It's the most ridiculous decision I've heard in my life.' Tanner gave Doctor Patel a look of disgust. 'Mandy Jones and Susan dead and she allows him to come here again. Words fail me.'

'I had no choice, Tony.'

Medical opinion versus political considerations – what a terrible position she'd been in. Grant knew how hard it must be for her and her team after they'd lost two of their own. And with Tanner on her back too.

'I think that's quite enough, sir,' he said firmly.

'If anything happens today, it's on your heads,' Tanner said.

Mr Tanner was to give a small address to a posse of press clustered in the foyer. He paced at the back, consulting his notes. He was dressed in an expensive navy suit and shirt and his tie was askew. Every time Grant saw him he wore smart clothes, yet he somehow never looked polished.

When Tanner walked to the front and cleared his throat, the press fell silent. Tanner kept to his professional line, not his personal one. He talked about how it was a human right to receive pain medication and treatments to prolong life, and it was a human right to end life in comfort. This was the situation with any cancer patient, regardless of whether or not they were a felon.

A uniformed officer came up to Grant and spoke close to his ear. 'The prison van's twenty minutes away, sir.'

Grant gestured to Mr Tanner it was time to wrap it up. Then he left it to the uniformed officers to get the press out. Grant had hoped the Hospital Manager would have other business to attend to but Mr Tanner had clearly decided to make himself a nuisance for the whole visit. Tanner joined Grant and Doctor Patel as they headed for the treatment room.

'Tony, there's no need for you to follow me around,' Doctor Patel said.

Tanner looked offended. 'I have responsibilities too. You can't push me out.'

Delaney came hurrying towards them.

'What is it, sergeant?' Grant asked.

'Sir, I just got news. The pathologist has got preliminary results on...' Delaney's eyes flicked towards Tanner and Patel. Doctor Patel nodded and continued walking down the corridor.

'If you would excuse me a moment, sir' Grant said smoothly as he walked a few steps away. He could tell from Delaney's face the news wasn't good.

'Has Luke got the DNA results from the latest victim?' Grant asked in a low voice.

'Yes boss, and it's not what you want to hear.'

Delaney cupped his mouth and leaned closer. He wanted to make sure only his Inspector got the information.

'He found a partial match to Travis's DNA on the secretary.'

Damn it. The secretary had been nowhere near the hospital nor the prison. She worked from an office in town. She never had direct contact with Travis. Ever. It was the worst it could have been. Grant's mind went straight to the lost little boy. Travis' son.

Tanner was watching. 'Bad news, Inspector?'

Grant called over his shoulder. 'A few routine issues with the perimeter.'

'What are we going to do?' Delaney whispered.

'Keep it to yourself and don't let it throw you off course. I'll warn Inspector Mainwaring. Let's concentrate on getting through the next couple of hours.'

Chapter Twenty-nine

Tom Delaney thought Travis looked much worse than before. The man's skin was greyer and his prison overalls were soaked in sweat. Travis' limbs were shaking so badly he had difficulty climbing onto the bed and had to be assisted by the prison officers.

The stink from the man was worse too, and this time Delaney thought he caught the whiff of decay. Travis was deteriorating quickly.

Doctor Patel was serious and concentrated.

They were crammed around the bed – Delaney, the four prison officers, Inspector Grant, Doctor Patel and her members of staff. Two police officers were outside the door. Four more were stationed at each end of the corridor and six along its length. Use of treatment rooms on the floor had been cut down to a minimum and patients were being escorted via a service stairwell and a secondary corridor where possible. But a few people would need to have access to the corridor, it simply could not be avoided. The situation was far from ideal.

Grant had left Ruby Silver with Collins because Ruby had simply looked too ill at the thought of entering the same room as Travis.

Mr Tanner was still making problems. He said he had supervisory responsibilities and therefore it was necessary for him to have access to the area. Grant was finding it difficult to keep his patience with the man. At least Doctor Patel had made it clear Tanner had no right to enter Travis' treatment room. That was her domain.

Grant was waiting to question the prisoner. This time he wanted to focus on what happened to Travis' son, Ryan. But when she finished, Doctor Patel shook her head.

'I'm sorry, Inspector, I can't allow it. My patient is much too weak. We're having difficulty stabilising him and it will take time for the regimen I've put into place to have its effect. I can't agree to your request.'

'I respect your judgement, doctor. However, with three women dead, I've important questions only Travis can answer.'

Grant used all his charm and his tactics of calm persuasion and managed to squeeze a couple of minutes out of her.

'Two minutes only, Inspector. And I'll be waiting outside.'

Travis locked red snake-like eyes on to Grant.

'Are you going to threaten me again, Inspector?'

His voice was weaker.

Grant tutted and shook his head. 'Now, now, Travis. We both know the real threat you're facing is destruction by disease.'

Tom caught the characteristic curl of Travis' lip.

'Tell me about your son,' Grant said.

'Have you found his remains yet?'

'I'm looking for Ryan alive.'

'Ah, and how is your own son? Daniel. I hope he's well. So many risks young people take these days. I'd hate something bad to happen to him. And that's not to mention your lovely daughter Chrissie.'

Grant gripped the rail and leaned over the bed. 'Have you been in contact with Ryan?'

Travis opened his mouth as if to reply and then his eyes rolled and his body started to shake.

'Convulsion!' Tom shouted.

One of the prison officers yelled for Doctor Patel. She rushed in and Grant stepped out of the way.

'Leave now, Inspector,' she said, as she ripped open Travis' shirt.

Tom wondered if Travis might die on the spot and a part of him hoped he would. Travis talking about Grant's family shook Tom up. In this job, he'd often been told being single was an advantage. How could Grant stand it?

Travis didn't die. He stayed under the doctor's supervision for several hours and then he was taken back to the prison.

During that time, Grant kept in constant contact with Inspector Mainwaring. He also kept in contact with Sergeant Wilson at the station.

By the time the prison van left the premises, there had been no reports of incidents. Uniform had no problems with the protest group and nothing happened to the other patients nor staff at the hospital. Patrol had been on high alert across the whole of Himlands Heath. No major incidents were reported and Wilson had no call-outs to dead bodies.

'How did it go in there?' McGowan asked.

'He mentioned the inspector's adult children by name. It sounded like a threat,' Tom said. 'And then he had some kind of fit and almost died.'

'Shame he didn't,' McGowan said.

'Any results with the public?' Grant said.

'I didn't get the eyeball on anyone outside. Most of them were over sixty and I'd not rule out an older killer but none of them had the vibe. Same for my patch inside.'

'Ditto,' Collins said. 'Nothing on the floors I was patrolling. Everyone seemed normal. But sir, your family…'

'I know how he operates. He likes talking about them. He's done it before so don't get distracted. It's his style to throw stuff out left, right and centre to see which ones he can make you run after.'

'Feeling so ill and right before a convulsion?' Delaney said. 'Boss, are you sure?'

'Shouldn't we check to see if–?' Collins said.

'We need to stay on track.' Grant's voice went up a notch. 'Do not allow yourselves to be distracted by *anything*. I cannot stress it enough. Delaney, you pick up on anything?'

Delaney shook his head. 'I don't think so. No one seemed to stand out.'

'You sure about that, sergeant?'

'Certain, boss. We were together most of the time.'

'Most of the time but not all of it.'

'If you've got something to say spit it out,' McGowan said.

'It's nothing. I didn't see anything, but, I dunno, I kept getting an idea someone was watching on that third floor and then when I scanned around I couldn't see a thing.'

'All non-essential personnel were cleared out,' Collins said. 'It was cut down to the bare minimum.'

McGowan slapped Delaney on the back. 'You see! The bastard must have blended in. He was like part of the wallpaper. Maybe it was a member of staff. Or it might have been a patient or a relative. And he got in very close, he was right on top of you.'

'It's a skill certain killers perfect over a lifetime,' Ruby said. 'They merge in. Nothing seems odd about them and so the attention rolls off them like water off a duck's back. Nothing sticks. The mind is fooled but sometimes the subconscious isn't.'

'Which is why Delaney got a vibe.' McGowan slapped Delaney on the back again.

Collins nodded. 'He was here. Amongst the chemo and the radiotherapy patients and essential personnel. Dr Patel would not allow those appointments to be rearranged.'

'Make a list,' Grant said. 'Split it up between you and start background checks.'

Who the hell could it have been? Grant felt on edge. He was waiting for the next blow. For the next photograph. The next murder in the chain.

As the crowd control barriers came down and the hospital returned to normal, he sent his team out for a proper lunch.

'Shouldn't we start on the checks straight away?' Collins asked.

'Take an hour out, you deserve it.'

Ruby looked as if she was going to her own funeral. 'Are you joining us, Inspector?'

'I've some catching up to do.' He was glad Ruby had Collins and Delaney as a buffer. McGowan could be too hard sometimes. The problem was Ruby needed to learn to stand up to him.

On the way back to the station, he grabbed a sandwich and ate it at his desk. He sent an email to Daniel and exchanged texts with Chrissie, glad they were both living their own lives and no longer children. He understood why his team felt protective. Having a family who could be threatened was one thing he would never get used to. Yet he felt certain in his own mind it was a bluff. And the team was stretched so thin, he could not allow any loss of focus.

Then he went to see Luke Sanderson – they had things to discuss.

On difficult cases, David Grant had several habits which helped. One of them was having a heart-to-heart chat with the pathologist. Grant had spent many a session in the morgue mulling over the details of a victim. It was a tradition he had started early in his career with Luke's predecessor, who became his firm friend. And somehow, it had been natural to continue with Luke.

The young pathologist sat at his bench, peering down a microscope. With boyish good looks and blonde hair, Luke couldn't have been physically more different from his predecessor. Strangely, he had a similar manner and a similar quiet reflection to the man he replaced. Grant thought Luke must have an old soul inside a young clubbing-and-partying body. How was that even possible?

He knocked on the open door and went through. 'I hope I'm not interrupting?'

It was quiet. Luke's staff must be at lunch. All Grant could hear was the hum of the air-conditioning and the tap of his own footsteps on the tiles.

'I was just finishing up,' Luke said. 'Have you come to inspect the victim?'

It was how they always started. As if a tour of the body said it all and from there, they could spin out ideas and find avenues to explore which hadn't yet occurred to anyone. The seed which solved many cases had been planted in Grant's mind down there in the morgue.

Luke checked the labelling on the giant metallic drawers. He gave one of them a tug. The tray slid out, coming to a smooth cushioned stop. Luke folded back the covering and they both stared down at the body of the killer's third victim.

'You've read my report?'

'Of course.'

'Then you know this crime scene was as clean as the others. The killer is careful to not leave trace evidence. All we've got is a couple of fibres which come from a wool coat, black. They're different from the husband's coat or hers. There's nothing new. Except for this.'

Luke walked to his bench and held up a key fob. 'You see this little thread?'

It was a single strand of blue.

'The break is fresh. According to the husband, she had a tiny dream catcher. He remembers seeing it on there until recently. He won it for her at the fun fair.'

Now that was interesting.

'The doctor's daughter said her mother kept a goldfish ornament on her desk,' Grant said.

Luke raised his eyebrows. 'And?'

'There was no goldfish there after the murder. Flora bought it for her mother when they were on holiday and she was adamant her mother still kept it in the same place. She's only four years old and the husband wasn't so sure, he thought the doctor might have put it somewhere else. Their disagreement gave it less credibility.'

'But the daughter could have been right. And what about the nurse? Was anything missing from her?'

'The husband said not.'

Grant thought back to Ruby's comments. She said the house photographs this killer sent were personal. What if the daughter was right and the goldfish had been taken? And they had a dream catcher missing. Did it mean their killer was taking personal items from the victims? This was important. He would have to get Collins to check with Mandy Jones' husband again.

Luke waited, not rushing in with his own speculations. It was another thing Grant liked about coming down here. It gave him space to think.

Grant took a seat at the bench. He thought back to the two killers he had convicted who collected body parts; Maloney who took fingers and Kurt who cut out his victim's tongues and stored them in a jar. They had both been gruesome cases. He could recall three other killers who collected mementos; Rogers, Flint and Bergerman. All three took personal items from the people they murdered.

'From the look on your face, you think the possibility of it being a memento-taker is important.'

'Trophy-takers are very particular types of killers.'

Luke tapped a keyboard and brought a screen to life. 'Do you want to talk to me about the DNA?'

Grant felt a dark shadow pass over him. It was the kind which people sometimes describe as someone walking over their grave. Then it was gone and he felt warmer again.

'You said it was a partial match?'

'That's right. Take a look at this, it shows my results. I got a full match with Travis' DNA on the first victim, then I found none on the second, and now a partial match on the third.'

'Did it definitely come from Travis?'

'It's definitely from a male and I don't have an explanation for why it's partial. The sample could have degraded, that's one possibility.'

'Travis had a son.'

'Right.'

'We never found him. Twenty-five years ago he was classified as missing presumed dead, though I was never convinced. Could this be from him?'

'It could be and so could the DNA taken off the first victim.' Luke spoke slowly, as he thought it through. 'But I couldn't say for sure without having a sample from the actual person and trying to do a match.'

The boy would be the same age as Grant's son. He had tried so hard – to get the evidence to pin on Travis for the five killings, to find Meredith and Isabella and then track down the missing child. He hadn't managed it. Events forced him to let the last one go – the missing child.

And the boy Grant failed was now a prime suspect. If he had succeeded in finding him, this might never have happened. Grant almost choked on the irony.

Chapter Thirty

Grant gathered his team. Each sergeant gave their update and Collins was the last to give her report.

'Eleanor Vickers worked as the prison psychiatrist's secretary for the last twelve years,' Collins said. 'She had access to confidential records. She made appointments. As such, she had a link with the prison Travis is in and a second prison down on the coast. The psychiatrist also saw private patients and she handled those appointments too. He emphasised she never had any direct contact with clients. It was all telephone and admin work.'

His detective constables were already following up inmates in both prisons who had been seen by the psychiatrist. The priority for interview was any who were now free men. Then they needed to get alibis for each one for the time of each murder. It was a lot of painstaking paperwork, phone work and legwork. Namely, it would take ages.

The psychiatrist had been unable to release his records on private patients due to confidentiality constraints. However, he told Grant if the police had a specific suspect in mind, he would be able to be more cooperative.

The pool of potential suspects was widening with each murder. It was the opposite of what Grant wanted. They needed to be focusing down and narrowing the field. The whole thing was spiralling out of control.

He stared at the team doughnuts and did his best not to take one. McGowan helped himself. Ruby was unreadable, sitting quietly, Collins was patient, sipping at her mug and Delaney was waiting for what was coming next.

'We've a new priority. A major suspect has come to light and location of this person takes precedence. Delaney and McGowan, I want you to lead on this.'

Grant took a photograph from his pocket. It was the one from his dusty, bottom drawer at home. It was the picture the original investigative team had of baby Ryan Travis. He pinned it up.

'This is Ryan Travis. The missing son of Mike Travis and Amy Travis. He was almost two years old at the time of his mother's murder. We need to find him. DNA evidence on victims one and three brings him into the frame. I want you to comb through everything from the original Ryan case files and come up with something we missed. Anything. We've got to track him down.'

There was utter silence in the room. They were hanging on his every word.

'Between the time of Amy's murder and when we caught Travis, there were four months when Travis was on the run. We never found out where he was. I always suspected he found a new girlfriend and she was harbouring him. You all know Amy was his fifth victim, found on the moors outside Himlands Heath. The injury she inflicted on Travis, namely the ripping of his ear-lobe, was the reason we were finally able to take him into custody.'

Tom nodded. He'd read it in the case notes. They'd found a tiny piece of skin and flesh at the scene of Amy's death. It had been discovered after a painstaking combing of the mud, the trampled heather, leaf mould and bracken. The finding had been little short of a miracle and was a victory for the investigative team. They didn't have DNA analysis back then but the pathologist surmised it came from the earlobe of the murderer. Amy had scarred her killer.

By then, Grant was convinced the killer was Travis. Travis had come up on the radar with two of the previous victims – as an old boyfriend of Edith and as a casual friend of Diane. Each time, Travis escaped prosecution due to lack of evidence, despite being brought in for questioning several times. Grant wrote in his reports how he believed Travis gave subtle hints all along. It was as if he was toying with the investigative team. He wanted to show them how clever he was.

When Travis went on the run after Amy's murder, the police put out an alert. The whole country searched for him.

Without the ripped ear, Grant thought that after murdering Amy the man would have returned home and pretended he knew nothing of his wife's whereabouts. It would have been in line with his character and his mode of operation. But his injury made it impossible.

For four months Travis became invisible. If he'd found another woman to take him in, who could it have been? It could only be someone vulnerable. Someone cut off from the flow of ordinary life because Travis was up on the nation's radar.

Four months later, an assistant in a dry cleaner's spotted a man with a tiny nick in his ear. It was healed and Travis had dramatically altered his appearance but she called the police anyway. It was the break Grant needed. When Travis returned to collect his dry cleaning, he was taken into custody. He was charged. He would certainly have been convicted of Amy's murder but, better than that, under Grant's interrogation, he admitted the murder of all five women. But he never told police where he had been living. Or with who. Or what happened to his son, Ryan.

In the notes Tom read, the inspector wrote how the man was proud of his sick achievements. Travis wanted the public to know he was clever. For years, he successfully hid his identity as a serial killer. He murdered, undetected and without restraint, while living in the disguise of an ordinary man.

Tom Delaney brought his attention back to Grant. The inspector was staring at the photograph of Ryan Travis.

'Travis took the child from the scene of Amy's murder,' Grant said softly. 'His half-sister, Rosie, was found in a state of shock at the roadside but we never found Ryan.'

McGowan cleared his throat. 'The son was believed dead, wasn't he?'

'Would Travis have killed his own son?' Grant turned to face them. 'It's possible. But no body was ever found.'

'Meredith Evans and Isabella Rees were never found either,' McGowan said. 'And he likely killed them too.'

Grant tried not to wince.

'If Ryan Travis is alive,' Collins said, 'by now he'd be...'

'Twenty-eight.' It was easy for Grant to know.

'Could Travis' terminal diagnosis and closeness to death have somehow triggered Ryan to go on a killing spree? Copying the chain of murders carried out by his father?' Collins asked.

She looked at Ruby.

Ruby did her best not to flounder. Not to let them know she was drowning. Of course, she should have known Ryan would come up as a suspect sooner or later. It was one of the reasons she was here, wasn't it? Under the desk, she curled her fists tight.

'We don't know anything about the son,' Ruby said. 'He would have spent very little time with the father. A year and a half when Travis was married to Amy and then potentially four more months after the father abducted him.'

'You don't think that's enough to have an influence?' Collins asked. 'I thought the early years were the most important.'

'In terms of serial killers, it's an unknown. Nature and

nurture both play their part in forming a killer. There are elements which are there from birth but it doesn't mean they're triggered to become part of the psyche. That was the whole basis of Professor Caprini's research – what makes a serial killer? We have a lot of data but we don't have a definitive answer. In fact, the balance fell slightly in favour of nurture being more important. Or, to be more precise, lack of nurture.'

'A couple of years with Travis doesn't seem like very long,' Delaney said.

Grant felt suddenly old. 'It doesn't matter. We need to find him. Period. It will either clear his name or implicate him.'

Everyone nodded and Grant left them to get on with it.

Back in his office, Grant swivelled his chair so he could stare out of the window. Every senior officer he knew had regrets and baby Ryan was his. It wasn't a mistake but Travis was right, he should never have been hailed a hero, not with a child missing.

He never fully understood the feeling he had towards the boy. The only explanation was the link with his own son. Two little boys of a similar age. One with all the chances and the other who could have had chances if only Grant had been able to find him. He'd be carrying this one to his grave.

Did he want to believe Ryan was guilty of the murder of three women? Grant didn't know what he believed. His secret wish had been to one day find the boy well and alive and happy. Grant ran his fingers through his hair and rubbed his face. He would have to put that hope away and stick with the facts. That was the basis of all good detective work. And so far, the facts said Ryan Travis was the prime suspect for this string of deaths.

Chapter Thirty-one

When Soraya received Ruby's message, she was doing the make-up for a man about to shoot his first part in a television series. It was a big break for him and a big break for Soraya's beauty business. For the next four hours, she found it almost impossible to concentrate. Lucky for her everybody else was so stressed they didn't notice. As soon as filming finished, she flung everything into the back of her car, unrinsed and unsorted and in a heap. Ruby never called for help. Which meant it was serious.

The car park at the climbing wall was half empty. Soraya jumped out and wrapped her arms around her friend. Ruby didn't say much. It was a bad sign. Soraya knew how Ruby operated. Probably she needed a hard climb. It would loosen her up and help her put into words whatever was troubling her.

'Fancy a climb?' Soraya said, trying to keep it light.

Ruby nodded and trudged towards the entrance, her head down.

They got changed and equipped. Soraya kept up a one-sided chatter about the filming and the show and the part the man played and the crew.

She watched as her friend worked her way up the wall. Ruby made the first moves quickly. Too quickly, Soraya thought. Ruby was usually a climber who paced herself and knew how to save her energy. In no time, Ruby was gaining on the top.

Soraya took up the slack in the rope and called up. 'So, are you going to fill me in on what's bugging you?'

Ruby screwed her eyes shut. She could see her little brother gurgling as she raced towards him on her pink scooter. She could feel him slipping off to sleep, his sweet breath on her face as he hugged his tiger and she hugged him. Then she saw her stepfather dragging her mother away. Ruby could see her mother stumbling. Her mother was sobbing and getting further and further away. Then Ruby heard Amy's screams going on and on and on. Ruby was clinging on to the climbing wall. She wanted to cover her ears with her hands. Her whole body started a violent tremble.

Her mother was screaming. *'Get out of the car! Run Rosie! Run!'*

Ruby's stepfather dragged her mother into the trees. She was out of sight.

Rosie undid her own safety belt and then tried to get Ryan out. He was too small to help her. He didn't know what was going on. He simply stared at her with big frightened eyes.

'It's all right Ro-ro, don't be scared,' she said. 'Mummy says we need to go.'

But the fastening on Ryan's seat held tight. Try as she might, Rosie's little four-year old hands didn't have enough force to get the clip to open. She tugged at it. She pulled on the straps. She got desperate, pulling at Ryan's clothing and at his arms and legs to try to get him through.

Then Amy screamed in the distance. It was a horrible blood-curdling noise. Rosie started to cry.

After a few minutes, something worse happened. The horrible screaming stopped. Her mother went silent.

'It's Ryan,' Ruby whispered.

Soraya had to strain to catch what Ruby said.

Ruby had frozen three-quarters of the way up the wall. 'Ryan? What about him, darling?'

The bottom fell out of Soraya's stomach. Oh God, surely not the little brother her friend had been searching for all her life? Soraya knew the whole desperate story. Soraya and Hawk were the only people in the whole world Ruby had trusted with the truth.

'Darling, what's happened? What have you found out?'

Ruby opened her eyes. She didn't really see the wall. She was still stuck on the heath, with the fog closing in and her mother screaming. Her right hand reached for a tiny hold and she swung her foot into place on a little ridge below it. Sweat was coursing down her back and she paused, trying to push away the memories and failing.

Ruby held on tight.

She had been too young to understand what happened to her mother. Yet in a primal way, little Rosie knew. She knew from the way her mother screamed. She knew from the way it all went quiet. It was death.

And then her stepfather was striding back to the car. Snot started running out of her nose. She was sobbing and pulling and pulling at Ryan to get him out and he was stuck fast.

When her stepfather got to the car, he made a grab for her. Rosie scooted out of the way. She scrambled free and ran.

It was getting dark and she was quick on her feet. She didn't run towards her mother. Instinct kept her away from that place. Instead, she ran across the moor. When she got to tall bracken, she threw herself down on the ground and crawled on her stomach as quickly as she could. She didn't stop until her body found a hollow amongst the heather. And she lay there still and very quiet.

She had always been good at hide and seek. Rosie

scrunched herself as tiny as she could go. She breathed in earth and plants. Her stepfather was shouting her name and thrashing the ground with a stick. He was coming closer and closer. She tried not to whimper.

And then a miracle happened – Mike stop hitting with the stick. Rosie kept her eyes screwed shut. Then she heard the car door closing and the sound of the engine. And Mike Travis drove away with her little brother still in the back.

Ruby tried to rub her eyes with the back of one hand. She pulled up her foot and dug her toe into a tiny depression. Then she pushed up on it to get to the next handhold.

'Inspector Grant thinks the killer is Ryan. They've got his DNA on two of the victims.'

'Shit.'

Her voice broke. 'If I hadn't left him…'

'Honey, you didn't leave him. You were a kid. You tried to get him out.'

Down on the ground, Soraya made doubly sure the rope was nice and tight. She had the horrible feeling Ruby might simply let go and plummet to the earth. In a state like this, what if Ruby did something crazy?

'It's my fault. I should have saved him, I should have… '

'Come down, Rube. Let's talk about this on the ground.'

'All this time I've tried so hard to believe he's not dead. To believe Travis didn't kill him. I've searched and searched. I've never given up hope. And now–'

Ruby was sobbing.

Soraya clung on and caught the eye of a male climber. She made wild faces and mouthed words at him. He nodded his understanding that Soraya wanted him to bring Ruby down. He came over with his climbing partner and began making his way up the wall.

'Hurry!' she hissed at him.

'It's all right,' Soraya said. 'Everything's going to be okay. We can sort it out together, you and me. Just like we always do.'

'It's too late.'

Ruby pushed up onto the next hold, then reached her foot to a crack and pushed up another half metre. She was almost at the top. The last move was the dodgy one. The one where you had to leap into space and grab a hold that seemed too far away. The one Soraya never managed. And Ruby always did.

The male climber was over halfway up and gaining on Ruby but he hadn't reached her yet. It was then Soraya heard a distinctive metallic *click*. Ruby had unattached herself from her safety harness.

'Don't you dare, honey. Reattach yourself right now! Don't you dare make that last move without safety.'

'What if it is Ryan?'

Soraya heard the torture. 'No! You always believed in him. You've spent your whole life looking for him. You've never given up on Ryan. Don't do it now.'

Her friend clung on.

'You believe in him. You always have.'

Ruby's hand strayed into space. Soraya saw the shift of weight as Ruby made ready for the final lunge.

'Don't do it.'

Her friend's arm was in mid-air.

'Don't do it! Don't give up on him now. He needs you. *I* need you.'

Ruby's arm stayed in mid-air for what seemed like an eternity. Then she pulled it back and brought her weight back. Soraya heard a *click* as Ruby re-attached herself. After a few seconds, Ruby abseiled down to the floor. The male climber followed her down.

'That was dangerous. She shouldn't climb in a state like that. I wasn't near enough to grab her,' he whispered in Soraya's ear.

'Thank you anyway,' Soraya mouthed to him. Soraya held Ruby tight. 'Don't you ever do anything like that again.'

'I wasn't going to... I was just being stupid. I'm sorry.'

But Soraya wasn't fooled. She kissed Ruby on the forehead and held her close some more. Just like she used to do at the children's home when Ruby had nightmares.

That night, at The Nag's Head, Ruby stared up at the sloping ceiling. She had told Soraya about the strange connection she felt to David Grant. What drew her to the inspector? Was it because he had the same desire which had haunted him for years, hidden away? Was it because they both needed to know the truth about what happened to her baby brother? How was that possible?

When Grant put up the picture of Ryan, the regret on his face had been clear. He had even been careful where he'd put the pin.

Of course, the inspector would not remember he'd met Ruby once before. When he interviewed her when she was Rosie. Rosie had spent a freezing night on the heath. She might have died of hypothermia, except the next morning, a passing motorist found her. She remembered how the woman wrapped her in a blanket and drove straight to a hospital. Inspector Grant came to see her there.

Afterwards, Rosie was given a whole new identity. Rosie became Ruby whose parents were killed in a car crash. She became anonymous. And she lived that lie ever since.

Ruby pulled the duvet up to her shoulders.

Ryan was her sweet little brother, with dimples and dark curls and with rosy lips shaped like a heart. He was the lost boy she had always loved. Like Soraya said, she had never given up on him and she could not do it now. Yet, to find justice for the murdered women, and prevent more deaths, she would have to find the strength to put aside her feelings and search for the truth.

The one thing she did know was she had to find him. And if the truth turned out to be the worst, she knew it might destroy her.

Chapter Thirty-two

Ruby gripped the steering wheel. Overnight, the weather had got a lot worse. Forecasters said snow was a certainty. The question was, would it fall before or after Christmas. At the station, bets were on for whether Christmas Day would be a white one.

Ruby was accompanying Inspector Grant to the prison to interview Travis. It seemed he was deteriorating so fast, this might be their last chance.

She kept her eyes fixed on the road. Before leaving The Nag's Head, she threw up twice, then once again at the police station. When Grant asked her to drive, she was glad because there had been a couple of icy patches and it demanded her concentration. It meant she could try to prepare for the man she was about to face. Her serial-killer stepfather.

Travis was the serial killer Ruby interviewed for Professor Caprini's research. He was the killer she had spent her life wanting to meet, and at the same time dreading ever seeing. In fact, he was the one killer she obsessively tracked for the whole of her life and the real reason she studied criminal psychology in the first place.

When the opportunity came to interview him for Caprini's research, she'd spent days vomiting in terror. Back then, Ruby believed it was her one chance in a lifetime to find out what he did with Ryan. Had Travis killed him? Or had he allowed Ryan to live? This was Ruby's second chance. She must make sure she got what she wanted.

Earlier, Grant spoke to Doctor Patel. The doctor warned him Travis needed to be admitted either to a hospice or to the hospital as an in-patient. He was entering his last weeks sooner than expected and the prison hospital was no longer an appropriate facility.

Inspector Grant was glad for the heads up. Doctor Patel told him she would not be able to give the police access once Travis reached the final stage. He got straight on the phone to the prison and the Warden granted them an interview for that morning.

'Any thoughts on our approach?' Grant asked.

Ruby took a double bend, noting the sign which warned of black ice. 'This stretch is treacherous,' she said. 'I hope it's been salted.'

'Me too,' the inspector said with a small smile.

'The killer is making a strong connection to the original murders,' Ruby said. 'With the names. And he selected a timing for the first murder which coincided with Travis being in the public domain. Why? Is this the work of Ryan Travis? Has he been in contact with his father? Or is this trail a smokescreen to hide the real reason for the killings? We need information to help us answer those questions. As for how to approach Travis...'

Her stomach did a flip. She gritted her teeth, willing herself not to throw up right there and then.

'You look a little green. Are you feeling all right? Let me know if you'd like me to drive.'

'Oh no, don't worry. Maybe I'm getting a bug or something.'

She hoped the inspector didn't start questioning her about the incident in the garage. Or wondering if she was fit to continue with the work. She *had* to continue. She had to find out the truth.

'Travis wanted glory for what he did,' the inspector said. 'He wanted admiration. I'm going to start by asking about Meredith and Isabella. This might be the last opportunity I get. As for his son, I know Professor Caprini questioned him at length on his family and Travis spoke about Ryan. I think we can pick it up with him again.'

Ruby nodded. She would be the best one to talk to Travis about Ryan. She was the one who'd questioned him for Caprini's research, though Grant didn't know it. She really should stop protecting Caprini.

'Travis and I have a long history,' Grant said. 'You'll be my extra eyes and ears. I want to know if Travis knows anything about what's going on.'

'He might have insights too. It takes a killer to know a killer. What he says might give away if he's been in contact with the murderer.'

Grant grunted his response. The time he took advice from Travis would be when he was ready to roll over and die – which would be never, or when he was ready to retire, and go on some damn-awful, boring-as-hell cruise with a lot of other old people – just like his wife Lily wanted them to do. And that most definitely wasn't today.

The prison hospital was spartan compared to the public hospital. There were three inmates on the ward and they all looked pretty ill. Travis was by far the worst. He looked as dreadful as he had at the hospital – ashen and sweating, his face gaunt and his jaw tight. It didn't look as if the pain had subsided much and the smell coming off him was awful.

Grant didn't feel much sympathy. He didn't see this person as entirely human. He couldn't, knowing what Travis was capable of.

Ruby had to rush off to the toilet to retch. This man was the monster from her nightmares. She wondered how she ever managed to face the interview for Caprini's research, though she supposed it had been easier without an eagle-eyed witness like Grant observing her. She remembered how Soraya and Hawk had spent days building her up to it.

This was it. Now or never. And she owed it to her brother, and to the dead women.

Grant sat down close to the top of the bed. A prison guard stepped back to give them space. Grant had already asked for the rest of the personnel and the two other patients to clear the room.

Travis' breathing rattled in and out of his chest.

The inspector carefully questioned him about the recent murders. Travis' eyes were red. For fifteen minutes he lay there as Grant talked and asked questions. Travis gave no response.

The man on the bed was incapable of posing a threat to anyone, yet Ruby did not feel safe. She felt in mortal danger. She could hear her mother's bloodcurdling screams. She could hear the sound of her stepfather beating the ground as he grew closer and closer to her hiding place. Terror crawled its way up her spine.

Then, the inspector took something out of his pocket and held it up. Ruby almost fell off her chair. Under her thighs, she clutched the seat with both hands, her knuckles tight.

'This is a photograph of your son, Ryan,' Grant said. 'He'd be in his late twenties by now.'

The blood was rushing from her head and she fought to not pass-out. Through the haze, Grant's voice rambled on in the background. Ruby talked sternly to herself, using brute willpower to make herself stay sitting there.

Then something even worse happened. Like an orange on a stick, Travis moved his head on the pillow. He was turning in her direction. He focused bloodshot eyes on her. Ruby wanted to scream.

The inspector was looking at her too. He gave an encouraging nod.

Travis seemed to have a lot of difficulty swallowing and she heard when he managed it.

'Don't I know you from somewhere?'

She had prepared herself for this. There was no way Travis recognised her as his stepdaughter. She knew it for sure because of the interview she did for Caprini. It had been the big risk she took then. But Travis had had no idea who questioned him that day. There had been no flicker of recognition, no memories stirred in his mind of a little girl. So he had no idea she was Rosie. He was saying it because he knew her from Caprini's research work.

'I interviewed you almost two years ago for Professor Caprini's research into serial killers.'

Travis took some time to mull this over. His mind had been quicker back then too.

'Ah, I read the final report online. That was some neat work you did. It made me sound almost… understandable.' Travis gave a nasty grin.

She flashed a look at Inspector Grant. He was solid at her side and it gave her a boost. This was the time to take risks and be brave. She screwed up her courage. She did have an idea how to get to Travis. He had one weak spot and she wanted to work her way towards it.

'Back then, we talked about your family life. You shared a lot of information about your parents and memories from your childhood. You told me how it formed you and dictated the choices you took as an adult. One example was your relationships. You told me how you purposely sought out weak women. You manipulated them into sheltering you, and used them to give you a semblance of an ordinary life. It was a carefully constructed camouflage for your killing.'

'That's correct. You're a clever girl.'

'They were like building blocks for you to construct a semblance of normality. You used them like objects.'

'Objects, items, belongings. You've no idea how easy it is to pick out women with so little self-esteem.'

'They didn't know you were using them?'

'Of course they didn't. There were three of them. All pathetic and needy. They latched onto me as someone to give them security.' Travis's red eyes fixed on her. 'Amy was the one I enjoyed the most.'

Grant was listening carefully. In all the interviews he'd had with Travis, and there had been many over the years, the man had never talked about *three* women. He only ever admitted to living with two – Amy, and Travis' first girlfriend, Edith. Both of whom he killed. In a few sentences, Ruby had taken Travis to a place he had never gone with Grant. The inspector felt a spark of excitement.

'You lived a life of lies,' Ruby said. 'You posed as an ordinary boyfriend and husband. And you were proud of how you escaped the police and were able to kill again and again.'

Travis gave a malicious laugh and Ruby was close enough to smell his fetid breath.

'No one suspects an ordinary man when they're looking for a monster,' he said.

'When you spoke to me, there was only one real thing you talked about. Only one element not part of your fantasy world. In all the pretence and fabrication, what stood out was how proud you were to have a son.'

She held out her hand and Grant passed over the picture. Her arm had stopped shaking. 'At first, you thought having a son would be a handicap.'

She was suddenly the adult criminal profiler who was second to none.

'You considered killing Amy there and then when she was pregnant and then you changed your mind because a family man is an even better camouflage.'

'It appealed to me to try it out.'

'And then something unexpected happened. Something you had never imagined possible.'

She held Ryan's picture, steady, in front of Travis.

'You felt something. Like a spark in the dark, you felt something. You, a psychopath, a person incapable of love, you *felt* something for the first time in your life.'

'Well, Professor, you know better than anyone how I am incapable of *any* emotion. I have no feelings. I have no connection to people.'

'I am aware of your pathology, Mr Travis. In fact, it was the main theme of my research.'

A new confidence was flowing in her. She felt stronger than she'd ever felt. The more she spoke, the more Travis diminished in front of her.

'Yet you felt something towards Ryan, didn't you? You felt a connection you've never felt to any other human being.'

Travis swallowed.

'You always denied you abducted Ryan. You wanted the police to believe you killed him. But how could you kill the one real thing in your life? I don't think you did.'

'Are you so smart you think you can answer your own questions?'

'It's too late for evasion, Mr Travis. Time has run out. Where is he? You never expected to feel any connection to your own child, did you? But it happened. Like a marvel. And then when you murdered Amy Travis, you took the boy. By keeping silent during your interrogation, you led the police to believe you killed him but I don't think you did. I don't think you could bring yourself to do it. You let Ryan live didn't you, Mr Travis?'

'Ryan was…'

She tried not to crane forward.

'... different.'

Grant held his breath. This was going better than he could ever have imagined.

'For a moment, I thought you were going to say he was special,' Ruby said. 'Because he was, wasn't he. You and I talked about it before. He was special because you felt a connection to him which you've never felt to any other person. He was the light in the dark.'

In fact, Travis had talked to her at length about Ryan. About his birth. About holding his son. He never mentioned Rosie. And try as she might, Ruby had not found a way to make him tell her what happened to her brother on that terrible night.

'You always pretended you killed him and you were clever at the deceit. But I think you allowed Ryan to live, didn't you. He's still alive.'

Travis didn't reply. His eyes held a strange glitter. It was an unexpected spark of life, Ruby thought. It was as if his dying body felt a sudden energy.

And it gave her an idea. If she could manipulate him down her path, it might work.

Ruby was locked on to Travis, in tune with his thinking, in tune with the man's psychology, in tune with every move he made.

'You don't deny it,' she said.

'Why should I?'

'Where is he? Where is your son, Ryan?'

'How would I know?'

'Is he implicated in the killings?'

Travis didn't answer.

'Have you been in communication with him? Has he been receiving tips from you?'

Again, Travis said nothing, his eyes boring into her. Then suddenly, his energy flagged and pain and disease took hold of him again.

Travis sank back into himself, though the man still kept his eyes on Ruby.

Ruby was nodding to herself, as if she had somehow got the upper hand. Perhaps she had. It was true, Travis hadn't denied Ryan was alive. Whereas Grant had told her how, with him, Travis always refused point blank to answer questions of any kind about the child.

Ruby felt in control. This man no longer had a hold over her.

'And what of the two other women, Meredith and Isabella?' she said. 'What happened to them? Two more killings makes you more formidable, doesn't it? You're sick and you're dying. If you want to sign a confession you have to do it while you're mentally able. What did you do with them? What did you do with their bodies?'

'It's strange,' Travis was shaking his head. 'There's something about you... I can't put my finger on what it is.'

She gave him a cold stare. She didn't care if he did recognise her. Nothing else mattered – all she wanted was the truth.

Travis blinked. It made her realise he hadn't done so up until then. He was as locked on to her as she was to him. She felt the tension between them and she didn't want to break it. In her peripheral vision, Grant hadn't shifted and neither had the prison officer. Their attention was riveted on Ruby and Travis.

'When you have feelings for someone those feelings are precious. They stay inside and they give you strength. Perhaps they give you hope. Warmth. Have you ever felt those things? Didn't you feel it with Ryan? If only for a moment. Wouldn't you like to feel them again? What if you could? What about if you could feel one more spark in your dark world. One more spark before you die.'

Ruby pushed the photograph closer. 'What if you could see Ryan again?'

Travis lifted his hand asking for it. She gave it to him.

'He would be a man by now. What would it be like to see your son? Once more before the end.'

She knew his psyche. She knew his past. Travis had nothing much to lose and something, perhaps something very worthwhile, to gain.

The silence stretched on, until she wondered if she had lost the gamble.

It was Travis who spoke next. 'I'd like to see him.'

It was so unexpected, for a moment the room went out of focus. The words made her mind and her emotions swim. Oh God, he was talking about Ryan. He was finally admitting it. He hadn't killed his son. He was telling her Ryan was alive.

'You're saying you'd like to see your son, Ryan, again.'

'Before I die. Yes.'

She didn't know where the words came from. They seemed to float out of the air and into her mouth. She had absolutely no authority to make promises. 'Tell me what happened with Meredith and Isabella and I'll see what we can do.'

Travis reached out a skeletal hand. They handed him a paper and he wrote with painstaking slowness.

When he handed it back, she stared at the two words. It was a name.

'What's this?' she asked. 'Irena Nowak. Why is this significant?'

'That's who had him.'

She met the inspector's steely eyes. Oh God, it was the third woman. In her hand, Ruby held the details of the person who harboured Travis after he murdered Amy. The person who might have kept Ryan? Grant had been right. When Travis disappeared, he had latched onto another woman to take him in. Had she still had Ryan when Travis was taken into custody?

When it rose, the anger took Ruby by surprise. 'Tell me about Meredith and Isabella.'

Then Travis spoke in spurts, swallowing loudly and with difficulty between broken sentences. She could hear his breath wheezing. He had diminished. He was no longer the monster who could get her. He was simply an old and very sick man. And someone to be despised.

Grant didn't show his excitement. He listened as Travis told them Meredith Evans and Isabella Rees were his first two victims. Travis said he killed them while he was living with Edith. He'd dumped their bodies in a local landfill site. Ruby had squeezed information from Travis which Grant had never got close to. After twenty-five years of silence, this was a bloody breakthrough.

Grant knew the landfill site. It was one of the old-style dilute and disperse facilities which were no longer in use. Garbage from Himlands Heath had been dumped there for several decades, one load on top of another in an open eyesore.

'I don't think so,' he said. 'We searched the landfill. Nothing was found.'

It had been an impossible task. Officers had carried out a visual inspection, walking amongst the decaying refuse. Dogs had been of no use because of the smells and gases from the putrid general mass.

'I put them there.'

'I'll need you to pinpoint exactly where you put them,' the inspector said.

'If you're playing some kind of game...' Ruby's voice was like ice.

'No, no, I'm not. I want to see my son.'

Grant marvelled at how Ruby had played him. And her connection to Travis was so intense, Grant felt he could reach out his hand and almost touch it. Her skills in latching on and opening him up were second to none.

When Ruby passed him the paper, he felt like kissing it.

Inspector Grant couldn't wait to report back to DCS Fox. She'd have to bring in extra resources for the search of the dumpsite. And now they had a lead on their main suspect, Ryan Travis. All thanks to Ruby Silver.

When they left the prison, Grant thought Ruby had an odd look on her face – a mixture of triumph, and a new confidence.

'There's something I should have told you,' she said. 'It's about Professor Caprini.'

'Oh yes?'

'It's a bit awkward but it was me who interviewed Travis for the serial killer research. The professor isn't well and Mark and I covered his work.'

'I think you did more than that, didn't you? Weren't you the one who masterminded the entire report?'

'How did you...? I didn't think anyone would guess. I'm sorry, Inspector, it's complicated. Professor Caprini isn't the man he used to be.'

'I understand. And he's not found the courage to step down, has he. What's more important than the professor are the decisions you make for yourself, and about your own future. I think we both know it's time for you to stop hiding behind other people.'

She nodded and Grant laid a kind hand on her shoulder. They walked back to the car, each occupied with their own thoughts.

The tyres crunched as she pulled out of the drive and they headed back to the station.

'Congratulations Ruby, you were top class. I couldn't have dreamed of anything better. Travis latched on to you and you opened him up like a can of beans. Well done, really well done. You've got us the break we need.'

She blushed. Gosh, how she liked working with him and she could tell he valued her.

Grant got on the phone to DCS Fox to report the good news and he smiled across at Ruby. She really was the gem in the pile.

Chapter Thirty-three

When Inspector Grant and Ruby walked back into the incident room, a glance passed from person to person. One by one people fell quiet. Fingers stopped tapping on keyboards. Papers were no longer shuffled and telephone calls were terminated. Everyone turned to Ruby. And it wasn't with smiles of congratulation for a job well done at the prison.

What the hell was going on? Her pulse accelerated. Had somebody found out by accident who she really was? Her legs threatened to turn to spaghetti.

Grant took in the situation, striding over to Tom Delaney. 'Tell me exactly what's happened.'

'Boss–' Delaney indicated the table in front of him and stepped back. The circle of onlookers at Delaney's sides did the same.

Grant stared down at a used pair of gloves and a house photograph sitting in a tray. It was a fourth photograph from the killer. Another night-time picture. This time of a room on the skyline. He stared at the one window and the crooked roof. There was no mistaking the outline because it was a local landmark. He was staring at The Nag's Head and Ruby's top floor guest room. Goddam it.

Detective Chief Superintendent Fox marched into the room.

'I see you've finally got back from your trip. Your team sent me the bombshell,' she barked at Grant. 'And I got your text. If you've got a lead on Ryan Travis, Inspector, what are you waiting for? Get him into custody!'

The rising body count, a lack of progress, and now one of the team singled out as the killer's next target – it was driving Fox to lose her cool.

Ruby came to stand by Inspector Grant's shoulder. As she stared at the picture, Grant set about allocating priority tasks for the next twenty-four hours. He wanted the search of the landfill to start. They still needed to check out alibis from the psychiatrist's patients. Work would continue following up calls from the public reporting suspicious night-time activity around the victims' houses. He gave the orders and people scuttled to get on with it.

He wanted Collins to interview everyone coming and going from The Nag's Head over the last two weeks. And DS Delaney and McGowan would take on their number one priority, following up the new lead they had on Ryan Travis.
He left the most difficult task to last. He wanted Ruby protected and he felt sure she wasn't going to take it well.

It was a relief to no longer be the focus of people's horror and sympathy. Ruby watched the room swing back into action. Everyone else already had an urgent task to be getting on with and she was the only one left out.

'Ms Silver, I'm going to place you in protective custody.'

'What! No, you can't.'

The inspector said it in a caring, almost fatherly way, only she didn't want protection. What she wanted was to keep working. What she wanted was to work with Delaney and McGowan in tracking down Irena Nowak and Ryan.

Minutes earlier he'd been telling her how great she was and now he wanted to get rid of her? No way. She had to be at the heart of it. She couldn't allow herself to be pushed aside.

Ruby felt like she was falling. She grabbed on to the edge of the desk. 'That's not what I want, Inspector. You still need my contribution. I have key expertise. I've proved myself this morning and it's why you asked me to come on-board in the first place. One stupid photo doesn't change anything.'

'I'm afraid it does. I never take risks with my people.'

The inspector gave her a straight look with those piercing eyes of his. It was a warning. She felt the weight and the authority of it. It was almost enough to stem the tidal wave of fear for Ryan, dread about him, fear about the house photo and a lifetime of anger at all the injustices which had been heaped on them both. In just one glance, Grant reminded her of the respect she felt for him. But she had no choice, the truth about Ryan was her priority, not her feelings towards Grant.

'In my office please, Ms Silver,' he said.

Ruby had spent a lifetime backing down. Not this time. She followed the inspector along the corridor. There was no question, she couldn't sit around in some safe house while McGowan and Delaney tracked down the lead. She couldn't let the inspector get rid of her. Whatever it took, she must fight to stay on the team.

She lacked practice in handling conflicts, which is why she launched straight in and pitched it over the top. She started before they got to his office. In the team cubbyhole they argued for fifteen minutes. Or rather, she argued and the inspector remained calm.

Ruby accused him of not thinking straight. She told him he'd got his priorities wrong and that shutting her away somewhere wouldn't help catch the killer. She didn't believe she was the next target. To her, it didn't make any sense. There was no correlation with the names and she could see no link.

What she didn't tell him was how it would only make sense for her to be the target if someone knew her true identity as Rosie. Then the killer would have to be Ryan coming after her.

Her mind refused to go there. It went counter to every sisterly instinct she'd ever had. It would deny and destroy every precious feeling she nurtured towards her adorable baby brother. No, it simply could not be true. Ryan was not coming after her. And if he were. So be it.

Grant saw her struggle. She was as invested in this investigation as any of them, perhaps more so. And she'd finally overcome her timidity and it was too bad but he was going to have to disappoint her. David Grant kept to his first line. He wanted her protected.

'The killer has sent three house pictures so far and all three women have turned up dead. This is a risk I'm not willing to take.'

'You're wrong, Inspector, because they were dead before the photos arrived. This is different. The killer had gone off pattern. My instinct tells me his next target is the one he's been heading for since the beginning. The Nag's Head is a smokescreen.'

'If you're not the target, then who is?'

'I don't know. And you're making it your priority to find Ryan but what if he's not the killer? The killer is playing a game. What if he's using Travis and his son as cover for him to get as near as possible to whoever is his *real* target?'

'I'm sorry, I don't have a choice. If you don't agree to protective custody, I shall have to let you go.'

'I'm not going back to the university. Inspector, you're pulled back to Ryan Travis because of your own past with him. What if there's another suspect we haven't even discovered yet? I can help.'

'We're keeping all avenues open on the investigation. Ryan is my priority. There's no question about it.'

'I know, but what if this is some kind of diversion? It doesn't make sense. You're going to get someone else killed.

Another woman is going to die and it won't be me.' Ruby was shouting. 'But it *will be your fault!*'

'Enough.' Grant thumped his hand flat on a desk to stop her from going any further.

Ruby immediately regretted it. Her emotions had got the better of her. She'd insulted him. She'd criticised him. She had gone from wanting Grant to admire her and respect her to hurling abuse. There was part of her which regretted ripping herself from him, and she pushed that right down. She grabbed her bag and clutched it tight to her chest.

'I'm out of here.'

Then she rudely turned her back on Inspector Grant. She walked out the door and as soon as she was out of sight, she ran from the building.

Chapter Thirty-four

It's very quiet at my house.

I've lived here alone for a long time, with the same dusty furniture and the chipped cups and plates which I have no desire to ever replace. I took them from my parents' house. I miss not having a mother and a father around, but I especially miss my father. Following in his footsteps makes me feel close to him.

I'm savouring the thought of another job well done. Planting Travis DNA at two of the three scenes was a masterly touch. I'm sure it will have them running in a circle right back to where they started.

I enjoyed blending with the crowd and watching Grant and his puppy sergeant as they plodded around at the hospital. They really are incompetent. And it was good fortune how it gave me the chance to observe Grant with a new young woman. She was tender and delicate. He seemed particularly attentive to her, like some kind of idiotic guardian. It solved a problem for me because I'd been puzzling over who I could highlight with my next photograph. All the Sandras were so boring. She'll be ideal to keep the inspector's mind in a spin, while I manoeuvre the final pieces of the trap into position.

This morning I deposited The Nag's Head photograph.

Now I'm rewarding myself by spending time with my mentor's trophies. Did I tell you he had a liking for jewellery?

Rings, necklaces, brooches. I suppose women wore more of it in his day.

My favourite in his line-up of mementos is a diamond ring. I pick it up and feel its weight. Holding it between forefinger and thumb, I put it up to the light. At least, I presume it's a diamond from the way it sparkles. It's beautiful. The first keepsake he ever took. I sniff it and I smell the last sweat and fear of its owner. She was wearing it when he killed her.

Caressing each item and contemplating the women my father killed used to satisfy my own urges to take life. It kept me tame for years. Like a dog gnawing at a bone that has long since lost its real flavour. I've spent days of my life admiring and crooning over them. Today, it's no longer enough. I need fresh meat.

Is it because I've begun my own journey? Crossed the line into the dark world of those who take life? And I can never go back. I must continue until I reach the end.

I put down the ring, carefully positioning it as the first in the line. In my blood, I feel a terrible restlessness.

Soon the trap will be sprung.

Is this how my father felt when he lined up his next victim? Did he anticipate their final moments? Their pleading? The dribbling of body fluids? Did he find it hard to stick to his own rules?

I roll my head to stretch out my neck muscles and I take one more look at the jewellery before I go back upstairs. It's no good. These objects have lost their lustre.

I've talked to you about my rules – about planning and about the need to keep ahead of the lawman. Well, the third unbreakable rule is perfecting the game plan. Because, you see, this is all a game. A wonderful vile and inspired game in which I reel my final victim in like a fish on a line. I want him to suffer. I want him to know others have died because of him. I want him to reflect on his sins.

Strangulation will be too good for him. I have something much more suitable in mind. Much more drawn out.

Part of me wishes the detective knew what was coming. And part of me wants it to be a surprise. The type of surprise where every cell in his lying deceiving body is filled with dread. Either way, I'll be the one to savour the look on his face when Detective Inspector David Grant realises the truth.

Chapter Thirty-five

Carys Evans felt so much pain, it was difficult not to whimper. She gasped for air, taking in tiny rapid breaths. It was her hips which were the worst. It made it difficult to think of anything else. She had to press her eyes closed to bear it.

She lay in the dark. She was on her side on a cold gritty floor. What had happened? Had she fallen? Been attacked? Mugged and left for dead?

When Carys tried to move, stabs of agony shot down her legs. Then she really did whimper. Carys tried to concentrate on surviving, breathing, and on enduring until help came.

Then she remembered there would be no help coming. Panic threatened to shut her down and she clenched her jaw and ground her teeth together, trying to fight it off.

It was absurd but all she kept thinking of was her favourite winter hat. It was made of thick dark blue felt with a yellow flower on the front and it was very warm. It had been so windy she had used one of her old-fashioned hatpins to keep it in place. Why did she keep thinking of that silly hat?

She saw herself standing in front of the mirror in her own hallway. She was in her coat and her warm, winter shoes. Around her neck was a cosy scarf to keep out the draughts. Then she had pinned on her woolly hat.

That's right, she had been getting ready for the anti-Travis group. A meeting with the press was organised and they invited her along. Travis was due to be moved to a hospice and the group wanted her to join them to give a statement of disapproval to the media.

They sent her an address for the meeting. She took the bus to get there and arrived at an innocent house on a middle-class housing estate.

Now she remembered. At the door, she had been greeted courteously. It was only when she stepped inside she had been hit. It must have been right in the face because her cheek and one eye were throbbing. The fist came so fast she'd not even seen it coming.

The blow must have knocked her out. And then she awoke in agony in the dark.

Not a soul knew where she was. No one knew her plans and there was no one to notice a missing old woman. How silly she'd been.

Carys Evans wondered if she was going to die.

If she was honest with herself, a part of her hoped she would, just like a part of her had always wanted since she lost her older sister, Meredith. In fact, when she was younger, Carys spent years dreaming of dying and meeting her sister in heaven. That way, she wouldn't have to look at her parents' haunted faces every day. She wouldn't have to live with the agony of never knowing. She wouldn't have to face all the unanswered questions. Except it hadn't happened – Carys continued living. She had no choice except to keep going.

She lay on her side and grit from the floor got stuck on her lips as she cried.

Chapter Thirty-six

'I hear your new woman has walked out,' Luke said.

David Grant was down in the morgue. Luke was in the process of preparing tissue samples. Grant watched as Luke worked methodically and carefully, his hands deft and accurate with the scalpel.

'I know news travels fast but I count that as supersonic,' Grant said.

Luke tapped out a few cells onto a slide. The instrument he used made a small *tac* as it contacted the glass. The pathologist didn't say anything. That was another thing Grant liked about Luke, Luke always gave him plenty of space to think.

Grant leant against the worktop and summarised the case for himself. Ryan Travis was their main suspect and good detective work demanded they make Ryan their top priority. The team were still pursuing other avenues of investigation thrown up by the three murders. New leads could turn up at any time. If, against the odds, Ryan turned out to have a cast iron alibi then they wouldn't have lost time.

'I wanted Ruby Silver in protective custody and she refused. But she was right about one thing – the killer was going in a straight line with the names of the first three victims and he's veered off course by sending a photo of Ruby's room. She's got no matching names. Which means he's taken a new direction. I don't know why.'

'And it's worrying you.'

'She accused me of my thinking being off.'

'Did she now? She must be coming out of her shell. I thought you wanted her to be bolder?'

'Yes. But not exactly like that.'

Luke smiled. 'Come now, Inspector. We can all go a little too far sometimes and it's usually with the people we like the most. And trust the most.'

'This case hasn't stacked up from the beginning. We're running in a hundred directions at once and getting nowhere. And it's not just the change of direction. It keeps bugging me how the killer didn't take anything from his first victim. I feel he *should* have. And if he had, it would all make sense. I'd be able to see him for who he really is.'

With all his slides completed, Luke went to wash his hands at the sink.

'I've already asked Collins to go through it again and the husband is adamant nothing was missing. If this had been a trophy taker–'

'Then you'd have something concrete on him?' Luke said. 'After our last conversation I had another look at our first victim.'

Water rushed down the plughole. Luke grabbed a paper towel from a dispenser, dried his hands on it and lobbed it into the bin.

'Let me show you something.' He tapped a few keys. Close-up photographs of Mandy Jones' body came up on the screen.

'Here we can see the markings from the strangulation. It's heavy bruising, which is what you'd expect. Look, can you see a tiny line here? It's only two millimetres long and falls on the collar line. It could have been made by the killer pulling at her uniform and that's what I thought the first time around.' Luke Sanderson looked at Grant. 'But when I examined it again, I have to say it's entirely possible it wasn't the collar. She could have been wearing something under her uniform which left a tiny snag. For instance, when it was removed.'

'You mean like a necklace?'

'It's possible.'

'And if the killer removed it roughly it might have made this type of mark when he did?'

Grant spoke almost to himself. 'I don't want to ask the husband to go through her things a third time. Although I know she has a sister. If there was a necklace... perhaps a fresh pair of eyes might make a difference.'

Luke smiled. 'Looks like you've got one of the answers you came for.'

Chapter Thirty-seven

Ruby pressed the buzzer. By her side, Soraya shifted a cake box from one hand to another. The name "Hawk" was the only thing written alongside the intercom. It was the nickname they had given him in the children's home and it was odd to think it was the name he went by.

Back then, the name had come from Hawk's passion for the work of Stephen Hawking, the renowned physicist. Hawk's amazing brains and his geeky interest in technology made him a perfect target for the children's home bullies. At only eight, Hawk hadn't been equipped to defend himself. He was another lost duckling Soraya tucked under her wing and the three of them had formed an unbreakable trio.

With an automatic *click*, the door popped open. They pushed their way in and Ruby caught the delicious scent of a chocolate topping.

'Thanks for bringing the goodies, Soraya. I didn't have time to even think straight.'

'No problem. It's the stickiest and gooiest I could find. Perfect for a chocoholic like Hawk.'

Ruby couldn't manage to dredge up a smile and Soraya gave her nudge.

'Forget about Inspector Grant. He's a big man. He'll come round.'

Ruby didn't think so. Not after the way she'd treated him.

'Hi Hawk,' Soraya called out.

Hawk sat in his living room surrounded by computers. He was wearing jogging pants and a ludicrous oversized striped jumper. He never did have any sense of style. Data scrolled continuously across several screens. Hawk took off headphones and swivelled his chair. His eyes went straight to the cake.

'Oooh, wonderful. Is it my favourite?'

'Of course it is,' Soraya said.

They gave Hawk a hug and Soraya tutted, mother-duck-style, about how thin he was. The cake came before business and Soraya trotted off to find plates and a knife. Ruby perched on the edge of a chair and chewed her nails.

Hawk was a recluse. He lived in a massive apartment with his cat. Most things, like regular food deliveries, were deposited at his door. Hawk didn't seem to know any actual people apart from Ruby, Soraya and the middle-aged woman in the flat opposite who had multiple sclerosis. She and Hawk kept an eye out for each other.

Hawk had come a long way since their days together as kids. He made literally piles of money working freelance as a technology mastermind. He did work off-the-grid and off-the-record. Not even Ruby and Soraya knew the details, though they knew Hawk had strict principles about stuff he would and wouldn't touch. Hawk worked for individuals and he did contracts for plenty of big-shot organisations, including the CIA.

And since he was old enough to know how, Hawk kept feelers out on the web for Ruby's little brother. He'd searched diligently for years and come up with nothing.

'Give me twenty-four hours,' Hawk had said, when she'd called him to pass over the name of Irena Nowak. 'And make sure you bring cake.'

Hawk gave her a lopsided grin. 'Don't worry, I found something for you.'

Soraya came back holding three loaded plates. Their friend

flicked his hair out of his eyes and, with his plate balanced on one hand, reached across to open a data file.

'I think you're going to be pleased, Rube.'

'Good,' Soraya said. 'Shoot. Who is this Irena Nowak?'

Hawk had located information on Irena Nowak and on another woman called Irene Newark. When one disappeared, the other appeared.

Irena Nowak was Polish. She got married young and had a baby in Poland. The baby, a boy, died soon after birth. Hawk found hospital records but no official death record for the child. There were no records of burial or cremation.

Soon afterwards, a single woman named Irena Nowak appeared in England. There were then no flags until two years later when an Irene Newark turned up in Brighton, Sussex, less than an hour away from Himlands Heath. Irene had signed her child up to a pre-school playgroup. The child's name was Jacob Newark, the same first name as the baby who had died in Poland.

'You think it's the same woman and she altered her name?' Soraya asked.

'I'm certain. Irene Newark didn't exist up until that point. The one became the other. It can be done because the anglicisation of Polish names leaves some wriggle room for change. And whoever the child was she signed up to pre-school, it sure wasn't her own son, 'cos he was dead.'

'Unless she got pregnant again in the UK,' Soraya said.

Hawk was stuffing himself with his slice of cake. 'Unlikely. Jacob was registered at the pre-school when he was two years old. There wasn't enough time for a second pregnancy.'

'Meaning Irena Nowak got together with Mike Travis. He latched on to her because he saw she was needy,' Ruby said.

'Makes sense. She'd lost her baby and she was grieving,' Soraya said. 'And she was in a country foreign to her. It would make her vulnerable. And you think she came to England alone?'

'As far as I can tell.'

Ruby's hands were sweating and she wiped them on her jeans.'All right, so she grieved for her own lost baby. Something goes wrong with her marriage and she comes to England. Then Travis turns up and he's got his own baby. She takes him in. She looks after Ryan. She gets attached. Travis is arrested and she does a runner. She can't go back to Poland because she's got a stolen baby, so she goes to Brighton which is a big metropolis where she can get lost in the city.'

'And she changes her name to Irene Newark,' Soraya said. 'Ryan becomes Jacob Newark. She gives the baby the identity of her lost son.'

Ruby nodded. 'Yes, she begins a new l-l-life.'

'It's perfectly possible if she kept Jacob's papers from Poland. And all the timing fits in,' Hawk said. 'It's okay, Rube, please don't cry.'

Soraya came to sit by her. While Ruby tried not to sob, Soraya took away her plate and gave it to Hawk who started on the second slice.

'This is great stuff, Hawk,' Soraya said.

'That's not all. I mentioned the one record at the pre-school. I've hunted down the woman who was in charge when Jacob was there. She's retired now. These are her details.'

Hawk handed over a paper. Ruby couldn't read it because her eyes were swimming.

'After that the trail goes cold,' Hawk said. 'No Irene Newark, no Jacob Newark. Nada, zilch. But hey, leave it with me. I'll keep my searches going.'

They put their arms around her.

She'd spent her whole life trying to find Ryan. But not like this. She held on tight to Hawk's jumper and she could smell chocolate on his breath.

Soraya was stroking Ruby's hair. She knew how much Ruby had suffered for leaving her little brother behind. Over the top of Ruby's head, Soraya saw Hawk's mouth set in a firm line. He didn't want to say it. And neither did Soraya. But what if Ryan *was* the killer? What if, after all these years that's exactly what he turned out to be? And he sent The Nag's Head picture because he was coming after Ruby.

Chapter Thirty-eight

Detective Sergeant Tom Delaney got Ruby's text asking for an urgent meeting.

He thought Ruby probably didn't realise the walls of the team cubicle were paper thin. Ruby should have waited until she was in Grant's office with the door closed. She might as well have argued with the boss in the middle of the incident room because her shouting had drifted through the walls. The whole team had caught it, in tone if not in actual words. No one spoke to Inspector Grant like that, not even Detective Chief Superintendent Fox. Tom decided he certainly wouldn't be embarrassing Ruby by letting her know how much they'd heard. After all, she was an academic and not used to the chain of command. She'd been speaking her mind, not being deliberately insubordinate.

Ruby Silver was waiting outside the hotel entrance

'Hello, Tom, thanks for coming. The inspector didn't get back in touch.'

Her arms hung stiffly by her sides and she gave him a questioning look.

Tom brushed aside the awkwardness. 'Don't take it personally; he's inundated. I'm sure he'll call as soon as he can. And I can't think of anything I'd rather do than take a stroll in freezing temperatures amongst a crowd of frenzied shoppers,' he said with a smile. 'And I sincerely hope we're going to be bombarded by mind-numbing festive music, otherwise I'm not coming.'

Ruby reached to squeeze his arm and Tom was surprised at how much he liked it.

Ruby had tried twice to contact Inspector Grant. She hoped to apologise but he didn't answer. Had she burned her bridges with him? Or was he off pursuing a hot lead? Either way, she felt a responsibility to pass on the intelligence on Ryan. There was no time to waste if more deaths were to be prevented.

Tom was his usual friendly bear. Ruby was grateful and she reached to squeeze his arm. She was surprised at herself for the sudden gesture of friendship.

Tom told her they'd found details on Irena Nowak in Poland but not about her reappearance as Irene Newark in Brighton.

They walked amongst the crowds. It was the big push before the holidays. The high street was packed with people lugging full bags. Music came out of every doorway and there were even Carol singers.

'You see, you got the music you wanted,' Ruby said.

Ruby told Tom everything she'd learned at Hawk's – how Irena Nowak's son died in Poland but there was no trace of a death certificate. How an Irene Newark then turned up in Brighton with a son named Jacob Newark who was the same age as the missing boy, Ryan Travis.

Tom listened carefully. All the background bustle died out as he concentrated on the details. He had searched the police databases himself and come up with a blank. How on earth had Ruby done it?

If this information was accurate, it was exciting. The odds of the boy being Ryan Travis were high. Especially since Mike Travis had been so determined to meet his own son before he died. Travis had given them Irena Nowak's name for a reason.

He didn't ask where Ruby got the intelligence. Every detective had their own sources. Though it seemed odd how a university researcher would have contacts of such quality. Ruby was certainly turning out to be more than interesting.

'You trust your source?' he asked.

'One hundred percent.'

'I'll have to do some quick checks. If it pans out, McGowan and I will head down to Brighton to meet this pre-school teacher.'

Ruby frowned. 'Not McGowan. You and me and we go right now. That's the deal.'

'I don't think the inspector will agree to–'

'Then don't tell him. That's the deal or I don't share the name of the pre-school teacher or her address.'

Tom hesitated. She'd already given him Irene Newark's name and Jacob's. He should be able to trace the pre-school himself so he didn't strictly need her input. 'Listen, Ruby, I'd like to pull you in on this but–'

'My source has the expertise to erase records. If I ask him, he'll wipe all traces of Jacob in Brighton.'

Was she bluffing? Tom could not tell.

The two of them were standing still, staring at each other, Ruby looking up at Tom's face. They formed a little island in the sea of shoppers. A woman banged her bags against Tom's legs and apologised. Automatically, he wished her a good holiday season as she moved on.

'Is that a threat?' he asked Ruby.

First and foremost, Tom Delaney was a good detective. There was something different about Ruby. There was an edge in her voice. And this was deeply important to her.

'There's one other thing you need to know.' Ruby looked him in the eye. 'I'm not the target.'

'The house photograph says you are.'

'It makes no sense. My name has no link to the names of Travis' victims. I'm just plain Ruby.'

'Come on, the professor works with murderers and serial killers. There could easily be a nutter with a vendetta against you.'

'You think so? Someone angry enough to kill three women in the run up to a hit on me? No. Why go to all that trouble? Why not kill me on the spot? It doesn't feel right.'

Tom had to admit, he couldn't see that one exactly panning out. 'Inspector Grant was pretty clear he wants you somewhere safe.'

'Yeah, I know. If you ask me, a much more likely target is Inspector Grant himself.'

Tom shook his head. This was going nowhere and he didn't want an argument. It would achieve nothing. Besides, he liked her. He'd come there to see if he could help get her back in the station. One other thing he realised was you couldn't protect someone who didn't want protection. That was called an infringement of liberties.

'Listen, let's you and me go find this woman in Brighton and see where it takes us,' Ruby said. 'And please, no McGowan on this one.'

Tom shoved his hands in his pockets. Ruby and McGowan hadn't been getting on. She didn't stand up to him, that was the problem. Finding Ryan Travis needed to happen fast. And it would certainly be quicker with only him and Ruby.

'Okay. But you stick by me and you do exactly what I say.'

Chapter Thirty-nine

Ruby had never seen so much traffic heading down to Brighton. It seemed half the population of Sussex was heading there for a last-minute spending spree. It started to rain and then the rain turned to sleet. The motorway conditions were dreadful.

Tom told Ruby he could feel the tyres losing grip. If it turned to snow, the road would quickly become treacherous.

'We've got to get there,' Ruby said. 'We've no choice.'

It took over an hour to get to the retired pre-school teacher's house.

According to her neighbour, Mrs Peterson was a busy woman. She led an active retirement, spending most mornings working as a volunteer at the local library. They sat in the car waiting. There was nowhere nearby to get a hot drink.

By the time Mrs Peterson got off the bus at the end of the road, Ruby was so cold she couldn't feel her fingertips.

Tom told Mrs Peterson they were searching for Ryan Travis in connection to a current case. It seemed Tom had something of Grant's golden touch because Mrs Peterson accepted the explanation with a smile and invited them inside. Ruby didn't say much. She wished it had been possible to come there alone or with Soraya. But it was essential this was professional and part of the official investigation.

'You'd both better have a cup of tea,' Mrs Peterson said. 'You look chilled through. I could do with one myself. I've been on my feet all morning.'

Mrs Peterson was sprightly and alert. She set about organising a tray of tea things and she and Tom made small talk in the kitchen. Ruby stood at the kitchen door. In her pocket, her hand curled around Grant's photograph of baby Ryan. Part of her felt like screaming at Tom and Mrs Peterson to shut up and she had to stop herself from simply thrusting the picture in front of Mrs Peterson's face.

In the living room, Mrs Peterson pulled the curtains back more.

'There's not much light today,' she said. 'With a grey sky and the way it's sleeting out there, they might be right about snow before Christmas. Now how can I help you, officers?'

The picture crackled. Ruby smoothed it out on the table.

'This is Ryan Travis. You might have known him as Jacob Newark. We think he went to your pre-school.'

'This boy is only a baby. I'm not sure I'm going to be much help to you, I'm afraid. The children who came to me were much older. And my memory for names isn't as good as it used to be. What did you say he was called again?'

Ruby curled her hands into fists. She sensed her nerves were about to fray.

'Jacob Newark,' Tom said.

'I'm so sorry,' Mrs Peterson said. 'That name doesn't ring a bell. Two sugars or one?'

'None for me,' Tom said. 'Of course, we understand it's a long time ago. Perhaps you kept records or lists? I mean of the children's names. Or perhaps the details of the parents?'

'It's a long time ago, you're right. And I knew so many little ones over the years. In those days, all the regulations weren't what they are today and I'm afraid I haven't got anything written down. But I tell you what, we always had an end of term photograph of the whole class and I kept all of them. If you know the year we could have a delve up in the loft. My grandson put them in a box for me.'

Tom went up into the loft He brought down a big cardboard box and carried it into the living room. Mrs Peterson produced a pair of scissors and slowly cut through the brown tape sealing it closed. Ruby had to sit on her hands to stop herself tearing it open.

Tom must have sensed her frustration because he gave her a couple of reassuring glances.

The photographs were in date order. Ruby let them find the one corresponding to the year Hawk told them about. She was about to crack and she didn't trust herself to be able to keep it under wraps. When Mrs Peterson laid a picture on the coffee table, they all edged in close.

There were around twenty children, arranged in three rows. Mrs Peterson found her glasses and peered at the picture. Her finger hovered and she told them the children's names out loud, working her way along each row.

It was painstakingly slow. Ruby began to feel as she sometimes did in her very bad moments. As if she floated outside her body, powerless to stop events. She started breathing more deeply and slowly, as she'd been taught, trying to ground herself and bring herself back to the here and now. Anxiety had her in its grasp, as she followed Mrs Peterson's finger along the top row.

It was quite remarkable how good Mrs Peterson's recall was. Contrary to what she said she had a good memory of the children's first names. She paused for a few seconds before confidently proclaiming each one. Sometimes she gave a little smile or a nod as memories of each child returned. Ruby leaned closer. She could smell Mrs Peterson's perfume – a light flowery old-person's type of fragrance. And then she saw him.

Two children ahead of Mrs Peterson's finger was a little boy. He had dark, curly hair and a mouth she remembered. She thought she might pass out.

'That's Robin… and then Shelley…'

Time stood still. Mrs Peterson licked her lips.

'… and then… Jake.'

The woman lifted her eyes.

'I'd forgotten we called him Jake. I remember now it was short for Jacob. Is this him? Is this the boy you're looking for?'

Ruby couldn't stop herself. She reached and picked up the photograph and stared at her brother.

There was no mistaking Ryan. Part of her wondered how she could tell. The last time she'd seen him was when he was less than two years old and it was so long ago. In the photograph he was four. But his face was the same. He had the same eyes, the same lips, the same everything.

She nodded.

'Well, my dear, I'm glad I could help.'

Mrs Peterson was giving her a strange look. Ruby nodded again and forced herself to hand the photograph to Tom.

'So this is Ryan Travis,' Tom said. 'If you could tell us whatever you know about him and his family, that would be very useful.'

Mrs Peterson was sitting back on the settee. She took her cup and saucer and stirred her tea.

'Are you all right, my dear?' Mrs Peterson asked Ruby. 'You've gone very pale.'

Ruby didn't trust herself to speak. Instead, she flapped a hand, as if to waft some air across her face. She knew it was futile.

'Perhaps it's too hot in here? Shall I get you a glass of water?'

Mrs Peterson pottered out and came back holding a glass. Ruby politely took a few sips. After all this time. It was surreal. It was Ryan. He wasn't dead. She was one-hundred percent certain. This was a picture of her little brother. Travis had allowed him to live.

'We're on an active murder investigation, Mrs Peterson,' Tom said. 'Anything you can tell us could prove to be invaluable.'

Mrs Peterson produced a tin of biscuits and told Ruby to take one in case she was a bit low on sugar. Then she told them how she had got on well with Jake's mother. Irene was Polish and a single mother. Mrs Peterson said there'd been some kind of family rift and Irene was on her own with her son.

'I remember Jake as being a quiet boy. He often played on his own rather than with the other children.'

'Did she love him?' Ruby couldn't stop herself blurting it out. It sounded odd and she caught Tom's twitch of surprise.

She had to know if he had been happy. Loved. Cared for. In a professional sense it was also important. It gave key pointers to the nurturing, or lack of, which might have taken place in his life and the consequences for his psyche. If he had grown up in an emotional vacuum, things might have turned very bad for him.

'Oh yes, my dear, she loved him very much. It was obvious. And he loved her. They had a very close bond.'

Mrs Peterson told them Irene was a devoted mother.

Ruby felt a huge lump in her throat. She took gulps of water in an attempt to force it down. Tom would surely think she was a nervous wreck and unfit for work.

Part of her didn't care. Ryan was alive. He had found a mother and a home. He had been loved and looked after. But the next thing Mrs Peterson said was the one which kicked her feet from under her.

'Like I said, Jake spent a lot of time playing on his own and he had an imaginary friend. It's not unusual at that age. As I recall, he had a pretend older sister.'

Neither the water nor the biscuits helped. Ruby started hyperventilating. In the end, Tom had to ask her to put her head between her knees and he told her to take deep breaths until her head cleared. She was glad because it helped hide she was crying.

Mrs Peterson fussed and offered this and that – another biscuit? An open window perhaps with more fresh air? A lie down in the spare room? It really wouldn't be any trouble.

Ruby refused as politely as she could, wishing for Soraya and Hawk and their understanding.

Back in the car, Tom started the engine. Ruby told him she thought she might be coming down with flu.

'There's a lot of it around,' Tom said kindly. He was sure she'd been crying earlier. It had made him want to put his arm around her. He hadn't done it because he hadn't felt it would be entirely appropriate or professional.

Tom watched as Ruby sent a text. He was dying to know what about and who to, but it was impossible to see the screen and he didn't want to ask.

He hit the steering wheel in triumph. 'And now we know where Ryan Travis was until he was four and we even have an idea where to continue the search. This is fantastic.'

Mrs Peterson told them Irene was a gifted linguist who spoke Polish and English and she also spoke fluent French. She earned her living by doing translation work from home. If Irene wasn't in England, the retired pre-school teacher felt she would not have returned to Poland and her estranged family. Instead, she might have gone to France.

They were going to find Ryan Travis and they were going to nail him. Tom felt sure of it.

'We're going to get him before he kills again. This has given us a chance.'

Ruby didn't say anything. And then they were heading for the motorway and Ruby was leaning back with her eyes half-closed. Tom gave her a look of admiration. Her cheeks and lips were flushed red, maybe from the cold air or from a fever. She looked very attractive. Tom had to drag his eyes away. Every way he could see it, this woman was an asset to the investigation. She was the one who had got Irene Nowak's name out of Mike Travis and now she was the one who traced a lead on Ryan. Ruby was something special.

Chapter Forty

Carys Evans felt woozy. She sat propped against the wall. A while ago, he injected her with something which took away the pain and it made her feel sick.

She never thought of herself as a weak person, even as the years crept up on her, sapping her strength. Carys had been the strong one of her family.

Losing Meredith had taken her family to hell and back. Her mother closed down and became a shadow of herself whereas her father struggled with the pain of Meredith's loss every moment of every day until his deathbed.

Then there had been Carys' brother who became a criminal, vandalising property and then, before they knew what was happening, he emigrated, cutting contact. Her parents blamed it on the loss of Meredith. Carys hadn't heard a word from him in over twenty years.

Whereas Carys, younger than Meredith, grew into a young woman who never forgot her sister. Carys vowed to find Meredith and to uncover the truth. And she had kept going all these years.

Carys came back to the present and she tried to drown out the voice of her captor. She hated the sound of it, so gloating and arrogant, dripping with self-importance.

He was reading out a letter. He said it was written for him by his father. She tried to block it out. Tried to think of happier thoughts. But none would come to mind.

...and so, my dear son, I hope when you read these letters you'll realise I am not what they say I am. I am so much more. I am so much greater than they can ever imagine. They call my acts crimes and I call them acts of compassion...

Carys' stomach started cramping. He had been reading the damned, sick letter for what seemed like hours. The earlier part had been about what this man's father did to his victims. The father was a mad man. She could hardly bear it. Listening to the details made her physically ill.

When she tried to block her ears with her hands, her captor threatened to hurt her. Carys slumped, desperate.

Her own situation made her think about Meredith. It had been impossible not to make a link between her own plight and that of her sister. Had Meredith been captured? Had she felt frightened and alone? Had she been trapped in the hands of a maniac?

If I'm not careful the woman will expire before I've made use of her. She's frail. Capturing her had been easy. Dealing with her snivelling was proving more of a challenge. When I see her sprawling like that, I'm tempted to kick her, but common sense prevails, after all, I need her alive, at least for now.

I finish reading. As I fold away the pages, I'm in a buoyant mood. I know all twenty-three letters by heart because I've read them so many times. Sharing them with Carys is turning into a pleasure because I like to see how she squirms.

'And if you're good, I'll read you another one tomorrow. Now isn't that something to look forward to.'

A while later, I go upstairs to check the news feeds. Mike Travis is soon to be transferred from the prison to hospice care. The moment I've been waiting for will soon be here. I must make sure everything is in place.

After I've checked and double-checked my plans and made sure I've left nothing to chance, I jog back down to the basement. I've still some time before I strike so I take out my special polishing cloth. One by one I clean the row of trophies, removing every speck of dust.

It takes a while. Once they are all pristine and shiny, I kneel down and speak slowly and clearly close to Carys' ear.

'Stop that noise or I'll make you stop.'

She nods and presses her lips together.

'We're going to call your friend, Inspector Grant, and you're going to deliver him a nice Christmas message.'

Carys squinted up at him. Her eyes were watering. She'd lost her glasses and she couldn't see properly. The man's face seemed ugly and distorted and blurred. She wanted to refuse, but all her resistance had long since evaporated.

As he held the phone to her mouth, Carys could smell soap on his skin. Her captor dialled. She waited, hoping the inspector would not answer. After a few moments, Inspector Grant came on the other end of the line. And Carys repeated as best she could the words her captor had told her to say.

Chapter Forty-one

One of Grant's trademarks was being meticulous. Paying attention to detail had won him success on many cases. And he kept being pulled back to the idea of the killer collecting trophies.

He dispatched Collins to meet with the sister of Mandy Jones. Luke said it was possible she had been wearing a necklace. The sister could go through the nurse's jewellery and find out if anything was missing.

Grant knew mistakes are often made in investigations right at the beginning. Closing the door of his office, he sat down and scrolled through page after page of notes written by his team. He allowed his mind to scan over the details, not knowing what he searched for. He had missed something, he knew it. He could allow himself a little time to backtrack on his line of thinking.

He picked up Ruby's research report and flicked through it. Ruby had documented several killers who collected mementos. Of the killers from his own past who collected jewellery from their victims, he remembered all three very well. Rogers targeted prostitutes, Flint was a taxi driver who charmed his passengers, dropped them home and then returned later to kill them, and Bergerman murdered elderly women. Rogers and Flint were still incarcerated and Bergerman had committed suicide in prison. Grant pushed aside his sandwich, his appetite gone. As he took a drink of cold tea, his phone buzzed.

He glanced at the caller identification and didn't recognise the number.

There came a few seconds of silence, then he strained to catch a voice. It was a woman. Oh God no, it was Carys Evans.

She told him other people had died because of him. More would die if he did not do exactly as she said. Grant held his breath so he didn't miss a word. Once the connection was cut, Grant sat with the phone half way to his ear.

Carys said people had died because of him – Mandy Jones, Doctor Hawthorne, Eleanor Vickers. More would follow. Did she mean Ruby Silver?

Carys had been full of fear and he could hear someone else in the background. Which meant she was being held hostage. She was being used as a bargaining chip. And he was the price of her freedom. What choice did he have except to follow her instructions?

Could he risk alerting Fox? Carys had been clear she would be dead if he did. Grant's mind went cool and clear. He'd been involved in too many hostage incidents. So many things could go wrong. And if this was their killer, Carys was being held by a madman.

Poor Carys. Grant owed her more. She had been through so much. Grant knew what decision he was going to make. It was the only one humanly possible. The only option where more lives would not be at risk. Except his own.

He was the end target of the killer.

If he got up front and personal, might he stand a chance of outmanoeuvring his opponent? Of turning his own hand of cards into a winning one? It was a slim chance. But it was a chance he had to take.

For a moment, David Grant hesitated. He would not risk endangering his family, and yet he felt the need to speak to his wife.

Lily answered on the second ring and David told her he

expected to be home late and she should not wait up for him.

Lily Grant knew immediately something was wrong. For the last thirty years, her husband had been home late and for the last twenty-five, on mutual agreement, he stopped bothering to tell her.

She recognised the underlying message and knew David was in danger. And for him to make such a call, surely it could only mean others were in danger too, not only him. Lily could not risk alerting anyone in the same way he had not been able to risk alerting her. She thought of her son and her daughter and other innocent lives.

Lily leaned against the kitchen counter and closed her eyes. Their daughter was driving down the motorway. Chrissie was due to arrive that evening for the holidays. Lily didn't want to disturb her. Instead, Lily phoned their son, Daniel, in the States.

Daniel heard the wobble in his mother's voice.

'What's happened! Is Dad okay?'

'Yes, everything's fine. I'm just calling to say... We're looking forward to seeing you, my dear.'

Daniel almost dropped his mobile. His mother never phoned to say things like that. As soon as he hung up, he called the airline and brought forward his reservation, taking the next available plane to London.

Chapter Forty-two

Detective Chief Superintendent Fox was sitting at her desk when there came a knock at her door.

She glanced at the computer screen. It was quarter to ten in the evening. What the h-! No one in their right minds disturbed her at that time of night. The only people Fox saw after nine o'clock were those she summoned herself. And that was generally to leave them black and blue, metaphorically speaking.

The person knocked again.

'Whoever the hell that is, you'd better have a damn good reason for interrupting me,' she shouted. 'Come in.'

Ruby Silver softly closed the door behind her. *Ah, the criminal profiler*, Fox thought. She'd heard all about the woman's work from Inspector Grant. Fox turned to face her visitor full-on and she interlocked her fingers on the desk in a power pose.

When Fox had first met Ruby in the incident room, she had been expecting someone older and who looked more experienced. Ruby was sensitive-looking, with a slight build. One puff of wind and Fox thought the young woman might keel over. Still, appearances could be deceptive, and Grant spoke very highly of her.

Fox started the conversation with her signature narrowing of the eyes.

'I'm sorry to bother you, Detective Chief Superintendent,'

Ruby said. 'I couldn't get hold of Inspector Grant so I thought it best to come straight to you.'

Another sore point. Grant hadn't replied to Fox's last text. He really could be awful at keeping her in the loop.

'Detective Sergeant Delaney and I have followed up the lead given by Mike Travis. It took us down to Brighton and we met a woman who was kindergarten teacher to Ryan Travis. We're getting closer to finding Travis' son.'

Fox sat perfectly still and waited for more.

'We're missing key details. I'd like permission to question Mike Travis again.'

'You were the one to get the name of the woman who harboured Mike Travis, weren't you? Inspector Grant told me, last time he bothered to check in. What makes you think Travis will tell you more?'

'I think I know how to get to him. It's hard to explain, except to say psychology is my thing and I believe it's worth a shot.'

'And what's the real reason?'

Ruby didn't know what to say.

'You've got some balls coming in here. In fact, didn't Inspector Grant send you home?'

'I realise the timing's awkward.' Ruby went rather red. 'I came in to apologise to the inspector and when he wasn't available... we can't wait. Finding Ryan is top priority.'

Fox tapped her pen on the desk. Ruby was an unusual young woman. She was stronger than she seemed on the outside and she was candid. Clearly, she also had useful ideas. Inspector Grant told her how Ruby had locked onto Travis like a guided missile. She'd got information out of Travis which Grant had never got close to.

'I like a bold approach but with the inspector unavailable, I'm not sure it's a good idea to send you there.'

On a case like this, the inspector was usually at his desk in the evening. A small doubt and a worry planted itself in the superintendent's mind. She decided to send an officer over to his house to check.

'Ryan was looked after by a Polish woman. We believe the two of them have moved to France.'

In Fox's book, presenting new concrete information was always a winning tactic.

'Very well. I'll call the prison warden and get the visit approved for tomorrow morning. In the unlikely case I can't get hold of the inspector, take Detective Sergeant McGowan with you.'

'DS McGowan? Wouldn't DS Delaney be a better choice?'

'Are you deaf, Ms Silver? Please don't try my patience. Now get out of my office and make sure you bring me back a result.'

Chapter Forty-three

Inspector Grant didn't come in the next morning. There were murmurs and speculation Grant hadn't been home the evening before. Patrol had been sent around at ten thirty and then at midnight and he wasn't there. Lily Grant had been reluctant to answer questions. Collins knew something was wrong and Fox sent her over to find out what.

Which meant Ruby found herself driving to the prison with McGowan.

Mike Travis was sitting up in his bed, with a small tube under his nose which delivered oxygen. The prison doctor explained it was to help relieve his problems with breathing and lessen the build up of fluid in his lungs.

The ongoing pain was being managed by Doctor Patel's current regime, though bouts of breakthrough pain were still causing a problem. It meant they would only be allowed a short time with the prisoner. Otherwise they risked fatiguing him too much and it might bring on a period of breakthrough pain the prison hospital would struggle to deal with.

Ruby made a few polite noises and nodded as she listened to the explanation. By her side, McGowan didn't bother to pretend to be interested. He paced up and down, excited at the prospect of meeting Travis and Ruby was grateful Superintendent Fox had the foresight to tell McGowan to keep his mouth shut and let Ruby take the lead. Actually, Fox had used exactly those words and McGowan's response had been a meek, yes ma'am.

Ruby had eaten breakfast and she hadn't thrown up. She barely felt queasy at the prospect of meeting Mike Travis again. Something inside her had changed. Because, in their head-to-head, she was the one who came out the strongest. Mike Travis didn't hold power over her anymore. She was free. And now the priority was Ryan.

The other two inmates on the hospital ward had been cleared out. It left McGowan, Ruby, Travis and one prison officer. Travis smelled much cleaner and his muscles were more relaxed. McGowan started the recording and gave her a nod.

'I understand you've only got a few minutes, Mr Travis, before fatigue overtakes you,' Ruby said. 'So I'll be brief.'

Travis' eyes were still bloodshot. 'I can't eat anymore. My body's closing down. Did you find my son?'

He didn't rasp and struggle for breath. His breathing was easy. And he wasn't grimacing, which suggested he was not in so much pain. Yet, he had diminished. As if the life energy was slowly leaking out of him. *The cancer cells must be taking it all from him*, Ruby thought. Her emotions were hard and cold. She was glad Travis was dying and she didn't feel one tad guilty for it.

Oh no, Travis, she thought, *we have a narrow time slot and we're not going to start by talking about Ryan*. No, she wanted Travis to stress he would run out of force to speak. That he would end up so drained he would have to slump back and rest to regain his strength for another day. It wasn't cruelty – she was simply clear on her strategy. She had to make him answer her questions first.

'Let's start with Meredith and Isabella. We have officers and equipment excavating the landfill site at the spot you indicated. They've found no remains so far. I really hope you haven't been misleading us.'

Travis shook his head. 'You'll get the remains. They're right where I told you.'

McGowan cracked his knuckles. 'Then why haven't we found them? And why have I got a nasty feeling you're wasting our time?'

Ruby shot McGowan an annoyed look.

'Where's Inspector Grant?' Travis asked.

'He's got more important things to deal with,' Ruby said.

'Like finding his precious Meredith and Isabella? He was always so obsessed with those girls. The inspector's going to have a surprise on that one.'

She felt McGowan tense up at her side.

'What kind of a surprise?' she asked quickly.

'You'll see.'

Travis left the taunt hanging in the air. Like McGowan, she didn't like the nasty twist in his tone when he spoke about surprising the inspector. What did he mean? Travis' breathing had already become more rapid. She'd not expected him to fade so fast.

'If you're deceiving us about the location of the bodies, I won't help you meet with your son.'

She said it as a statement of fact. Then she opened the envelope on her lap and handed Travis a copy of Mrs Peterson's photograph. She pointed to Ryan Travis sitting in the bottom row, in his little blue shorts and T-shirt.

'This is your son at four years old,' she said. 'He went to kindergarten in Brighton.'

There was no way she wanted to tell Travis the trail had gone cold. What she needed to do was trick him into giving her more.

Travis studied Ryan's face. Then he looked up at her. Ruby suddenly realised Ryan was around the same age she had been when Amy was killed – the last time Travis saw her as Rosie.

'Yes, this is Ryan,' Travis said. 'And it's strange but there really is something familiar about you...'

'We talked about it before. I interviewed you for Professor Caprini's research.'

'I know you did.' Travis was shaking his head. 'It's something else I can't put my finger on.'

Ruby really didn't care anymore. 'If you've nothing else to tell us, then I think we're done here.' She stood to leave. 'We're done here, sergeant,' she said to McGowan.

McGowan managed to hide his flicker of surprise. He played along and made a show of closing down the recording.

Travis was alarmed. And he was too ill to be able to mask it properly. 'Wait. What about Ryan? Did you find him? Is he still in France?'

France. Good. That tied in with what Mrs Peterson had said about Irene Newark being fluent in French. The pre-school teacher had already pinpointed France as being a likely location. And it was obvious Travis had no idea Ryan was a suspect for the murders. He didn't know of their interest in Ryan nor how they were as desperate to find him as he was, but for different reasons. And the way he was clutching at Mrs Peterson's photograph made it clear Mike Travis and Ryan were certainly not in contact in some kind of co-conspiracy.

'Oh yes, we didn't get around to following up the France thing yet. Ryan Travis isn't exactly the inspector's priority. What was the name of that place in France we were going to check out, sergeant?' She clicked her fingers a few times at McGowan as if she was trying to remember.

'Paris?' McGowan offered.

'Cizay,' Travis whispered.

'Yes, that's it, Cizay,' she said. 'No, we haven't found him there yet. A bit like we haven't yet found Meredith and Isabella. But we'll let you know when we do.'

Under the stress, Travis had started to sweat. It brought with it the pungent smell he'd had at the hospital. Ruby imagined a pain spike was due any moment. Travis was panicking because he anticipated dying before they brought him Ryan.

McGowan was already standing and turning away. Ruby reached to take back the photograph. Travis' eyes locked onto hers and Ruby withdrew her hand, instead she leant towards him.

'You can keep the picture if you want, Mr Travis,' she said. Then in a whisper, 'Oh yes, I almost forgot, Rosie says she's looking forward to seeing you dead.'

Travis opened his mouth to say something but nothing came out.

She waited.

She saw that he knew.

Ruby signalled to the prison officer she had finished and she left the room.

Chapter Forty-four

Carys Evans wondered if Inspector Grant would come alone, as her captor had told him to. And would she then be allowed to go free? Or would the inspector stay away? Or bring armed officers who would shoot her captor dead on the spot? And maybe her too in the process.

Her captor had given her another injection to dull the pain in her hip. It was the best painkiller she'd had in her life. When he went upstairs, Carys crawled around the floor of the cellar trying to find her glasses. She could hear him moving about upstairs and she took the risk of using a chair to drag herself to standing for a few moments. In the dim light, she saw a row of glittering objects arranged in a showcase. Then the effort and the fear of him returning and punishing her for moving became too much and she sank again into her corner.

He was spending a lot of time upstairs listening to what sounded to Carys like news snippets.

How long had she been here? Perhaps twenty-four hours? Perhaps longer? She had no way to mark time. He had given her food twice and injected her twice. Would that be once a day or twice a day?

In her call to the inspector, Grant was instructed to arrive at a precise time. Carys realised Inspector Grant must soon be expected, when her captor came downstairs and took the precaution of securing her wrists.

'I need you to stay alive a little longer. Don't die of shock on me, will you? Our guest will soon be here.'

Sitting in the dark, Carys strained for every sound.

A while later, she gave up hope and was drifting into a daze, when she heard a front doorbell. It jerked her awake. She had the instinct to shift onto her knees, in case it might somehow help her.

The front door opened. Then it slammed shut. Footsteps sounded inside the house as one person walked slowly along a hallway. Was it Inspector Grant? Where was her captor? If it was the inspector why had he come on his own?

But she knew the answer. Because he'd been told to. She somehow knew he would. Was it because David knew she was in danger?

She imagined him in his smart suit with his grey searching eyes scouring around him. Her heart sank. Should she give a warning? Swallowing hard, she tried to shout. Except nothing came out apart from a mouse-ish whisper of fear.

Grant was coming closer to the entrance to the cellar because the footsteps were getting louder. Then she heard sudden voices. Her captor's and David's. Followed by a thump and one man's voice sharply calling out. She couldn't tell whose. Then came scuffling and scraping overhead. Carys clutched her knees tight. Had David concealed some kind of weapon? Had he overpowered her captor? Was he triumphant? Please, please, let him be the victor.

The basement door flew open. Carys' faith in the inspector, which she had held on to for all those years, finally failed her. Her hopes were destroyed in one blow as her captor came down the steps, dragging the inert body of David Grant behind him.

Chapter Forty-five

Detective Inspector David Grant was officially missing. Superintendent Fox announced it to the staff in the incident room and there was a silence. Fox told them she was assigning her next best inspector to find Grant, Detective Inspector Sharp.

Delaney spoke immediately. 'Permission to transfer to DI Sharp's team, ma'am.'

'Denied.'

'Ma'am, permission to transfer to–' Collins started to say.

'Denied also,' Fox snapped. 'And please don't bother me with the same futile request, McGowan. You will all remain with your current duties.'

Grant's team would continue with the three murder enquiries. They would continue searching for Ryan Travis as the main suspect. From now on, Grant's team would be under Fox's direct supervision.

Afterwards, Delaney shook his head. 'No body found so far. He's not been home. And he called his wife to say everything was fine. Which meant, obviously, everything was not fine.'

'There are only three options I can see. The inspector is dead or seriously injured, he's tracking Ryan, or he's been captured,' McGowan said.

'And this isn't a deep undercover case,' Delaney said. 'Why

would he need to drop off the radar if he was after Ryan? And why keep us out of the loop?'

'We've got to assume Grant has been captured,' Collins said.

'You mean you don't want to face the fact he's been murdered?' McGowan asked.

'Listen, McGowan, you really get on my nerves sometimes. You think what you like. We've got to believe he's alive. And we've got to get to him.'

Delaney was nodding. 'Agreed. Finding Ryan will help us with that, I'm sure of it.'

'Did Grant have some kind of warning he was in danger?' Collins said. 'Maybe he was contacted by the killer. What do you think?'

'That's not the pattern. Our killer doesn't make contact with his victims beforehand,' McGowan said. 'He takes them by surprise.'

Tom crossed his arms in front of his chest. 'Looks like you were right, Ruby. You said the inspector was the target. I should have listened to you.'

McGowan pointed at Ruby. '*She* said that?'

'Yes, McGowan. Ruby told me she suspected Grant could be the final target of the killer.'

'Bloody hell,' McGowan said.

'I'd say the killer has gone off pattern because he's reached his target,' Ruby said. 'What he's going to do with Grant I've no idea.'

McGowan grimaced. 'But it won't be something pleasant.'

'Why the trail of murders?' Collins asked. 'If it's Ryan Travis, was it because he wanted Grant to suffer? To punish the man who put away his father?'

'It could be,' Delaney said. 'And Fox has given us an order we shouldn't get involved in Grant's disappearance. That's for DI Sharp.'

'Which, naturally, we're going to ignore,' McGowan said.

They all nodded.

'Well done for sneaking the trip past Fox,' Collins said. 'You did well, Ruby.'

It had been an opportune moment to get the superintendent's approval for a trip to Cizay. Only one place of that name existed in France – Cizay-la-Madeleine. It was a small village in the Loire Valley. Neither Hawk nor the police database had come up with any information for Jacob Newark and Irene Newark in Cizay which meant the only option was a direct visit.

'Yeah, I don't know how you got away with that one,' McGowan said.

'Because she's got diplomacy and tactics which you totally lack,' Collins said.

Tom was far from happy. His instinct was to stay close to the station and to DI Sharp. To be around should any leads come in about Inspector Grant. It was impossible for him to stay away.

'We've got to go, Delaney,' McGowan said. 'Let DI Sharp run with it. I know people on his team. They'll keep me up to date.'

'You three need to get over there,' Collins said. 'If there's any news on Inspector Grant, I'll let you know. And I'll start my own snooping about his final movements, phone records and so on, see if I can retrace his steps. And we know him the best. Maybe I can pick up a clue DI Sharp might miss.'

'Is Inspector Grant's passport gone?' Delaney asked. 'Can you check with his wife? It's a long shot but maybe there are travel records linking him to France?'

'I'm on it,' Collins said.

'Good,' McGowan stroked his moustache. 'If Ryan Travis has got the inspector, let's face it, Cizay is the only lead we've got. We've nothing closer to home. Come on, Delaney, let's go and do what we're good at and bring that bastard in.'

Ruby, McGowan and Delaney travelled over to France on the Eurostar. A train ride from Paris and a car hire later, and they were in Cizay-la-Madeleine. The village was in the middle of the French countryside. Tom could smell ploughed fields and he couldn't hear a single car.

After walking around the hundred or so white stone houses and finding the place deserted, an old man directed them to the cemetery.

Ruby got down on her knees to take photographs of Irene Newark's memorial plaque. It was modest – with simply a name and dates. Weeds had grown high. Ruby wiped her hand over the gold lettering. It was pretty clear no one visited to look after it.

'We need to find out why she died so young,' Tom said 'She was only fifty-seven.'

Ruby knew Tom was thinking Ryan Travis might have killed Irene. It twisted her guts, but she knew he could be right. 'Agreed.'

'We need more local information on her,' McGowan said.

'Ruby, can you talk to the gardener or handyman, whatever he is. You see him over there by the fence?' Tom said.

'It's a good job I'm here. You both speak awful French.'

Tom's French was basic. As for McGowan, Ruby wondered now how he'd dredged up the name for Paris at the prison hospital. He was certainly no expert on France. He knew nothing beyond bonjour and merci – both of which he pronounced terribly.

The man over the other side of the cemetery was cutting the hedge. Ruby did her best to explain they were there for information about Irene Newark. They walked him over to look at the plaque. He didn't really understand their questions.

Tom brought up Inspector Grant's photograph on his phone.

'Has anyone else been asking questions about the Newark family? Do you recognise this man? Has he been here?'

The man shook his head. He seemed to sense their exasperation and took them to a friend of his in the village. The friend gathered a small crowd of neighbours. Everyone was friendly and curious, though no one could actually help. One of the neighbours finally took pity. She drove them to a golf course, about twenty minutes away.

McGowan was losing patience.

Tom was starting to think it was a big waste of time and they'd be better off contacting the local gendarmerie and asking for assistance there. He was itching to get back to the station. But it turned out the manager of the golf course, Sebastian, spoke good English.

'I understand you wanted to know about Irene Newark? Ask me what you like. I was at school with her son, Jacob.'

Tom noticed how Ruby locked on to Sebastian. She led with the questioning. Ruby was a different woman to the one who accompanied him to Mrs Peterson in Brighton. She was sharp and focused and knew exactly what she wanted to ask. She also built a good rapport with their helper.

'Let's sit down,' Sebastian said. 'I love visiting England. My wife and I have been over a few times. Can I offer you coffee? Or lunch?'

Tom tucked into a massive baguette stuffed with soft French cheese and salad and a huge bowl of soup. McGowan ordered a steak and chips. While the two of them ate, Ruby questioned Sebastian about the Newarks.

Sebastian told them he knew Jacob through primary, then secondary school and then lycée, which was the equivalent of English sixth form college. After that, Jacob took off to go backpacking. The last he heard, Jacob was in Vietnam.

'He was restless, and I guess he got that from his mother.

She lived in Poland and then England and then France. I think there was a breakup with her family and it was only the two of them. That's strange around here where family is so important but they fitted in really well.'

He told them Jacob played the bass guitar and he and Jacob played together in a band. Apart from with his music, Jacob wasn't very social. He liked to keep himself to himself.

Irene Newark died of a heart attack. She'd had a heart condition for many years and Jacob was a devoted son, doing everything around the house, even renovating it during his summer holidays.

'Jacob was a pretty good handyman. One of their neighbours used to show him the basics and then he kept their little place in top shape by himself. I remember he always had a project going during the holidays, like repainting the shutters or rebuilding the front wall.'

Tom thought the mother's death was highly suspicious. She and Ryan lived alone. Ryan could have been messing around with Irene's medication. Perhaps he even kept the woman dependent on him. They would have to request the medical records, to check for any signs of foul play. Also, Ryan was quiet, and in Tom's experience, that was often a bad sign.

'Any girlfriends?' Tom asked.

'You probably wouldn't believe it but he only had one I can think of. Though with his looks lots of the girls liked him. His old girlfriend is married now and she works in town, actually, she works with my wife. Would you like me to contact her?'

McGowan stopped chomping. 'Only one girlfriend? You've got to be kidding me.'

'Has anyone else been asking?' Tom showed Sebastian the picture of Inspector Grant.

'Not that I know of. I'm sure someone would have mentioned it. This is a quiet place.'

'We need to find Jacob as soon as possible,' McGowan said.

'Could this old girlfriend help us?'

It didn't take long for Sebastian to get the woman's phone number. After a long conversation in French, Sebastian gave them a smile.

'I think I've got something you might find useful. She says he wanted to join the Army. Although I have to say he never mentioned it to me, but then, like I told you, he was quite private. Also, she said he preferred his middle name. I didn't know that either. After his mother died of course he was pretty shaken up, and she said he decided to change it around. So maybe you should be searching for a Ryan Newark instead of a Jacob Newark?'

McGowan was on his feet. 'You've been very helpful, sir. Very helpful indeed. We need to speak to Mrs Newark's doctor. Can you help us with that?'

Sebastian made an appointment.

When they got to the doctor's office, they met a young woman, roughly the same age as Ruby. The doctor who treated Irene Newark had retired a long time ago and she had no idea how to contact him. She said it was a lengthy paperwork procedure to gain access to old medical records which were all held on archive. The best thing would be to send in a request from England.

'This was a visit worth making,' McGowan said. 'But we've done all we can. It's not going to be easy to find an evidence trail if he killed his mother.'

'Do you think he fits the profile, Ruby?' Tom asked.

'There are some flags but the picture isn't clear cut.'

'It's as clear cut as it's going to get,' McGowan said. 'There's the suspicious death of his mother. He was a loner and a drifter. What more do you want? Seems clear to me. We might even be looking at the possibility of young women being buried on the Newark's old property. Remember he told us Ryan took charge of maintenance, building walls and stuff. Burying and then cementing in bodies and body parts is a known disposal method used by serial killers.'

'Good thinking. Let's ask Collins to check for reports of missing persons in the area,' Tom said.

On the train back to Paris, McGowan spent most of the time online, sifting through the notes from the incident room and sending emails to his pals in DI Spark's team. McGowan reported back there was no progress from DI Spark. And Collins hadn't sent any news on Grant.

Tom looked gloomy.

Ruby spent most of the time staring out of the window. It was near impossible for her to make a professional assessment because little things kept sending up flares of hope. Serial killers were isolated as children, living with cold and emotionally cut-off parents. It was one of the common traits. Ryan having a loving mother didn't fit the profile. Neither did the fact he played in a band. He was creative, liked music – both way off target for psychopaths and sociopaths. Not to mention the roller-coaster ride her emotions took whenever she thought of Ryan inventing an imaginary sister. Every time she thought of it, it made her break out in goosebumps. Then again, it was suspicious Irene died young and also suspect how private he was, with only one girlfriend. She mustn't allow herself to be hopeful.

Ruby suddenly felt exhausted. McGowan and Tom's inner drive to find Ryan was powering them on. McGowan was like a hunter on the trail. It was obvious they were both convinced of Ryan's guilt. She really hoped she was up to the job. She would have to stay clear-headed – for Grant, for the dead women, for Ryan and herself – there was so much riding on this. She must stay professional and not allow herself to be emotional. It was the only way to make a clear independent decision.

When McGowan went to the buffet car, she allowed herself

to drift to sleep. The motion of the train nudged Ruby's head to settle on Tom's shoulder.

Tom could feel her hair against his neck and occasionally little wafts of sandalwood scent drifted towards him. Tom didn't allow himself to study the curve of her cheek, though he wanted to. He didn't feel it was appropriate, and they were facing enough complications without him adding more.

Chapter Forty-six

McGowan, Delaney and Ruby arrived back from France to find a heavy atmosphere in the incident room.

'DI Sharp hasn't made any progress,' one of the constables said. 'We've still no news about Inspector Grant.'

Ruby heard a choke in the constable's voice. Tom was the one who walked across the room to reassure her. Everyone's eyes were on him and he did a short tour of the desks to check on what the constables had been working on, but really to give them all a small boost. Just like the inspector would have done, she thought.

Collins looked like she might have been crying. The team doughnut tray lay empty next to her desk. Remains from yesterday hadn't been cleared out. It was a sure sign things were going quickly downhill.

'You didn't get Ryan Travis, did you?' Collins said.

Delaney shook his head.

Collins seemed to pull herself together. 'Thank goodness you're back. I haven't come up with anything on the inspector. Office phone records, his computer, his family – none of them give any ideas.'

'Shit,' McGowan said.

'There was one thing the inspector left me a note about,' Collins said. 'He wanted me to check with Mandy Jones' sister to see if any of the victim's jewellery was missing. I did and it turns out an amethyst necklace is gone. Mandy Jones may have been wearing it when she was killed. Luke Sanderson agrees.'

Ruby was unloading her laptop. As she reached to plug it in, she stopped. 'Wait! The dream catcher, now a necklace and maybe a goldfish, which means... Diane, were there any results from the missing persons search around Cizay?'

'Nothing.'

Superintendent Fox marched in.

'The neighbour living next door to Carys Evans has called in to say she's concerned. Carys Evans hasn't drawn her curtains for a couple of days. DS Collins please get over there with patrol and check it out.'

'Delaney, McGowan, I see you've got back from your *holiday* in France. Please tell me Ryan Travis is in the custody of the French gendarmerie or that you know exactly where to find him in our green and pleasant land.'

'Ma'am,' McGowan said, 'we believe Ryan Travis may have joined the Armed Forces. Also, the death of the woman who pretended to be his mother may have involved foul play.'

'That's too many maybes in one sentence, McGowan. I want facts not supposition. Find Ryan Travis and find him quickly. That's all I'm interested in.'

'We'll get straight on to it, ma'am,' McGowan said. 'Any news about Inspector Grant?'

'None,' Fox snapped. 'What are you waiting for, I thought you had an Armed Forces check to run?'

McGowan and Delaney left the room at a jog.

The Superintendent turned her glare on Ruby. 'What have you got to say for yourself?'

Ruby spoke slowly and carefully. 'I'm not certain the information we're piecing together on Ryan Travis fits the profile of our killer.'

Fox's eyebrows went up.

'Ryan had a strong relationship with Irene Newark who he

regarded as his mother. He was creative, he played in a music band. Everything we know about serial killers tells us they're loners. They're people cut off from society, brought up in emotionally stark homes.'

Fox walked up to Ruby. 'I hope this is a rational conclusion, Ms Silver.'

'I believe it is. I've thought it over thoroughly and this is my professional judgement. The problem with the information we found is it's not a clear picture. In fact, it's mixed, and there are a couple of red flags in Ryan's profile, only I don't think they're enough to tip the balance.'

'Please explain why you're telling me something which runs counter to your colleagues.'

'Ryan Travis is our only suspect. Until I can find another name it's natural they–'

'Exactly, Ms Silver. Then I suggest you make it your business to find another name.'

Fox was already moving to the front of the room. Ruby called after her.

'There's more, Superintendent.'

One of the constables gave Ruby a look of alarm as Fox stopped mid-step and turned, theatrically, in Ruby's direction.

'The killer sent a photograph of my room at the pub. It's got to be a ploy. I believe Inspector Grant is the real target. He has been all along and we didn't see it. What if, from the beginning, someone has been using Ryan Travis as a cover? What if they want to frame him as the main suspect to keep us looking in the wrong direction? I think it's likely the killer is someone else from Grant's past.'

Fox narrowed her eyes. It was disconcerting. 'As I explained before, Detective Inspector Sharp is looking into Grant's disappearance. If there's a link, he'll find it.'

Ruby felt it would be wise to keep her mouth shut and Diane's report on the amethyst necklace had given her an idea.

Superintendent Fox rapped her knuckles on the desk. 'Listen up, everyone. I didn't come down here to mollycoddle you. I came to inform you Travis will be transferred to the hospice this afternoon. In fact,' Fox consulted her watch, 'in two hours' time.'

'Oh no, that's all we need,' someone said.

'Yes, it's shit-hits-the-fan time,' Fox said. 'We've got anti-Travis protestors out in force. We've got Christmas crowds and we've the dropping off of a serial killer at the hospice close to the town centre. I'll be overseeing the transfer myself. Half of you, detective constables, and I don't care which half, get yourselves to the briefing room in five minutes. I'm calling in all available officers from uniformed division and half of you lot for maximum bodies on the ground. The rest, carry on here. And you, Ms Silver, continue working on whatever you were working on.'

The tension in the room rocketed. People scurried to pack away their things. Fox marched out.

Ruby's mind was already racing.

Chapter Forty-seven

He was reading out another of his father's hateful letters. Behind her back, Carys screwed her fists as tight as she could. She was not allowed to cover her ears nor close her eyes, otherwise she would be punished. Nothing could keep out the twisted words. Before he started on the letter, her captor had told her his father died in prison and Carys had felt glad; father and son, they were both monsters.

Inspector Grant lay where he'd been dumped. Carys dreaded the inspector might be dead, until he made choking noises.

By the time the man finished reading, David was trying to sit up. Folding away the pages, the man crouched by Grant's side.

Grant coughed, trying to clear his throat.

'Have you worked it out yet, old man?'

The inspector was staring at the show cases. 'I know who you are,' he croaked.

'After all those times you've acted superior around me? I doubt it. Aren't I simply the stutterer everyone thinks of as an idiot and a nuisance?' The man laughed. He started removing Grant's jacket. Grant didn't resist.

'You're Doctor Bergerman's son.'

'Very clever. And do you know how long it takes for a man to die of starvation?'

'It was suicide. Your father Doctor Bergerman committed suicide in prison.'

'Wrong. My father went on hunger strike and starved himself to death to prove his innocence.'

David Grant remembered the case well. Doctor Bergerman had been responsible for a trail of stealthy murders and the scope of it had been sickening.

Doctor Bergerman worked as a rural general practitioner. His area was full of old people who often lived alone. His elderly patients relied on him and he visited them regularly. He was only convicted when one woman bequeathed the doctor money in her will and the woman's son filed a complaint. Grant led the investigation. It turned out Bergerman had been injecting his elderly patients with morphine and then registering it as a natural death. He had been at it for years. Grant brought ten cases to court and Bergerman was convicted. He suspected the death toll was much higher but there was insufficient evidence to bring the other cases.

'You didn't answer my question, Inspector. How long does it take for a man to die of starvation?'

'I don't know.'

'Around sixty days. At first, the body burns up its fat storage, then it starts on its own muscles. That stage takes a while.'

He tossed Grant's jacket aside.

'Then, once the body begins attacking its own bone marrow, starvation becomes life-threatening.'

He knelt down low, bringing his face close to Grant's.

'My father lasted sixty-one days. Can you imagine the force of will required for him to hold out so long? In his last days when he became unconscious, my mother asked the authorities to intervene to save his life. They agreed, but my father contracted pneumonia. He died, despite last-minute medical assistance. That's it, look at me, Inspector. You killed him. You murdered my father. And for that you are going to suffer.'

Bergerman's son took out a syringe.

'I saw what he did. Bergerman was guilty. He was convicted by a jury. He was calculating, he abused his position of trust. He used elderly people to feed his own–'

'Shut up.'

The man was shaking with rage. 'Ideally, I'd have liked you to go the same way he did. I'd have liked to keep you in a cage and starve you to death. And I hope you've been appreciating the victims I've selected so far. Those young women gave their lives for you.'

'There's no way you'll get away with this. Give it up.'

'I said, shut up! Unfortunately, I don't have time to wait sixty days. So, to ensure a torturous death, I've decided to improvise.'

Carys watched as he rolled up Grant's sleeve and stuck in a needle. Grant didn't seem able to resist. His muscles weren't working.

'The shot I gave you upstairs was a tester so I could work out the dosage. Death by morphine poisoning is a horrible way to go. As the amount is slowly increased, the victim can retain awareness of their demise, and yet be powerless to stop it as their heart and organs slowly close down. I'm looking forward to watching you suffer.'

'Is that what your father did to his victims? Did he do it the sadistic way?'

Carys knew from the man's letters that he had.

'Let her go,' Grant whispered. 'You've got what you wanted, you promised you'd let her go.'

'I'll let Miss Evans go when I'm good and ready. Assuming, of course, she survives that long.'

He patted Grant's arm and laughed. 'Sweet dreams, *Inspector* Grant.'

Grant could feel the poison working its way through his system. He watched the man's ankles as he made his way up the stairs.

'Carys–' Grant's voice was weak.

She crawled to his side. David was losing consciousness.

'Listen,' he said. 'Your sister. Travis gave us information. We've officers searching a new location. You've got to keep strong. You've got to survive, we could be close to a breakthrough.'

Grant could feel his heart slowing down and it was getting laborious to draw each breath. Tremors started along his back and legs. He knew he would soon be passing out as the effects of the morphine took hold.

He had recognised the killer at the front door. If Carys was to come out of this alive, he must give her every reason to live.

'They've found human remains. We don't know yet if….'

'Is it Meredith?' Carys said. 'Is it Meredith?'

She shook him. She wanted to scream at him but his eyes were already rolling up into the top of his head. Carys held onto his shoulders.

His wife was lucky. In those early days, perhaps if things had been different… Carys often wondered if something might have happened between them… but with Meredith gone… and then David Grant met Lily…

David Grant had been a handsome young man. He was still good looking. She noticed his age for the first time. Back in those days, she sensed he liked her too, but the years had all gone past them.

'Oh David, you should never have come here for me.'

Carys put her hand on his chest. He was solid and dependable. He always had been. His support had kept her going in the bad times.

At least she wasn't alone with this psychopath and she was

grateful for it. Carys rolled Grant onto his side so he wouldn't choke.

Chapter Forty-eight

Ruby shut herself off from the other activity in the incident room. She cleared her mind and made herself think it through step by step.

Taking a whiteboard, she wrote up her hit list on the killer. If she ignored all the false information linking him to Travis, his first characteristic was he targeted women. Then there was a hospital or medical connection. And the most important information had been provided by Collins – he was a trophy collector.

The nurse's missing necklace was the crucial factor. He was a killer who collected from his victims.

Ruby was willing to bet this person expected to get away with their crimes by keeping the police running after Travis' son.

'Hang on a sec,' she said to herself.

Yes, might that mean the killer was also the child of a killer? It was an inspired thought and a long shot but yes, it could be an unintentional, subconscious link to why they'd chosen Ryan Travis as a scapegoat in the first place. That was how the mind worked. It made mysterious connections which people were barely conscious of.

And what about motive? Why would someone go to all this trouble to target Grant? And to lay a trail of murder before honing in on the inspector? The obvious motive was revenge. A vendetta. And to make him suffer. Yes, this killer wanted David Grant to suffer and they had used the deaths of Mandy Jones, Doctor Hawthorne and Eleanor Vickers to that end – to make Grant feel responsible for their lives being taken.

She added "child of a killer" and "suffering" to her list.

'Impressive. I like the way your brain works,' Luke said. He'd come into the room without her noticing.

'If I'm going to trawl through thirty years of Grant's cases, I need some pointers. Using these as keywords will save time. Assuming, of course, I'm right in my thinking.'

Luke came and sat next to her. 'We're all worried about Inspector Grant. I don't suppose you know, but he's been a good friend to me. He helped me fit in. Before he disappeared, he came to see me and we talked about going back to find if the nurse was wearing a necklace. His little chats are something I look forward to.'

The pathologist sounded sad.

'Don't worry. I'm working on it and we're going to find him,' Ruby said. 'The necklace is what clinched it in my mind. Trophy hunter is our biggest clue. And the type of trophy they like to take is important. Killers are very specific about which items attract them.'

She was busy setting up the search parameters 'What brought you upstairs?' she asked.

'Someone told me you were on a one-woman mission and you might need a little company.'

'Tom, I suppose?'

'It was Superintendent Fox. Yes, I thought that might be a surprise but she's not as bad as she makes out. I think she's taken a liking to you.'

'This could take hours,' Ruby said, 'and we don't have hours. Let's hope I'm on the right track. Inspector Grant won't have much time.'

'Oh no, you think the killer's got Grant. And he's already

making his move?'

'Yes.'

Luke's face became even more serious. 'I'd better not distract you. Can I get you a coffee?'

Ruby hardly heard; she was already on a manual trawl of the files, starting from the very beginning of Grant's career, while her search program ran in the background.

Chapter Forty-nine

Delaney and McGowan sent off requests, searching for a Ryan Newark or a Jacob Newark in the Armed Forces of the UK, France and Poland. They also targeted Australia, the US, Canada and New Zealand. After all, Ryan had gone travelling. He could have ended up anywhere. The two of them waited impatiently, McGowan pacing and cracking his knuckles and Delaney fretting about Inspector Grant.

It seemed to take ages. It turned out the searches for Europe came up blank. But their luck was in because the Canadian Army had a listing for a Captain Ryan Newark.

It meant they had to make a call to Captain Newark's commanding officer, and they rushed upstairs to get the authorisation.

Twenty minutes later, Delaney and McGowan burst into the incident room.

'We got him!'

Ruby jumped to her feet, her eyes wide. 'Ryan Travis? You found him?'

'He's a Captain Ryan Newark in the Canadian Army. We had to go through the top brass, the Chief Constable no less, to get permission. The Chief Constable spoke to a Major Jefferson. Jefferson says Ryan Newark's mother was Polish and he lived in France in Cizay-la-Madeleine. It's the same person,' Tom said.

Ruby clutched at the back of a chair. The room was spinning.

'Come on, sergeant, tell us,' Luke demanded. 'Where is he now? Is he the killer? Does he have an alibi?'

'Major Jefferson says Ryan Newark has been on active duty in Afghanistan for the last twenty months,' McGowan said. 'It can't possibly be him.'

Ruby made a small noise. She felt the blood draining from her head, her legs buckled under her and she fell.

'Help me get her away from the furniture,' Luke said. 'Stay calm, Ruby, everything's okay.'

Tom was staring at Ruby's screen and struggling to read it. 'What's she searching for?'

'She trawling Grant's old cases,' Luke said. 'That's her list up there.'

Tom read the whiteboard. Women victims. Medical setting. Trophy hunter.

His mind turned it over. Tom had listened to most of Grant's old case files. And his memory was second to none.

'Wait a minute,' he said. 'I think I know who fits that.'

'You can't possibly–' McGowan started to say.

'Bergerman!' Tom shouted. 'It's Doctor Bergerman. That's the only one of Grant's old cases which fits all those criteria.'

Ruby was coming around. She could see the screen of her computer and it was flashing a red message. Her program had crashed. They'd never make it in time. There was no way they could read all Grant's files. It would take days.

'We need to start a manual search of Grant's old cases. Get started you two. There's no time–'

'It doesn't matter, Ruby. It's all in here.' Tom tapped the side of his head.

McGowan gave Tom a slap on the back. 'Come on, man, spit it out.'

'I know who it is. Bergerman was convicted some twenty years ago by Inspector Grant. I listened to the files. I know the details. He was a doctor. He was convicted for the murder of, I think, ten elderly women. They were all his patients. Bergerman killed them by injecting them with morphine, then he registered their deaths as natural. He took items of jewellery, personal stuff, from each one.'

Luke was helping Ruby to her feet.

'Go on,' she said.

'Over the years, a few colleagues raised questions about the high death rate of Doctor Bergerman's patients but their concerns were dismissed. He was finally convicted when one elderly woman left Bergerman money in her will and her son complained. Grant was assigned to the case. He found out Doctor Bergerman had been silently murdering his elderly patients for years. And there was something else...'

'Tom you're a genius. What an amazing memory,' Luke said.

'...and Bergerman starved himself to death in prison years after he'd been convicted. No one knew why he did it.'

'Did he have any children?' Ruby asked.

'I don't know,' Tom said.

McGowan was logging on. 'But we can find out.'

Ruby was suddenly crying. She hoped they all supposed it was to do with the tension of the moment and identifying Bergerman. It wasn't. It was to do with Ryan. She'd found her little brother at last. He was alive and well and working in Afghanistan. He was innocent. Oh God, he was innocent. She could hardly believe it. She wanted to hear his voice. She wanted to see him. To speak to him, and tell him how much she... But she had work to do.

She stood behind McGowan and focused on the screen.

'Bingo,' McGowan said. 'Bergerman had a wife who's now

dead. And he had a son. The boy was ten years old at the time of Bergerman's conviction. Boy's name was Anthony. Like you said, Bergerman went on hunger strike and died in prison.'

'What about the trophies?' Ruby said.

'Relatives testified Bergerman took significant items of jewellery his victims had been wearing at the time of their death, but the items were never recovered. You think this is our man?'

Ruby concentrated as McGowan scrolled through the details.

'Stop.' She pointed. 'Look at the wife's name. She was called Kathleen Tanner.'

'That's it!' Tom said. 'Unbelievable. He took his mother's name. It's the hospital manager, Mr Tanner.'

Chapter Fifty

When David Grant next regained consciousness, the first thing he heard was the voice of the killer. Tanner was reading another letter. As the words slowly made sense to him, Grant realised it was a letter sent to Tanner by his father.

Tanner stopped mid-sentence. 'So glad you could join us, Inspector. I was hoping I'd get an opportunity to share my father's thoughts with you.'

The man's voice was twisted with hatred. Grant tried to push himself up to sitting and he managed it on the second attempt. His heart felt like it was racing and he wondered how much morphine was still in his system. How long had he been out for?

Carys was sitting to his left, her mouth slack with horror. Grant didn't know if it was due to the contents of the letter or his own appearance, maybe both.

'I see you've inherited your father's stolen trophies.'

The jewellery was neatly arranged in a glass showcase. Grant's attention was caught by a diamond ring. It was so long ago, yet he remembered it. Grieving relatives had passed a photograph to the police except the ring had never been found at Bergerman's house. The rest of the jewellery on display in Tanner's basement must have been stolen from Bergerman's other victims. All of it ripped from elderly people after their lives had been ended by their own doctor injecting them with morphine. Grant felt his anger stirring.

Beyond the showcase was another shelf. On it was the amethyst necklace and Doctor Hawthorne's goldfish in its glass sphere. Yes, their killer was a trophy collector. Just like his father.

'Bravo, Inspector. At long last, your dim brain has managed to piece together the puzzle. Shame it took you so long.'

Tanner crossed his legs and smoothed his hands over his smart trousers. There was no trace of his stutter nor his hesitancy. He was a different man. Cold and sharp and deadly.

Grant took notice of the cool precision in Tanner's movements. He was just like his father. Calculating and dispassionate. Doctor Bergerman had gained the trust of his elderly patients. He picked out women who lived alone, and who had a range of symptoms associated with the latter stages of life – severe arthritis, diabetes, dementia, heart conditions. Bergerman had been clever enough to escape scrutiny for years. He had fooled his fellow health workers and the relatives of his victims.

'It was clever to frame Ryan Travis,' Grant said. 'The son of a killer framing the son of a killer.'

Tanner smiled. 'Meticulous planning always leads to success. That's what my father taught me in his writings. Mike Travis coming to the hospital was an opportunity too good to miss. Strange to think it was his illness which threw the two of us together. Again. Did you know my father sent me a letter once a year up to his untimely death?'

That Bergerman had corresponded with his son surprised Grant.

'Do you actually remember me, Inspector? I was there when you put handcuffs on my father.'

David Grant gave a small nod, though he had no recollection of a boy being present. What he wanted was to make sure he created as little friction as possible between him and the killer. This was all about survival. And finding opportunities. Like knowing this man's proper name was Anthony because the father called him that in the letter.

'When I saw you at the hospital talking to Doctor Hawthorne about Mike Travis, it all came flooding back. I was transported to the moment of my father's arrest. And all the hatred I've felt for you came alive again.'

Yes, Grant thought. And Mike Travis gave Tanner cover for murder, even providing the perfect suspect in Travis' missing son. Even providing DNA. Grant had to admit the plan had been inspired, right down to leaving a trail of women with names matching Travis' victims. Of course, it meant Tanner thought he could get away with it. Just as his father had professed his innocence even as he was led away from court. Anthony Bergerman-Tanner thought he would walk free.

'Why Ruby?'

'Would you believe how boring all the Sandras are in Himlands Heath? There was so little choice and nobody I could count on to distract you for more than a moment. And then I saw your ghastly shielding and protection of Silver at the hospital. I almost gagged. Isn't she a bit young for you?'

Tanner's phone buzzed and he checked the screen. Whatever he read there, Grant knew it was important. Tanner put away the letter, folding it carefully back in the envelope.

'Events are marching forward. Get up, both of you.'

Tanner moved quickly and dragged Carys to her feet. The woman gave a squeal of pain as he jerked her upright.

Grant's mind was turning over the possibilities. The tempo of the situation had suddenly sped up. What had happened to spur Tanner into action? Were his colleagues searching for Carys? Or for Grant? Had some outside event kicked things up a gear?

What Inspector Grant didn't know was that the ambulance carrying Mike Travis had arrived at the hospice and his colleagues were struggling to contain a crowd hell-bent on making sure Travis never set foot in the place.

Grant stood slowly. He felt shaky and drained of power. He had to hold on to the wall to steady himself. 'Where are we going?' he asked softly.

Tanner ignored the question. Then he signalled for Grant to start up the stairs. The man was agitated. Or excited. Tanner dragged Carys behind him.

'The trial turned my father's name into one loathed by the nation. For that and for his death, you are about to pay dearly. Reflect on your sins, Inspector. You don't have much time left.'

Chapter Fifty-one

Tanner lived in a three-bedroom property in a tidy suburb of Himlands Heath. His neighbours had three plastic reindeers as decoration in the garden. They were dotted with Christmas lights.

There was no back-up because every available unit had been called to deal with the situation at the hospice.

Around the back of the house, Tom Delaney looked the other way while Ruby used a rock to smash a window in the kitchen. She put her arm inside to undo the latch.

Despite his six-foot frame and rugby-player physique, Tom didn't like it. He didn't like having Ruby alongside him. He couldn't help thinking how easy it would be for someone to injure her.

McGowan went to go in first. 'Keep it tight, Delaney. Ruby, you wait here.'

'No way. I'm part of this whether you like it or not. You need me.'

'We're wasting time.'

'Exactly, so let's get on with it.'

Ruby ignored McGowan's scowling. Stepping over the glass, she followed him inside. They tiptoed across the kitchen and into the hallway. All was quiet, except for the pounding of her own pulse. She kept her eyes on McGowan's sizeable bulk in front of her, trying to see around him when she could. The house smelled of food – takeaways and stale fish and chips. Tom was right behind her.

They checked each room, moving as stealthily as they could. Tom stayed so close, she could feel the heat coming off his body. All the downstairs rooms were empty, the upstairs bedrooms too. The only place left to check was the basement.

For this one, Ruby was sandwiched between the two officers. Her knees started shaking. She really didn't fancy the idea of walking into the dark. With a psychopathic killer waiting for them. And neither did she like the idea of the sergeants leaving her at the top. What if something happened to them? Or if the killer managed to creep up behind her while they were below?

The door made a small noise as McGowan swung it open and Ruby winced. She still had the rock in her hand and she raised it higher, ready to punch it out with all she'd got.

They were halfway down the stairs when it occurred to her to throw the light switch. She went back up, squeezed past Tom and then groped around on the wall.

They were blinded when she flicked it on. McGowan almost lost his footing, flailing for his balance and sprinting down the rest of the steps to regain it.

What they found was emptiness. No one was in the basement. But there were signs people had been there. And there were trophies.

Tom stared into the showcase and pointed. 'This is from Doctor Hawthorne's desk.'.

She went to join him. 'And these are Bergerman's. From all those old people.'

McGowan picked up Grant's jacket. 'It's definitely Grant's. And what's this?'

He held up a lace handkerchief. It was old-fashioned and feminine. It had been in one of Grant's pockets. McGowan put it to his nose.

'It smells of a woman's perfume.'

'Carys Evans?' Delaney said. 'Collins has reported her missing. She might have been held here too and Grant put it there in case we came searching. Might that be why the inspector came here in the first place? Because she was being held hostage?'

'Makes sense,' McGowan said. 'That call Grant made to his wife was odd. Like he knew what he was about to do. And hasn't the inspector always kept in touch with Carys Evans?'

Tom was examining the floor for more clues. 'They were at school together.'

'Tanner has been several steps ahead of us all the time. And now he's taken Grant and possibly Carys Evans someplace else,' Ruby said.

'Wait.' Tom smashed his fist into his palm 'Think about what's happening in town. Tanner is the bloody hospital manager. He'd know it's time to move Travis to the hospice. Wouldn't that be a great moment to get them into a car?'

'You mean, if he wanted to kill Grant and not do it in this house?' McGowan shrugged. 'Just being realistic.'

'I think you're right. He's been planning this. He's in control. And he's moving them so he isn't implicated. They have to be murdered elsewhere,' Ruby said.

'But where would he take them?' Tom said. 'It could be anywhere.'

McGowan started pacing. 'Shit.'

Ruby was working through Tanner's strategy. Tanner believed he could murder them and get away with it. He'd pointed them at Ryan all along. Going as far as taking DNA from Mike Travis at the hospital to plant at the scene of the crimes. He was counting on them never finding Ryan and he anticipated walking away scot-free.

Tanner had neither moved his trophies nor destroyed them,

which meant he had no idea they were even on to him. It had been the killer's first, and perhaps only, error.

'He's made a mistake,' she said. 'He didn't hide his trophies. Tanner didn't know we'd be coming here. He thinks he's in the clear.'

McGowan stopped pacing. 'We've got to work out where he's taken them. And fast.'

'Let's get back to the car,' Tom said. 'They've already got a head start.'

Where would Tanner take them, she thought? He didn't know they were on to him. He didn't know they had found Ryan and Ryan was in the clear. Therefore, Tanner would still be working on his plan to frame Ryan.

And the way to do that would be to kill them somewhere connected to the original Travis killings. And there was only one place with enough significance. Only one place convenient. She knew where Tanner would choose – the spot where Travis killed Amy on the heath.

'He's still working on his plan to frame Ryan. Which means he'll choose a place linked to the murders committed by Mike Travis. Tom, where were each of Travis' victims found?'

Tom reeled out the details, checking off each one on his fingers.

It came out like she knew it would. Of all the places Tom listed, there was only one likely location and they all knew it.

The pit of Ruby's stomach felt like it dropped out of her. 'It's got to be the heath.'

Chapter Fifty-two

Grant felt sick and drowsy. His legs were heavy and he kept stumbling. Was the ground uneven? Or were his legs not working properly? Everywhere was misty.

Tanner had brought them to the heath. It was foggy and freezing. As he plodded after Tanner and Carys, a strange thing happened – David Grant's wife came alongside him. Lily was dressed in a long black dress. She wore a black veil and would not turn to look at him. Grant tripped on a tussock of heather. He lurched forward, landing on his hands and knees. Lily could not be there. It had to be a hallucination. An effect of the morphine. Then he thought he heard his wife sobbing. *No, he told himself sternly, that's not Lily, Lily is safe at home.*

'Get up,' Tanner ordered.

His wife and his daughter were another two reasons why Grant had come to Tanner's house in the first place. He could well imagine what a maniac like Tanner was capable of inflicting on Lily and on Chrissie. Which is why he had not left that door open.

Grant got back on his feet. He took another couple of steps and almost fell again as his foot caught on another clump. He tried to fight off the vision of his wife. His daughter came to walk on his other side. She was howling with laughter, a bloodied knife clutched in her hand. *Another hallucination*, he told himself, *don't look at it and don't listen to it.*

Tanner was on a high. This was worth it. He felt like a god. This is what it had all been for. Grant was his to play with. He imagined how he would lay Grant out in a crucifix form, his life draining from him as he stared up into Tanner's face. Even the fog would add to the atmosphere. This would be a masterpiece ending.

It was a nuisance the woman was spoiling it with her snot and her snivelling. She was the fly in the ointment. Miss Evans had been a valuable lure but she had outlived her usefulness and Tanner didn't want any distractions. Time to put an end to her. He grabbed Carys' wrist and took her to one side to silence her for good.

While McGowan drove at full speed out of Himlands Heath, Tom Delaney called the station. It wasn't good news. Sergeant Wilson told him they were dealing with ongoing clashes and arrests at the hospice. The crowd had managed to break through the barricades and surrounded Travis' ambulance. Doctor Patel had been injured and there were several other casualties. The police were still trying to get the situation under control. Wilson said he would deploy a patrol car out to the heath as soon as he could. But he wasn't making any promises about how quickly that would be.

Delaney put in an urgent request, asking for an armed response unit. Sergeant Wilson asked if Delaney had sight of Inspector Grant. Was Inspector Grant or a member of the public in clear danger with an armed criminal in Delaney's sights? Tom couldn't lie and Wilson made it clear the top brass were unlikely to send the unit unless they were sure about the facts. Wilson promised he would do his best.

If Ruby was wrong about the location, they all knew the likelihood of finding Inspector Grant alive would be nil. Tanner was well ahead of them on all counts. Including timing.

A while later, they drew up to a nature reserve car park. The heath was shrouded in fog. It distorted the landscape and ghostly shapes loomed at them. Sounds were dampened down. One other car sat in the parking lot.

'Remember, this is not a last-minute impulse. Tanner knows what he's doing,' Ruby said. 'This has been planned out in advance, every step of the way.'

'Too bloody right,' McGowan said. 'Where the hell are we heading for? There's no path and we can't see a damn thing. He could be right on top of us or ten miles away and we wouldn't know the difference.'

'I know the way,' Ruby said.

Her colleagues looked at her in disbelief.

'Trust me. There's a stand of trees up ahead. That's where Amy Travis was killed. I looked up the layout when I read the files,' Ruby lied.

'Delaney, are you with her on this one?'

Tom nodded. 'She's right,' he said in a low voice. 'Amy Travis was killed around one hundred metres from the car park. Her body was found in a stand of trees.'

'Then let's go,' McGowan said. 'Quietly.'

Tom could tell Ruby was shaking. From cold maybe, and from fear. He wanted to keep Ruby close and safe. So did McGowan. The three of them advanced in a spearhead formation, with Ruby slightly leading the way.

McGowan shot him a look which said, 'I don't like this.'

Tom kept scanning ahead. The fog made everything strange. There didn't seem to be any track. They were stepping through the heather and going around clumps of bracken waist high and he wondered how Ruby could possibly know where she was going. They were blind. They were going to get lost, stumbling around in the middle of nowhere, while Grant was being murdered. Visibility was right down and that's how Tom almost tripped over Carys Evans.

He dropped to his knees. McGowan wheeled around and then swore under his breath when he saw the body.

Carys had been dumped amongst the heather. Her coat was flapping open and her skin was freezing to the touch. Tom felt for a pulse. How long had she been there?

He saw no obvious wounds and there was no blood on her clothing. At first, Tom thought her heart had stopped beating, then he realised she had a very, very slow pulse. But he wasn't certain she was still breathing.

'If Tanner moved them the same time as Travis arrived at the hospice, she can't have been here for long,' he said. 'Why is her pulse so slow?'

'Hypothermia?' McGowan suggested.

'Possible,' Tom whispered.

McGowan kept his back to the three of them, constantly scanning the mist on all sides. 'Or maybe she was wounded in the basement? At least it means we're on the right track.'

Tom carefully checked Carys Evans for injuries. When he rolled up her sleeves, he found puncture wounds.

'What's this?'

Ruby inspected the marks. 'Remember how Bergerman killed his victims using morphine? I think he's injected her. Tanner has used the same method his father used – morphine overdose.'

'We can't leave her,' Tom said. 'Her heart's weak. She could slip away at any moment. If she needs resuscitation there has to be someone with her.'

'You're right. You two stay,' McGowan said.

'Wait!' Tom hissed. 'You can't go on alone. We need to wait for back up.'

'And let Grant be killed? Wilson already told us it will be a while. There's no time to waste. I have to find Tanner and Grant. Where's the stand of trees?' McGowan said.

'You'll never find it on your own. I'll lead you. Tanner must be up there with the inspector.'

'No,' Tom said. 'Stay with me, Ruby. It's too dangerous.'

'Like McGowan said, we have to get to the inspector. This is about teamwork. Remember how Grant always tells us how important that is? And I keep telling you, I'm part of this. You need me.'

'Shit.' McGowan jerked his head to indicate for her to go in front of him.

The two of them left Tom behind.

The fog was playing tricks with her mind. Ruby started to wonder if she had veered off course and was heading in completely the wrong direction. The distances didn't seem right. They'd been walking for too long. Then she saw the outline of the first pine trees rising out of the mist. This was where her mother had been killed.

'We're very close to the spot,' she whispered.

McGowan's eyes were big and bright. He put his huge hand on her arm.

How many times had she visited this place in her nightmares? As she placed one foot in front of the other, she realised the hold it had over her had lifted. It was no longer the place she could never run from. It was no longer a place full of horror, full of Amy's bloodcurdling screams and then the terrible silence.

No, it was only pine trees. The spell had been lifted. It held no terror for her any more. On the contrary, it had been the killer's second error bringing Grant here because Ruby was on familiar territory.

She also knew a killer's mind. She understood Tanner's needs and motivations. She knew him from the inside out.

She thought she could see shapes in the mist up ahead. This was the culmination of Tanner's trail of killings. Likely it was the end of years, if not decades, of fantasising about how to end

Grant. Tanner would want to inflict death on the inspector with his own hands. He would want to taste it and savour it. This was his final move, and Tanner would want to linger until it was utterly finished. And it wasn't finished because Tanner's car was there. They still had time.

'I can see something. Stay here,' McGowan whispered.

McGowan took a step in front of her.

And then he screamed.

'It's just you and me, Inspector Grant. Or should I call you David?'

They stood facing one another. Carys had fallen by the wayside. Grant couldn't work out what had really happened to her. One minute she was there and the next she was gone. His mind had been invaded by hallucinations and strange sounds. It was no longer clear what was real and what wasn't. Grant had seen people in the fog. They had materialised from the mist and dragged Carys to the ground. As they crowded in on her, Grant was barged aside.

When Tanner dragged him away, Grant heard people screaming like demons, crowding around Carys and stabbing her to death. He saw the flashing of knives being lifted into the air and then thrust down. Or had that been made-up? It was impossible to tell. Nothing seemed real.

'I've been inspired, don't you think, David? I'm going to get away with it and you're going to die. And meanwhile the whole of the police department will be chasing the shadows hunting for Ryan Travis. The boy who will never be found.'

Grant had a sudden flash of reality. 'Doctor Bergerman was guilty and we both know it.'

'Liar!'

Spit flew from Tanner's lips and Grant thought he saw insanity in the man's eyes.

'Do you remember when you came to see Doctor

Hawthorne? The moment I saw you at the hospital, it brought back all your treachery, all the lies you heaped on my father. *You* are the murderer. My father was a great man!'

'He killed innocent people and for that he paid the price.'

'Wrong. You will pay the price.'

Tanner moved quickly before Grant could react, punching him in the stomach. Grant groaned and fell to his knees.

While Grant was down, Tanner calmly took a small box from his pocket. The first syringe he'd already used on Miss Evans. But the second one was ready and waiting for the infamous detective.

It was then Tanner heard a scream from the edge of the trees.

Ah, he had an intruder. Someone else had turned up to admire his ceremony. Good job he had been prudent and set a trap.

McGowan's scream had been short and ear-splitting. Now he bucked in agony, clutching at his leg. His ankle was caught in a set of metal jaws. It was some sort of barbaric animal trap. Ruby could see the jagged edges, buried deep in his leg. It was impossible to open. It had gone in far enough to reach the bone, she thought.

'F-! F-!' he shouted through clenched teeth.

McGowan controlled himself and stopped writhing. He was panting to deal with it.

Blood was seeping from his wounds. Ruby opened up his collar and wiped the dirt out of his eyes. McGowan needed urgent medical attention but he would live. Wilson would send a patrol soon. She didn't need to stay with him.

She realised just how much inner strength she possessed. She was resilient, she was strong. She always had been. Without it, she would never have survived.

Ruby turned to stare into the gloom. McGowan's eyes

moved there too. She saw a dark huddle in the middle of the stand of trees.

'Don't,' McGowan said. 'We don't need more dead bodies.'

'Give me some credit, or is that too much to ask.'

As she moved cautiously forward, she could see more clearly. The huddle became two shapes. It was one person bent over the other.

'Inspector Grant is a big man,' she said. 'I hope you haven't underestimated the dosage.'

Tanner was startled. His head came up so quickly it hurt the back of his neck. A young woman walked through the mist. Tanner felt a momentary confusion. Then a cold fury flooded his veins. How dare someone interrupt his moment of triumph?

He gave her a look of pure evil.

Ruby stopped well out of arms reach. Tanner recognised her as one of the police team. The delicate one.

'He'll get a shot big enough to down a rhinoceros,' Tanner said with a smile. 'Not even the wonderful inspector will be getting up after that.'

The syringe was in Tanner's hand. Ah, so he hadn't given it yet.

She thought quickly. The game of psychology was one she was good at.

'We've located Ryan Travis. You might be interested to know he has a watertight alibi.'

Tanner frowned. She had to be lying. 'Impossible. Aren't you that profiler?'

'We also found the mementos at your house – Doctor Hawthorne's goldfish, Mandy Jones' necklace. And I presume the other jewellery was collected by your father, from his own victims? That's quite a haul you've got there.'

Ruby was walking in a slow circle, keeping her distance from

Tanner. Keeping on the move helped her to think.

'I read about Doctor Bergerman,' she said 'He must have been someone you looked up to. Why don't you tell me about him?'

She knew Tanner was weighing up every word she said. Tanner would be searching for her weaknesses. Thinking out his next move. He had wanted to savour Grant's death and there she was, messing it up.

'I once interviewed a killer who kept trophies,' she said. 'He was very proud of his work.'

The woman was confident and Tanner thought it sounded as if she knew what she was talking about. It was almost as if she was someone who might appreciate his calibre.

The teachings from his father's letters came into Tanner's mind. 'The number one rule is meticulous planning,' he said.

The mist damped down other noises and made his words stand out. Tanner liked the sound of it.

The hairs on the back of Ruby's neck stood on end. She had been right. He had stayed to experience the completion of his work. This man didn't see the world as other people did. And he was only focused on one thing; taking Grant's life.

'Of course,' she said. 'A master at his game must plan if he's to be ahead of the opposition.'

Water dripped from the trees and her whole body buzzed. Adrenalin, fear, her own understanding of killers, alarm about the position the inspector was in – it all swirled around in a vicious cocktail. She had to draw the killer towards her. Use her psychological skills to manipulate him.

'My father was a great man.'

Oh God, she thought, his own belief in his superiority had led him to make a third error – which was underestimating Ruby. He had already allowed himself to be pulled slightly off course. Her mind against his. She was pitching herself against him, mind against mind, and she had to win.

'Of course he was. Why don't you tell me about him?'

Tanner was holding the syringe at Grant's neck. 'Stay back.'

Ruby crouched down and softened her voice. 'I'd like to hear about Doctor Bergerman. About how great he was.'

Tanner knew he should simply empty the morphine into Grant and finish it. But he had so wanted to linger. He'd wanted to savour every last drop of the inspector's death. Tanner wanted to taste Grant's last heartbeat.

He'd already played it out in his mind many times. He would administer the shot. He would listen to Grant's failing breath. Perhaps Grant's limbs would convulse and if they did, that would be a bonus. Then his breathing would dampen until it became non-existent and his heart would shake out its last feeble efforts. Then nothing. By the time anyone tried to revive him and certainly by the time any ambulance arrived to administer an antidote, it would be far too late. The inspector would be dead.

'You can't get away, Tanner,' Ruby said. 'And now I've spoiled your perfectly constructed ending, haven't I.'

'My father was innocent!' Tanner's arm was shaking with fury. He was about to do it.

David Grant felt the time was right. It was his opportunity. He twisted, taking out Carys' hatpin which he'd been concealing. He forced it into Tanner's testicles.

Ruby sprinted forwards. Tanner was screeching and clutching between his legs. He dropped the syringe and Ruby picked it up and stuck it straight into his body.

He reached for her as she pressed the plunger.

Ruby screamed as Tanner grabbed her hair. His hands were grabbing for her throat.

'You bitch!'

Tanner was snarling.

She stared into his face and he was like an animal. She felt his hands on her windpipe, and he squeezed, the force building up. Ruby's vision started to darken. She saw little dappled lights. Her legs were collapsing under her.

She reached for his face and gouged in her nails. Then he suddenly went limp and flopped to the ground like a rag doll. The drug had knocked him out.

She coughed and choked and kicked herself away from him.

'Carys,' Grant said.

'Tom's... with her.' She managed to say.

She could hear a siren. Thank goodness. A patrol car must be pulling up in the car park.

'The morphine,' Grant said, 'how much did you give him?'

'All of it, I think.'

David Grant laughed.

'I'm sorry, I'm so sorry I walked out.' And she threw her arms around his neck and held on tight.

Chapter Fifty-three

Inspector Grant received emergency antidote for morphine overdose. The nurses told him Carys Evans and Tanner had the same.

He was recovering in hospital when Ruby and Tom Delaney came to visit.

Ruby gave him a get well soon card which had been passed around the station. She was pleased he was looking better. Grant had lost the purplish hue on his skin which the morphine had brought on. Another twenty-four hours in hospital and he would be allowed home.

'The pathologist has got the results back on human remains found at the dump, sir,' Delaney said.

Grant took the card. He scanned the messages – some of them warm and lots of them funny and quite a few of them rude. He tried to ignore the horrible sinking feeling he felt in his stomach. He didn't feel bad because of the morphine messing up his system, it was because Carys was recuperating a few rooms away. He had not been able to see her yet. And he did not relish the thought of having to break the news they had found her sister's remains. But it was his job and he was her friend. He tried to console himself – at least she'd be able to put her sister to rest and it would be a comfort of sorts.

He hitched himself further up the bed. 'And?'

'It's Isabella Rees,' Delaney said. 'The search team couldn't find any other remains at the site and the Superintendent has called it to a close. Superintendent Fox visited Mr and Mrs Rees this morning to break the news.'

Grant let the shock sink in.

It was a few seconds before he spoke. 'Superintendent Fox went all the way up there?'

Grant was grateful she had done what he himself would have wanted to do. Most Superintendents would have delegated the task to the local force. It was a definite point in Fox's favour.

'She did, boss. Which leaves the question...'

There came a knock at the door and a nurse popped her head around.

'Another visitor for you, Inspector Grant,' she said. 'Seems you're popular today.'

In walked a young woman.

He stared at her face and was transported back twenty five years. To the two girls he knew at school and then as they became young women. The young woman in his room had chestnut hair and hazel eyes. She resembled the Carys and Meredith he knew from his youth.

'I'm sorry to intrude.' She had an Australian accent. 'My name is Kate. You don't know me but you once knew my mother, her name is–'

'Meredith.' It came out as a whisper.

'That's right. May I talk with you a while?'

For once, he was lost for words. Delaney offered his chair and he and Ruby quietly left.

'I think you'd better tell me everything,' Grant said.

'I don't really know where to start. It took me many years to find out my mother's story. It began when I stumbled across a letter in my father's desk. It had come from the British police and was enquiring about the whereabouts of an Edwyn Evans. He was my uncle.'

Grant nodded. It must have been one of the enquiries he sent to Australia himself. He'd sent three over the years. He only received a reply from one of them and it told him no one of that name existed.

'My father started out in Australia from nothing but he's good with people and he and my uncle went into business together. They made connections from the get-go. When I asked Dad about it, he said lots of people came to Australia to escape the past. The sheriff was a friend of his and he sent back a negative reply. It was only years later Mum told me the real story of why they'd left England.'

Kate had been persistent and badgered Meredith to find out about her past. She was finally told the truth when her Uncle Edwyn died.

Meredith told Kate how, as a young woman, she had fallen in love with her brother's best friend. Her parents had forbidden the romance because the boy was much older. Meredith's mother backed up her husband. Meredith's father refused to discuss it. So Meredith and Kate's father continued seeing each other in secret and hatched a plan to escape to Australia. Meredith's brother, Edwyn, helped them. In the end, Edwyn came along too because he was so disgusted with his parents' behaviour.

That was why Grant had always had a question about Edwyn Evans emigrating so close to Meredith's disappearance. It was the mistake which Travis had alluded to – Travis had killed Isabella but he did not kill Meredith.

'Mum told me her dad was super strict. He'd used his belt on Edwyn more than once. If he'd have found out she went with Dad to Australia, she was sure he would come after them and kill my father. She never meant for her disappearance to be linked to the South Coast Killer.'

'But when it did, it turned out to be convenient,' Grant said. 'So my enquiries got through to the right place, after all. And they made sure I never got a reply.'

'When I got the whole thing out of her, Mum broke down. I know she feels terrible about abandoning Carys and never letting her know. I've always begged her to contact Aunt Carys and Mum refuses. She says she left it too long. I found out everything I could about the South Coast Killer years ago and then I saw the recent case on the internet. When I heard what happened to Carys, I had to come. I hoped Mum would join me but she couldn't face it.'

'You mean she couldn't face her own sister.'

Grant felt like crying. For Carys. All the years she'd wasted on Meredith.

'What about when Meredith's parents died? Couldn't she have sent a letter? One single letter! Couldn't she have thought for one moment about her little sister?'

'She said Carys was too young when it happened. That Carys would forget all about her. My mother and father got married in Australia. They started afresh.'

Grant had to take a tissue. Meredith had lived a full life, whereas Carys…

'Mum has been terribly selfish, hasn't she. I've always known it.'

My god, Grant hoped he never got to meet Meredith face-to-face. He would never be able to stop himself telling her exactly what he thought of her. It was beyond selfish. It was unforgiveable.

'Is Aunt Carys all right?'

'Kate, you've done a brave and wonderful thing coming to England. I'm not going to hide the fact your aunt has suffered terribly from Meredith's disappearance. We believed her dead. Carys searched tirelessly for her.'

Kate was crying. 'I should have come sooner. I knew I should have done. Mum always found a way to stop me.'

Grant gave Kate a look of admiration. Carys might never be

able to forgive her sister, but he was sure she would find a place in her heart for her niece. And what a difference Kate would make in Carys' life.

'You're here now, and that's what matters. Please excuse my pyjamas and come with me, there's someone I want you to meet.' He swung his legs over the edge of the bed. 'Let's not waste another moment.'

Chapter Fifty-four

Hawk called in all the favours he could, in order to get Ruby a video link up with Captain Ryan Newark in Afghanistan.

Soraya and Hawk caught sight of Ryan on Hawk's giant screen. Ryan was wearing his uniform and he had dark, curly hair and a mouth just like Ruby's. Then they tiptoed out and closed the door. In the kitchen, Soraya clutched at Hawk's jumper and squealed.

'I can't believe it! It's him! Oh God, I hope it goes well.'

Soraya was so excited she couldn't eat any cake. So Hawk helped himself to half of it. He felt sure Ruby would find her way with her little brother.

In the living room, Ruby couldn't get any words out.

'I'm Captain Ryan Newark,' said the man on the screen. 'And you must be Ruby Silver. That was a cryptic request you put in for a face-to-face. It's pretty unusual for my commander to agree – which must mean you know some people in high places. I understand it's to do with a murder investigation in the UK. How can I help you, ma'am?'

Ruby opened her mouth again. Nothing came out.

Ryan was puzzled. He scrunched up his mouth, in exactly the same way he used to. 'It's funny. But do I know you?'

Ruby took a deep breath. Then she told Ryan she was his big sister.

Ryan blinked several times.

They only had ten minutes together. She launched into telling him how she had always been looking for him. That she'd believed he could be dead.

'It can't be,' he said. 'It's strange, but when I first saw you. I think I kind of knew who you were.'

The trickier part was telling him the truth about the woman who had raised him, Irene Newark. Ryan had realised she was not his birth mother, yet he had loved her and she had loved him.

'And what about our father?' Ryan asked.

Ruby already decided she had no right to hold anything back, however hard it was to say it. And so she told him about Mike Travis. That Travis was her stepfather and Ryan's biological father. That Mike Travis was incarcerated for the murder of five women. That a sixth victim had recently been found. That one of the women was their own mother, Amy Travis. Ryan went very quiet.

'Tell me, Ruby,' he said. 'Tell me everything.'

So Ruby told him what happened the day Amy was killed. That Ruby had seen Travis leading Amy away. That she had not been able to get Ryan out of his car seat.

'I know it's horrible,' she said. 'I'm so sorry.'

Ryan shook his head again. 'I had vague memories. Some nightmares and some suspicions. But it's not every day you learn you're the son of a killer. And that your father murdered your own mother. That's going to take some coming to terms with.'

'Sure,' Ruby said. 'I understand.'

He seemed a young man who was certain of himself and who he was.

'There's more, isn't there?' Ryan said.

'Yes, actually there is.'

Ruby felt honour bound to tell him Mike Travis was dying and wanted to see him.

'Yeah, that's a sucker-punch,' Ryan said. 'I'll give it some thought but my knee-jerk reaction is a no. My unit is involved in humanitarian work and reconstruction. It's important and I take my responsibilities here seriously. It's much more important to me than fulfilling the dying wish of a serial killer, even if he is my father.'

The last thing Ruby told Ryan was she had a new identity. She was no longer Rosie, she was Ruby Silver whose parents had died in a car crash. Ruby Silver was a name she had been given to start a new life. No one, except Soraya and Hawk, knew her connection to Travis. If she wanted to protect her career as a criminal profiler, she thought it best to keep it a secret.

'Got it,' Ryan said. 'So people can't know I'm your brother. It will be our secret, don't you worry.'

There was a silence. They were almost out of time.

'These link-ups have a habit of simply cutting out,' he said. 'There's no warning. So, I want to say I hope we can meet, that you want to meet, and thank you for getting in touch. The next time I get leave, maybe we can get together? And, you know, it's great to know I'm not alone.'

Ruby was crying. 'Yeah, it is, isn't it.'

Then the screen went blank.

Chapter Fifty-five

Tanner was in custody without bail and Grant's team was busy preparing for the trial. It meant they could spend time with their families at Christmas after all.

Ruby had the best Christmas Day she ever had. She, Soraya and Hawk spent it in London at Hawk's place, as they usually did. They cooked a giant meal and then they went for a walk in Regent's Park. It didn't snow. It was a sunny day and they went boating on the lake and Hawk almost fell in and she and Soraya laughed themselves silly over it.

Several days afterwards, Ruby was invited for drinks at Inspector Grant's house. Soraya came along too. There was quite a gathering, with Grant's family and plenty of people she recognised from the station. The atmosphere was relaxed and friendly. Ruby felt happier than she had ever felt before.

'Steve McGowan has no permanent damage to his leg,' Diane Collins told Ruby. 'He should be back to cycling in a couple of months' time. You did really well out on the heath. I read the reports. I don't know how you kept your nerve like that, you should be proud.'

Ruby felt herself blushing. 'Thanks. Inspector Grant coming to Caprini's office and this whole investigation has been one of the best things that's happened in my life. I've a feeling next year is going to be even better.'

Diane clinked her glass against Ruby's. 'I'll drink to that.'

'This is nice. I hear the inspector always hosts an after-Christmas drinks session.'

'It's been a tradition for as long as I've been around, and that's a long time. You know the inspector thinks of his team as a kind of family, don't you. I think that's why we work together so well.'

Gosh, her world was starting to open up. At last. Ruby felt a lump in her throat. To cover it up, she helped herself to some snacks.

'His wife is nice too.'

'Yeah, Lily is the best. And your friend Soraya is very attractive. She's your plus-one then?' Diane said casually.

Soraya was flirting outrageously with Grant's son and with Tom. Tom was laughing and so was Daniel. Ruby's heart flipped a little. How could any man resist Soraya?

Ruby sighed. Diane was fishing for information but she didn't have any to give. She'd been single for a long time.

'Soraya and I have been best friends since forever.'

'No boyfriend then?' Diane asked with a twinkle in her eye. 'And tell me to keep out of it if I'm being too curious.'

Ruby smiled. She'd been warned earlier in the evening about the dangers of station gossip. Sergeant Wilson had given her a little pep talk soon after she'd arrived.

'If you don't mind, I'm going to keep quiet about my private life.'

Diane winked. 'Very wise.'

A while later, Ruby went over and dragged Soraya away. 'Behave,' she whispered in Soraya's ear.

'I'm not doing anything wrong,' Soraya said. 'And you didn't tell me he was gorgeous.'

'Who?'

'Don't try to pretend with me. Tom, of course. He's lovely.'

Oh no, for sure Tom was just the type of man Soraya would fall for. Ruby should have known.

'If you say so, I didn't notice.'

'Yeah right, who are you trying to fool? He's the perfect man…'

'Then go for it. I hear he's single.'

Soraya rolled her eyes. 'He's the perfect man, *for you*, silly. Not me. Didn't you notice the way he keeps looking at you? The man can hardly keep his eyes off you.'

Soraya must have had too much to drink. She was imagining things. Ruby glanced over the other side of the room and found Tom looking straight at her. He quickly turned away.

'See. I told you.' Soraya giggled.

'Don't be crazy. And since Tom and I are going to be colleagues, I don't think it would be appropriate.'

To which Soraya rolled her eyes again. 'Boring.'

David Grant was talking with Luke and Luke's partner, Olivier. Grant was keeping an eye on Ruby at the same time. He still found her a curious young woman. And one he liked a great deal.

He found himself, more than once, speculating on her background. It was a well-known fact how children who had been caught up in the witness protection programme were given the cover story of their parents dying in a car crash. The same as Ruby. But it went further with Ruby, because Grant knew that once, when she ran away from her foster parents, she had been found wandering around the moorland, not so far from Himlands Heath. And not so far from where Ryan Travis went missing. Now wasn't that a curious thing?

Not to mention McGowan and Delaney both commenting in their reports how Ruby had been certain about where Tanner would take him and Carys. She also unerringly led them through the fog to the stand of pine trees, which McGowan said he found unbelievable. Another curious turn of events.

As if she had been there before, Grant thought. Three coincidences were three coincidences, or was it more than that?

And his mind wandered back to the little girl he once interviewed, all those years ago.

'Are you listening to a word I'm saying?' Luke said.

'Of course I am. Now come on you two, and meet my son Daniel. I'm sure you'll find a lot to talk about.'

Later, David Grant went over to Ruby. 'I'm glad you could come,' he said. 'And I'm even more pleased you decided to take up Superintendent Fox's offer.'

Ruby smiled. She was to be joining Inspector Grant's team on a permanent basis.

'It wasn't her idea,' he said.

'I know.'

He had been delighted when Fox accepted his suggestion. Fox thought having a criminal profiler on the staff was just the thing to improve the station's statistics.

'I was flattered, and thank you,' Ruby said. 'It's overdue for me to leave the professor and working on this case has given me a taste for being in the field. I think it's my thing.'

'I think so too. You've certainly a flair for it.' Grant raised his glass. 'And thank you for saving my life.'

She chinked her glass with his and took a sip of sweet white wine. She had wanted to tell him the truth about her past but the inspector had been recovering and then Fox had made the job offer and Ruby had not wanted to ruin it. What would they think of her if they knew she was the stepdaughter of a killer? And what did she think of herself? She wasn't sure yet, but what she did know was this was a new beginning.

Maybe one day she would be able to tell Grant. When she felt sure of the new her.

'You're welcome,' she said. *And thank you for saving mine,* she thought.

'I don't suppose you've heard the news about Mike Travis,' Grant said. 'He died in the night. Dr Patel sent me a text.'

Ruby felt a weight lifting. 'I can't say I'm sorry.'

'Me neither. I believe his son declined to visit him during his last days, even though Ryan Travis was given compassionate leave by his superior officer.'

She nodded. Her conscience was clear. She had passed on the message and Ryan had made his own decision.

'Glad to have you on board, Ms Silver.'

Later on, Chrissie, Grant's daughter, came and linked her arm with her father's.

'Mum said Carys Evans has gone on holiday.'

'She and her niece have written a wish list. They've jetted off to the Pyramids and next is Norway to see the Aurora Borealis. Carys told me they intend to travel the world.'

'It wasn't all bad news for her then.'

'Yes and no. It was a terrible shock to learn about Meredith's selfishness but Carys is more forgiving than I will ever be, though she told me she doesn't want to see her sister for a very long time. Meanwhile, she and her niece, Kate, are getting acquainted and they've made plans together. Carys sounded happy in Egypt. She told me they're having fun.'

In fact, Carys had been more carefree than he ever remembered her. He hoped it was the first of many wonderful times and happiness. Carys deserved it.

'I like the new woman on your team, Dad. She's interesting. Different. You always pick the best ones, don't you.'

David Grant laughed. Yes, he always did pick the best ones. He looked over to where Ruby was talking with Luke. Grant decided he would never ask Ruby about her past. And he hoped she would learn to trust him, and grow sure enough of herself, then one day she'd be able to tell him the truth.

******

A message from Ann Girdharry –

Hello,

Thank you so much for choosing Deadly Motives.

One of the things I love about being an author is hearing direct from readers.

So if you'd like to get in touch, please do. You might have a question about one of my books. Or maybe you have a general question about publishing. Or maybe you've spotted a typo or an error.

Whatever it is, feel free to send me an email. I'd be delighted to hear from you.

If you're an avid reader and you'd like to receive news and updates, I'd love you to join my Reader's Group. Don't worry, no spam. I'll only get in touch when I have something I think you might genuinely be interested in, like the release of a new book. I offer a free gift to new members and you can find details on my webpage – www.girdharry.com.

Happy Reading,
Ann Girdharry
Email – ann@girdharry.com

Deadly Secrets (Detective Grant and Ruby book 2)

How long can you get away with murder?

Mr Quinn whispers a secret on his death bed. Hours later, the person present when Quinn died, is murdered.

Detective Grant, Ruby, and the team, investigate. Himlands Heath is an idyllic Sussex town but all is not as it seems. Two children disappeared many years ago and they were never found and Quinn knew them.

Then a local person takes their own life. Or do they? What does someone want to hide? And what about the rich Watson family? Benefactors of the town and admired by many, are they victims? Did Sir Paul Watson's wife really drown on the night of the children's disappearance? Or are the Watsons too good to be true?

A dark twist

They must track a suspect who has been getting away with it for years. But when Grant realises senior police officers withheld information, the investigation takes a darker turn.

Corruption and secrets from the past are used against Sergeant Tom Delaney, as the killer claims another victim and turns their attention to one of Grant's own...

What readers are saying –

'Oh my! It just gets better and better! Loved it'

'Just finished this. It was amazing!!!'

'Loved this one'

Deadly Secrets hit the Hot New Release Top 50 in both Amazon USA and Amazon UK charts.

Get your copy today!

Deadly Lies (Detective Grant and Ruby book 3)

When six-year-old Emily and four-year-old Lisa are abducted from their grandparents' house, Detective Grant and criminal profiler Ruby Silver race against time to find them.

As they dig deep into the personal lives of the parents', they discover secrets from the past. It seems Jack and Alice have not been honest with each other nor with the police. And then there's the grandparents, who have their own fair share of enemies.

Everyone comes under scrutiny. But just when the team are homing in on a suspect, a murder throws the investigation into turmoil.

Is there betrayal within Grant's own team? Or within the family? With the parents desperate and one of the little girls dangerously ill, time is running out. As treachery and lies threaten to tear the family apart, nothing is as it seems...

Who is responsible for the abduction and why?
And could the answers lie closer to home than anyone ever imagined?

What readers are saying –

'One of the best crime thrillers I have read this year!'

'...could not put this down and finally turned the last page in the wee hours. Yes this book is that good!'

'...lots of twists and turns...'

'A 100% must read'

'Great characters. Great story.'

Get your copy today!

Good Girl Bad Girl (Kal and Marty Book 1)

The darkest crimes can't stay hidden forever…

A young body washed up by the river in London, and a matron murdered at a children's home thousands of miles away…could there be a link?

Only one person wants to find out – Kal. Why does she want to know? Because Kal's journalist mother was researching the story and now she's missing.

Kal's father was a criminal, which is why she trusts no one and least of all Detective Inspector Spinks. Kal takes on the investigation herself. She's going to need all the skills she learnt from her father, especially when she discovers there's a link between her own family and the crimes that have been committed.

Trafficking, deception and dark family secrets - she'll be forced to confront her own worst nightmares, and form an alliance with the police, if they're going to nail a twisted killer.

What readers are saying –

'A stunning read'

'On the edge of my seat'

'Loved the characters and the writing!'

'Great to have female leads who were strong but realistically vulnerable at times too. Can't wait to read about these characters again!'

Good Girl Bad Girl is an Eric Hoffer Book Award Finalist.
Get your copy today

Acknowledgements

Beta readers are really important to an author because they are the very first reader's eyes on a story.
A huge thanks to Priya, Terje, Kiltie, Kate, Greta, Claire and Carol.

Titles by this Author

Deadly Motives (previously published as Killer Motive)
Deadly Secrets
Deadly Lies

Good Girl Bad Girl
London Noir
The Beauty Killers

The Couple Upstairs
The Woman in Room 19

Made in the USA
Las Vegas, NV
26 March 2023

69724891R00157